SURRENDER TO ME

The Wolf Hotel #4

K.A.TUCKER

Editing by Hot Tree Editing

Cover design by Shanoff Designs

Published by K.A. Tucker

CHAPTER 1

The horizon is glowing with a faint pink hue as I step through the patio doors and take in the view of the Manhattan skyline, my eyes still half-closed thanks to terrible jet lag. It's promising another stifling hot day. "Record-breaking," according to the news. Thankfully, we missed the worst of it yesterday, our flight from France not arriving at the airfield until late in the evening.

I stroll around the rooftop pool—pristinely clean and so inviting—to the lounge chair where Henry is stretched out, wearing only his briefs, a glass of Scotch in hand, the half-finished bottle sitting on the concrete next to him. "Come to bed," I say softly, perching on the edge of the chair. "Get a few hours of sleep before the day has to start." It's 5:00 a.m. Henry has a meeting with the funeral director at ten to discuss arrangements for his father.

And he's drunk.

It's a long moment before his steely blue eyes break their lock on the sky to regard me, slowly drifting over the silky white sheet that I hug to my naked body. There's no hunger in that gaze though. "He was supposed to die of cancer, not while fucking a twenty-five-year-old," he murmurs, his attention drifting away again, to the city skyline this time.

When Henry shared the details about the cause of William Wolf's heart attack, I hadn't known what to say. It still feels like an awkward topic. "Did he have heart issues?"

"He had blood pressure problems, but he was taking medication for that. It was under control."

"And he was still feeling well?"

"As far as I know. He hadn't mentioned anything otherwise to me. And Scott said he hadn't talked to him all week."

I smooth my hand up and down Henry's muscular arm soothingly, fighting the natural urge for my fingers to wander over his bare flesh, memorizing each perfect curve. "Life isn't always fair."

"Don't get me wrong, of all the ways to go.... Just not yet," he mutters bitterly.

"How is the girl?" I can't even imagine what it'd be like to have the man you're having sex with die in the middle of it.

"Hysterical that night, but I'm sure she'll be fine."

"Did she know him well?"

Henry chuckles darkly. "Depends on your definition of 'well.' He'd been fucking her for a few weeks. She thought she was in love. Scott says she wasn't the brightest light bulb in the pack." He takes a sip. "Good for my dad."

"How old was he, again?"

"Sixty-three." He says that with a slight slur. I've never heard Henry slur, but then again he did crack this bottle of Scotch the second we walked through the door.

"He looked good for sixty-three." And dying of cancer. Granted, I only met him that one time, in Alaska for the grand opening of the Wolf hotel in Wolf Cove, and that was months ago.

Henry sighs. "When he told me about the diagnosis, he said he couldn't really complain, considering all the luck he'd been born into. He was bound to come up short somewhere. That was his logic."

All that luck he'd been born into.... A gold mine and the luxurious global Wolf hotel chain that has made Henry's family more money than they know what to do with. "It sounds like he had made peace with it, at least."

"He did. And I was getting there. I thought I had another few years with him. And then this happens." Henry's voice turns husky. "First my grandparents. Now him. He was all I had left and he's gone, just like that."

There's no point reminding Henry that he still has a brother, because Scott Wolf is a lecherous snake and not someone either of us wants around. And then there's his mother, but Henry's been estranged from her for almost twenty years, and it doesn't sound like there's any desire to reconcile there.

I swallow the lump in my throat. "You have me. I know it's not the same, but I'm here, whenever you need me. However you need me." I slide the glass out of his hand. "And maybe we should ease up on the Scotch for now."

Henry gives me one of those hard, unreadable stares for one... two... three seconds, and my stomach instinctively tightens, afraid of what dark thoughts might be churning inside that head of his.

And then he chuckles. It's a bitter sound. "You're right. I should save some for you. You'll be needing it more than I will...."

That's not the first time he's made comments about how the next few days will be an ordeal for me, which makes me more than a little nervous. I've already met—and now hate—his brother, who played a role in breaking us up with his lies and manipulation. But that was back when I was Henry's assistant and we had to hide our relationship from everyone, including Henry's father.

I no longer work for Wolf Hotels, and William Wolf is dead.

Abruptly, Henry leans in to grip the back of my head and plant a hard kiss on my mouth, the sweet, smoky taste of liquor on his breath. I half expect him to yank off my sheet and take me right here under the morning sky, but he pulls away just as quickly. Climbing out of the chair, he throws his arms above his head in a stretch. And then pushes his briefs off his hips, letting them tumble to the concrete. He's a little unsteady on his feet as he stalks to the edge of the pool, without so much as a glance around for onlookers. We're some eighty stories up in the Wolf Tower penthouse and it's still early enough that there *likely* aren't spectators in the few equally tall buildings around.

Not that Henry would give a damn if there were.

He smoothly dives in, sending a small splash in the air before emerging on the opposite side of the pool to grip the edge while thrusting a hand through his wavy chestnut-brown hair, pushing it back off his face. I consider dropping my sheet and climbing in after him, but then he begins swimming laps, his sculpted body moving swiftly and powerfully through the water.

And so I sit and quietly admire the indomitable Henry Wolf as the sun climbs the horizon beyond.

Wondering what fresh hell the next few days will bring.

I TRY NOT to fuss with the hemline of my dress as we step through the main doors of the funeral home. It's a modest black shift dress that I picked up at Saks yesterday, thinking it would be appropriate for the visitation. It, along with a pair of classic black pumps with a price tag that made me choke, complete the understated look I was going for. Still, I tried my best to look like I belong next to Henry, fussing with my makeup and hair for almost two hours.

Meanwhile Henry stands tall and sharply dressed—as usual—in a tailored black suit and tie. And matching socks, that I chose for him while he showered. "Ready?"

"Are *you?*" I peer up at his handsome face—a face that ensnares females of all ages instantly, I know because I've watched it happen from the sidelines countless times—and take in the steely mask. It's been firmly affixed since he swam some fifty laps in his pool and sobered up. That was the only time I've seen him let go of control. Since then, he's been in and out of the penthouse, but mostly out, splitting his time between the Wolf head office and making arrangements for his dad's burial. All business as usual, his emotions hidden from everyone.

Including me.

But I haven't pushed him to talk. I figure he'll talk when he's ready.

He slides a hand over the small of my back. I can feel the heat of it through the light material of my dress. With a heavy swallow, he leads me down the hall of the opulent funeral home in the heart of Manhattan.

Visitation hours don't begin for another twenty minutes, and yet there is already a stream of people of all ages milling about the entrance doors to Promenade Hall, where William Wolf's body awaits. I shouldn't be surprised. News of his sudden death made the New York Times.

Countless eyes veer our way as we approach, and my stomach twists with nerves. Most are watching the powerful mogul beside me, but more than a few curious onlookers are sizing me up.

"He knew a lot of people," I murmur, just loud enough for Henry to hear, as my cheeks begin to burn from the attention.

"There will be a lot of Wolf employees here today to pay their respects. Plus business associates and media." Henry offers a reserved smile and nod to a middle-aged couple closest to us as we pass.

"What do you want me to say if they ask how I knew your father?" A question I *should* have asked him *before* climbing out of the limo.

"The truth. That you didn't know him at all, but you know his son *very* well."

"Is that a good idea?"

"Of course it is." Henry looks down at me, his eyebrow spiking with annoyance that I'm even questioning him.

"I'm just not sure you've thought this through." While we haven't been hiding our relationship, we have been keeping it low-key. But with a room full of Wolf employees, plus media, news of the woman striding in with "one of the world's most eligible bachelors," according to many—his ex-assistant—will spread like wildfire. Is Henry ready for that?

Am I?

"I'm quite sure that I have." The slightest smirk touches Henry's lips as he slips his strong, calloused hand into mine and leads me through the throng of watchful gazes to the set of heavy oak doors being manned by a solemn attendant.

I can't help the giddiness that surges through my limbs with this simple action, despite our surroundings. I know Henry. He wouldn't have done that if he didn't have serious intentions about me.

The doors close behind us with an ominous thud, sealing us inside the hall with William Wolf's body.

And Scott Wolf.

My tiny thrill vanishes instantly as I spot Henry's older brother standing at the far end of the cavernous room, where an elaborately carved wood coffin sits on a brass stand, surrounded by at least fifty elaborate bouquets—everything from the typical funeral white lilies to arrays of colorful sunflowers.

I fully expected Scott to be here and yet I can't help the visceral reaction at the sight of him. I haven't seen him in months, since the day he stormed out of Penthouse One at Wolf Cove, bleeding from several well-deserved punches delivered by Henry's fist.

Scott turns to watch us approach now, his gray-blue eyes widening at the sight of me by Henry's side.

"Huh," Henry murmurs.

"What?"

"I was sure he would have heard about you by now." There's amusement in his tone.

Unfortunately I can't match his joy as I watch Scott's face —not nearly as chiseled or handsome as Henry's—harden with the knowledge that he was duped.

Henry must sense my trepidation. He hand squeezes mine once in a sign of comfort. "Scott, you remember Abbi Mitchell."

"How could I forget?" An easy—fake—smile curls Scott's thin lips. "You're a better liar than I gave you credit for, *Abigail*."

I'm assuming he's talking about the day he cornered me in an elevator and tried to manipulate me into admitting that Henry was screwing me, his assistant, in the midst of legal issues over screwing his last assistant. While he failed at that, he did manage to plant such toxic seeds of doubt and outright lies about Henry that I convinced myself that Henry was sleeping with other women. It was without doubt the worst day of my life. A thousand times worse than the day I walked in on Jed cheating on me.

I clear my throat. There are so many things I'd like to say to this asshole—hell, I'd like to pick up that giant bouquet of white roses behind him and smash the heavy-looking white clay vase over his head—but this is not the time or place for vengeance. "I'm sorry for your loss."

His eyes shift to Henry. He isn't so adept at hiding the anger in them as his brother. "You son of a bitch."

"Now, now...."

"You have the nerve to bring your *whore* to his funeral?"

All amusement slips from Henry's face. "Call her that again, and you'll be joining Dad in that box," he warns, ice in his tone.

But Scott isn't so easily deterred. "You lied right to his face about fucking her."

"I told him about Abbi before he died. My conscience is clean. How's yours?"

I feel my own eyes widen with surprise now, as my attention veers to the left, to where the distinguished man lies. Still regal, even as a corpse. I didn't know Henry had told his dad about us.

Scott's eyes narrow as he regards his brother for a long moment, as if trying to read something between his words. "You lied right to Dad's face and yet I'm the one who took all the heat."

Henry releases my hand and steps forward. He's easily six inches taller than his brother, and now he towers over him. "You took heat from Dad because you tried to have me framed for rape so you could take over Wolf Hotels," he hisses through gritted teeth, his fists clenched at his side, looking ready to punch Scott again.

"I was just making sure Dad knew what kind of man his precious boy really is," Scott throws back, puffing out his chest to compensate for their size difference.

"A man who will run the family business with integrity?" Henry takes a step forward until they're toe-to-toe. Scott refuses to give ground. "Who has no problems keeping the women in his life satisfied? Who's always honest with them?"

The two Wolf men have somehow managed to fill this cavernous hall with tension. I'm torn between jumping between them to stall the explosion, and hiding behind the casket to avoid the shrapnel.

The door behind us creaks open and a man in a suit passes through. "Excuse me, but the crowd outside is quite large. Would you mind if we begin moving people in now to help clear the lobby? If everyone is ready?" He sounds skeptical. He must sense the impending doom in the air.

"Yes, we're ready. Thank you." Henry takes a deep breath and then two steps back, muttering under his breath to Scott, "Stay the fuck away from us."

I breathe a sigh of relief. Belinda, Wolf Cove's general manager and a woman who seems to know the Wolf men well, once commented on how Henry and Scott can't be in a room for more than five minutes without erupting.

Now I understand.

It's going to be a *long* three hours.

I SETTLE a hand on Henry's shoulder, grabbing his attention before the next well-wisher steps up. "I'm going to get you water. I'll be back in a sec." We've been standing in this same spot, to the left of the casket, for two and a half hours now, greeting countless people. All strangers to me, though I smile and accept their condolences as if I'm a part of the family, because what else am I supposed to do, standing next to Henry?

"Thank you," he answers, his voice hoarse from talking.

I edge my way through the crowd, happy to be moving my legs, though my feet throb from these heels. Thankfully, Scott has stayed on the other side of William Wolf's body, some distance away and suitably occupied by visitors and unable to cause more problems. Right now he's consoling a sobbing Becky, the woman William was with the night he died. The woman is everything I would expect of a rich older man like William, and yet at the same time not. She's stunningly beautiful and young, with evenly tanned skin, plump red lips and high cheekbones, and an hourglass figure. I'm 90 percent certain her waist-length platinum blonde hair is the result of high-end extensions.

She is the reason William apparently took a Viagra pill the night he died, something the preliminary autopsy report revealed. Henry threw a glass across the living room to hit the wall and shatter into a hundred pieces when he found out. William knew he couldn't take those pills because of his blood pressure issues, Henry said. But he must have taken one anyway, the need to enjoy his twenty-five-year-old plaything outweighing the dangers. He obviously didn't expect the consequences to be so severe.

I find a service area outside the hall, near the lobby, stocked with carafes of hot coffee and tea, along with a fridge full of cold beverages. I fish out two bottles of cold water, cracking one for myself and taking a big gulp.

"Is working for Mr.Wolf always so chaotic?" Miles asks from behind me, making me jump.

I offer Henry's assistant a sympathetic smile through my swallow. "Yes. It is."

He heaves a sigh and takes a sip of water from his own bottle, only to catch a dribble as it escapes his mouth and runs down his chin. "You'd think he'd slow down, with all *this* going on." He gestures toward the visitation room. "But the guy's actually working *harder*."

"It's just his way of coping. He'll ease up soon." *I think*. Henry has been sliding into bed after I've drifted off every night, and is either sweating his tension out in his home gym, or on the phone when I wake. The only proof I've had that he's actually slept is his gold watch sitting on the nightstand and the delicious smell of his cologne on his pillow.

We've shared nothing more than tender kisses since France.

For Henry to go four days without sex, with me ready and willing to give him whatever he wants?

He's hurting.

Miles runs a hand through his mop of curly brown hair. "He asked me to do, like, a *thousand* things and now I have a thousand follow-ups for him. I don't want to bug him, but at the same time, I know he's going to ask for a status update as soon as he walks into the office and expect it to be taken care of, and I'm not going to have any answers for him and he's going to think I'm an idiot and fire my ass. I don't want to get fired. I *like* working for him!" His face is pinched with stress.

I remember this feeling too well, back when I didn't think I could do anything right where Henry was concerned. "I'll ask him to carve out some time for you as soon as he's ready, so you two can sort out any questions you might have."

Miles sighs with relief. "Thank you. I guess it must have been a lot different for you, working for him. You know, because you two were...." His gaze drops to my ample chest, which, while it's well-covered by this shift dress, is still noticeable. "I mean, because he obviously had a hard on for you so.... No, wait! I mean...." His face screws up.

I can't help but laugh. I've only ever talked to Miles when he's confirming Henry's schedule or booking flights for me. On email and text, Miles seems so professional and smart. I wonder if he's always so frazzled in person, or if it's just because of the current situation. Something tells me it's the latter, because Henry wouldn't tolerate a bumbling fool assistant for long.

He gives me a sheepish smile. "I think it's cool. You know, that Wolf would fall for you. He could have *anyone* he wanted. Gorgeous women are throwing themselves at him *all* the time, but he's completely into *you*. I mean, not that you're not gorgeous, because you *are*, too. Like, *really* hot. But you're different than all the others. You're normal. Fuck, I need to stop talking. Please don't tell him I said anything. He'll fire me."

I giggle. "He won't hear it from me."

Miles sighs. "Fuck, I'm going back to the office. He can find me there."

I watch the tall, lanky guy speed away, amusement on my face.

"He's certainly in a rush."

I turn to find an attractive older woman—mid-fifties, maybe—filling a mug with coffee beside me. She's dressed in a well-cut black pantsuit, emphasizing a trim waist and appealing curves. Her hair, the color of spun gold, settles on her shoulders in a sleek bob.

"He's just a bit overwhelmed right now. He's Henry Wolf's assistant." I don't know why I add that last part.

The woman's piercing blue eyes flash with recognition. "He's not going to last long working for a Wolf if he can't find some decorum."

Something about her is so familiar, but I can't peg it. "Do you work for Wolf Hotels?"

"I used to, for a short time. A *very* long time ago, now." She chuckles as she stirs the sugar through her coffee, the metal spoon clanging softly against porcelain. "And you? Do you work there?"

"I used to. Also for a short time."

"Well, it's nice of you to pay your respects. Did you know William?"

"No. I mean, I met him once but I didn't know him. I know his son. Henry. I know him well." I stumble over the answer Henry prescribed earlier. I haven't had to use it yet.

The woman pauses in her stirring, her curious gaze skating over my features, as if really taking me in for the first time. "And how is Henry taking his father's passing?"

"As well as can be expected."

"Working a lot?"

"Day and night." I frown slightly. "Do you know Henry?"

"Not really." She smiles sadly. "I'm guessing he's a lot like his father, though."

"So I've heard." The water bottles are beginning to sweat within my grasp. I've been gone too long. "Speaking of Henry, I need to get this to him before he loses his voice." Somehow, "enjoy the visitation" doesn't sound right. So I simply hold up the water for emphasis and then, with a smile, I turn and head back toward the room.

The crowd has thinned out somewhat, with only half an hour left before the room closes to visitors. I weave through the staggered groups of two and three until I reach Henry's side to wordlessly hand him his bottle and set a hand on his bicep in comfort.

He abruptly stops talking. And suddenly I feel like I'm interrupting a private conversation.

When I turn to take in the woman's face, I'm *sure* I've interrupted a private conversation.

Whoever she is, she's stunning. Her long brunette hair hangs like sheets of silk over her shoulders to reach halfway down her back. Her eyes remind me of cat's eyes—wide, almond-shaped, and bright green. And her legs... they're obscenely long. Like, unnaturally so.

And the way she's looking at me from beneath that thick fringe of eyelashes, the corners of her full mouth turned downward with a hint of distaste? She's sizing me up as competition that she can easily squash.

Henry clears his throat. "Abbi... this is Kiera. Kiera... Abbi Mitchell."

My chest tightens.

This is Kiera? *The* Kiera. Henry's ex-assistant. The one who he had an affair with. The one who falsely accused him of rape. The one who is obviously still madly in love with him, by the look in her eyes.

My fingers dig into Henry's bulging muscle. "You have a lot of nerve," I begin in a whispered hiss.

"Abbi... remember where we are," Henry warns softly.

Right. At his father's visitation. Slapping her across her pouty face—as much as she deserves it, as badly as I want to do it—is the wrong thing to do.

So instead of that, I press into Henry's hard body and force a wide, fake smile. "Hello, Kiera. It's *so* nice to *finally* meet you." I sound like Tillie, the catty southern bell from Wolf Cove who is masterful at delivering sweet words laced with cutting bitterness. I release Henry's arm long enough to offer my hand.

She responds with a limp shake—which I squeeze—and a tight smile behind her wince. I notice there isn't a wedding band on her left ring finger. I guess her husband didn't stick around after finding out the sexual relationship she'd had with her boss was 100 percent consensual.

"Let me know if you think that could work," she purrs, her eyes locked on Henry, ignoring me.

"Thank you for coming," he answers smoothly, seemingly unperturbed by her presence.

Henry may be mine, but I still feel like vomiting as I watch her turn and stroll away, her mile-long legs emphasized by the tight black skirt. "I'll bet she can't even find pants for those things," I mutter.

Henry chuckles. "Don't be petty."

I sigh, reminding myself that Henry's not attracted to insecurity. "What does she need your help with?"

He cracks open his water and takes a swig. The line to pay

condolences has dwindled, and he has a break finally. "She wants to work for me again."

My mouth drops open. "For Wolf Hotels?"

He pauses, as if deciding what to say. "For me. As my assistant."

"Are you fucking kidding me? The nerve!" I blurt out, a touch too loud. "Well... you have Miles, so... you're good. You don't need another assistant." The last thing I care about right now is Miles's job. I don't want that woman anywhere near Henry.

"I do have Miles," Henry agrees, taking another long sip. I can't read his tone, and that makes my paranoia begin to grow.

I drop my voice to remind him, "And she accused you of rape."

"She did," he says too calmly.

"Henry!"

He turns to cup my cheek with his warm palm, his crystal blue eyes locking with mine. "I don't need a new assistant, and she accused me of rape, and I know you wouldn't be okay with it, so, no, there's no way in hell Kiera's coming back to Wolf in *any* capacity."

"Oh." I breathe a sigh of relief. "You handled her well."

"I humored her to get her the hell away from me. I wasn't going to cause a scene here." His lips curve into a sexy curve. "You, on the other hand.... I thought you were going to claw her eyes out."

I offer a sheepish smile. "Sorry, I saw red. I wasn't thinking."

His hand settles on the small of my back. "That's okay. I think I liked it." His fingertips slide down to trace the elastic waistband of my panties through my dress. "My money'd be on you, too."

I clear my throat and give him a cautionary look. There

are undoubtedly people watching. "By the way, you need to make some time for Miles."

Henry's brow rises in question.

"I ran into him in the lobby. He looked overwhelmed."

He sighs. "I've probably been overworking him."

"You've been overworking, period."

Another sigh. "I don't want him quitting on me. He's good."

I wonder what Henry would say if I repeated Miles's words. Either laugh it off or fire him. There's rarely an in-between with this man. "Just give him some of your time so he can ask his questions and do his job. Let him know that you appreciate him, and he won't be going anywhere. For some strange reason, he likes working for you," I add wryly.

Henry grins, the first real amusement I've seen on his face in days. "You sure you don't want your job back?"

"I'm positive. The boss can be a real tyrant."

"A tyrant." He leans in closer to me, and drops his voice. "Tell me... what kinds of things did he make you do?"

This is *so* inappropriate, but I'm guessing Henry needs this bit of reprieve. I bite my bottom lip in thought. "Well, there was this one time he tied my hands up and...." I sense a figure hovering, waiting for us to break our conversation. My mouth clamps shut and my cheeks burn, embarrassed at the prospect of being overheard, especially given our surroundings.

It's the woman I met at the service area earlier.

Henry leans into my ear and whispers playfully, "I remember that day. We'll have to reenact it later." But when he turns to greet his latest visitor, his entire body stiffens.

"Hello, Henry," the woman croons in that same soft voice. She's an inch or so shorter than I am, and is forced to tilt her head to peer up at him.

He doesn't answer for a few beats. When he finally does, his voice is curt. "Thank you for coming."

I feel Scott's beady eyes on us, but I'm unable to peel my attention away from this uneasy exchange.

She offers a wide smile, as if nothing is wrong. "How have you been?"

"Fantastic."

"Good. Well, I was hoping you'd be here."

"Of course I'm here. It's my father's visitation."

"Yes, I realize that. But I was hoping we could talk."

"So talk." Nothing about Henry's tone invites conversation.

After a moment of awkwardness, she turns to me and holds a hand out. "I'm sorry, I didn't catch your name earlier."

"Um...." I glance at Henry's stony face. "It's Abbi Mitchell."

"Hi Abbi. I'm Crystal McGuire." She meets Henry's gaze. "I'm Henry's mother."

CHAPTER 2

"Why are you here?" Henry has shed all politeness. His voice is ice.

"I saw the news." Her pretty blue eyes—Henry's eyes, I now realize; at least the same shape as his—shift to gaze over to her late husband's body. "And I wanted to pay my respects."

"Go ahead then. He's right there." Henry's arm curls tightly around my waist. He starts walking away and I have no choice but to follow, struggling to keep up with his pace.

"Slow down!" I mutter, my ankle shifting in these heels. Henry keeps me from falling and adjusts his stride once we're out of the hall. But he doesn't stop, leading me toward the front doors. "Shouldn't we stay?" The crowds have dwindled, but there is still a good number of people standing idly in circles, chatting.

"Scott can handle things."

The limo is already waiting for us outside. Henry doesn't wait for the driver, opening the door and ushering me in.

I settle into the seat and kick off my shoes, moaning with relief as I stretch my toes.

"Home to drop Abbi off and then to work," he directs the

driver, sliding in to sit across from me. He shrugs off his suit jacket and tosses it to the seat beside him. Then, unfastening his cuffs and loosening his tie, he pours himself a drink from the minibar at the side.

Tension radiates off him.

"Do you want to talk about—"

"No!" he barks, and I instinctively shrink into my seat.

He pinches the bridge of his nose. "What did she mean when she said she didn't catch your name earlier?"

I tell him about our exchange in the service station. "It was literally a minute, tops. I had no idea who she was." Now, playing back the short conversation, I can't believe I didn't figure it out. "I guess I didn't expect her to be there today."

Henry sinks into his seat and leans his head back to rest against the glass partition that separates us from the driver. "Why the hell did she come?"

"Maybe it's like she said, to pay her respects?"

His answering laugh is full of scorn. "Bullshit. What respect? She had no respect for us when she abandoned us twenty years ago. Why the fuck would I want it now?"

His tone is sharp, but I know him well enough to know that it's not directed at me. He's angry and hurting. And my chest aches for him. As domineering and narrow-minded—and hateful, sometimes—as my mother can be, and as difficult as she's made my life of late, there has never been any doubt that she loves me fiercely. That she would rather die than pack up her things and walk out of my life.

Henry's mother leaving him—abandoning him—the way she did has left gruesome scars.

"Maybe at least talking to her would help you move on, and get some closure," I say as gently as I can. "Help you open up."

"I'm fucking open!"

This is not the time to tackle this conversation. I climb

over to Henry's side to curl up next to him, resting my head on his shoulder while our car navigates Manhattan's gridlock and he broods silently.

"Why don't you just come home with me now," I finally suggest, smoothing my hand over his hard chest affectionately. "We can sit outside and stare at the sky."

"It's going to storm tonight."

"Fine. Sit inside and watch the storm. I'll make dinner." I'm far from the best cook, but I do know how to make a few dishes and well. But Henry wouldn't know that because I've never actually cooked for him. We always have our meals delivered from the hotel's kitchen, or we go out.

"I have too much work to do, Abbi."

Working day and night. That's what Crystal—Henry's mother—said when she asked how he was doing. She said it was just a hunch, but now I know that's not true. She knew because Henry is like his father, and obviously she thought William Wolf was a workaholic.

"You can't take a break, for just a few hours? Just one night?" My palm slides over his abdomen, a washboard of muscles, and further down, past his belt, to begin rubbing him.

His hand presses down on mine, stalling the movements. "It's not a good time for this."

"I'm sorry. I just—" I hesitate, letting my nose skim over his neck, inhaling the delicious smell of his musky cologne and soap. "I miss feeling you inside me." We've shared a bed for days and yet I feel like he's worlds away. Understandably so, but still.

Despite his words, there's movement against my hand. He's growing, hardening.

I manage to free my fingers from his grasp enough to curl around his impressive length.

"Is that what you want?"

I press my body into him in answer, sliding my thigh up and over his lap. I skate my lips against his neck. "Only if *you* want it." I know I'm being selfish for asking, given where we just left, but if there's one thing that puts Henry in a better mood, it's sex.

Henry reaches up to press the intercom button. "How much longer?"

"Three or four minutes," comes the response over the speaker.

"Thank you," Henry says curtly.

"We can go upstairs and...." My words drift as Henry flicks the lock to the divider window and adjusts the volume of the music up with ease. He slides my leg off his lap and then, unfastening his belt and dress pants, he unceremoniously pushes them along with his boxer briefs down to his knees, leaving him sitting in the limo with his dick standing erect.

And even though this wasn't exactly what I had in mind, heat begins to pool between my thighs at the sight, all the same.

"Take your dress off," he demands, lazily stroking himself.

It takes me a moment to slide my dress over my head and shimmy out of my panties.

"That too." He nods toward my bra.

Unclasping the back, I toss it to the opposite bench. And now I'm completely naked in the back of this limo and we're driving down a busy street with cars edging past us on either side. I glance at the windows warily, though I know they can't see us through the tinted glass.

"You heard him. Three or four minutes."

While this colder side of Henry isn't completely foreign to me, it's been a while since I've seen it. I gingerly climb onto his lap, fully aware that there's a man sitting just on the other side of that glass.

Normally, Henry would touch me first. He'd check to make sure that I'm wet enough. Now though, he simply lines up the end of his swollen cock, seizes my hips, and pulls me down.

I gasp with the sudden intrusion.

"I thought you missed feeling me inside you," he whispers, his eyes at least showing a flare of heat now as they focus on my breasts, as he adjusts his hips.

"I do."

He closes his eyes and lets his head fall back. "Well then, here I am, inside you. So, let's fuck."

This isn't *my* Henry, but this is the Henry I get right now —one that's hurting over the death of his father and the surprise visit by his mother. The closed-off Henry.

But I want to bring my Henry back to me.

Forgetting the oblivious world outside us, I settle my hands on either side of his chiseled face and lean in to place a tender kiss against his lips. I begin rocking my pelvis back and forth.

His mouth is unresponsive to me at first, but I don't relent, sliding the tip of my tongue against his seam as my body naturally opens up and he slides in deeper. "Look at me. Please, Henry," I plead softly.

After a few beats, eyes the color of a deep blue sea peer up at me. Into me. The veil normally over them is gone, showing me so much pain.

"I'm sorry," he whispers.

I press my lips against his mouth again. "It's okay."

"No, it's not." His arms wrap around my naked body and he pulls me tight to him, his mouth working against mine now, in that slow, tantalizing way he has of kissing that makes me forget everyone and everything.

I'm barely aware that we've pulled up in front of Wolf Towers when Henry hits the lock on the doors and tells the driver through the intercom that we'll be out in a few minutes.

My hair was pulled back in a tidy ponytail for the visitation. Henry works the elastic out with nimble fingers, giving him access to my thick mane of red hair. His hand weaves through it to seize the back of my head. "Have I ever told you how much I love your hair?" he whispers against my lips. "And your mouth. And your neck. And these...." He dips his head to gently clasp one of my hard nipples between his teeth. I gasp as he sucks, and grind my hips against him harder. After standing in heels for so long today, my legs are already tired. I can't help the sigh of relief when Henry lifts me off him to set me down on the opposite bench.

I glance to the window, where Wolf Tower's doormen stand just outside, primed to open the limo door and greet the building's owner. "They're *definitely* locked this time, right?" The last time we were caught in a compromising position in a vehicle, it was in the parking lot of the seedy Billy Bob's because Henry mistakenly unlocked the doors. I have no interest in repeating that night.

Henry kneels in front of me and hoists my legs up onto his shoulders. "Yes. And they know better." His heated gaze burns over my flesh as he studies first my breasts and then the space between my legs. He runs a finger through my slit a few times, teasing me. "Will you always get this wet for me?"

"Always."

He lines himself up and then thrusts into me so hard that I can't help cry out, more in surprise than anything.

One of the doormen's head jumps toward the window, and then he discreetly takes several steps back.

I bite my bottom lip to keep quiet as Henry starts pumping into me at a hard and fast tempo, so hard that the Scotch in the bottle sloshes around. I can't keep up with him, so I simply watch his beautiful face as it strains with concentration. Barely thirty seconds later, he lets out a deep groan and I feel hot liquid spurting into me.

"I'm sorry. I couldn't help it." He kisses the inside of one of my knees as he pulls out. I move to pull my legs down and get dressed, but he seizes the backs of my thighs and holds my legs up, pulling them farther apart.

Studying the view intensely as the sound of his ragged breaths compete with the music over the limo's speakers.

"What?" I finally ask, feeling a touch self-conscious.

"I was just thinking about Margo's tongue on you. About what that looked like." He says it so casually.

Blood flows toward my clit at the memory of the grotto beneath the French chateau we left. I still can't believe I agreed to that. I know I'm straight, and yet Margo Lauren is one of those sexual beings who could entice anyone to experiment.

And she wanted me.

"Did you like watching that?" I ask softly, daring to reach down and run a finger through my slit, now slick from Henry's seed.

"Yes." A devious smile touches Henry's lips, but it drifts off just as quickly. "Do you want it to happen again?"

"I'd much rather have *your* mouth on me," I answer truthfully. In the heat of the moment—like right now, as Henry holds my legs apart and I trail my finger over my wet, swollen clit—I'd probably agree to it again. That's how Henry gets me to agree to most things, when I'm too wound up to care. "But what do *you* want?"

"I want you to experience enough to know what you want. So you never have any regrets later in life."

"I already know what I want. You. Only you, Henry. Always." My hand stills as I try to convey my feelings through our locked gazes, hoping he can see what's inside my heart—utter adoration for him.

His eyelids shut with his deep sigh, as if suddenly too heavy to keep open. "Come for me."

I slide my fingers over myself again. Ever aware of the people outside.

"Abbi...."

"I'm trying."

"Try harder."

Even though he just came, his cock is still fully erect. "I need your help," I challenge in a playful voice.

With a smile, he shifts forward, close enough to lay his length against me, his tip reaching my clit. "Go ahead. Use it."

This is new. I grasp his cock with my fist and begin rubbing him against me.

He hisses, stalling my hand.

"No, keep going," he says through gritted teeth, unbuttoning the bottom of his dress shirt and pushing it out of the way.

So I do, reveling in the feel of his velvety smooth skin beneath my fingertips, trying to be gentle while I use his cock in place of my fingers to pleasure myself, keeping all my attention on Henry—and his plump pink lips that have touched every inch of my body, on his searing eyes that send shivers through me with every look, on his strong hands that grip my thighs almost to the point of bruising but not quite.

It's not long before that familiar tingle begins running down my spine. My breathing is coming in short pants and I feel the urge to stretch my hips as wide as they can go.

"Now?" he whispers.

"Yes."

"Thank fucking God." Henry pushes my hand away and thrusts his cock into me once again, letting me ride out my orgasm with him inside. Not five seconds later, he's releasing inside me again.

"Christ, Abbi," he mutters, his chest heaving. "What have you turned into?"

I smile. "Don't make me wait so long next time."

With a heavy sigh, he leans down to press a hard kiss on my lips that lasts five seconds. And then he's pulling out and reaching for the tissue box. He quickly cleans himself and me off before tossing the balled-up paper into the trash. "*You're* the one who told me to give Miles some time before he quits on me." He begins buttoning his shirt.

"I know. I'm sorry."

He chuckles. "Don't ever apologize for needing that. And you got my mind off things for a bit." With his words, that deep brooding look settles onto his face again.

I hesitate. "Has she tried to reconnect with you before?"

His jaw tenses, and for a moment I think I've ruined things by prodding. "Once, about ten years ago, around the time I got my trust fund."

"So you think she's after money?"

"I don't know. It could have just been a coincidence. She got a huge settlement in the divorce." He loops his tie around his collar and begins fussing with it.

I reach for my dress—because I need to get dressed—but I move slowly, hoping to get more out of him. "Did she ever give you a reason for leaving?"

"Does it matter? What kind of mother abandons her kids like that?"

"A horrible one," I agree. "I'm just wondering if there's more to the story. Maybe something that happened between your parents. Did your father ever say anything about why she left?"

"Because she wasn't happy." He yanks first his briefs on, then his pants. "Because she was a selfish woman who expected to be the center of attention all the time. And when he didn't give that to her, she started looking elsewhere for it."

"So she had an affair?"

"At least one." His fingers fumble with his belt. "And now my dad's gone and she's hovering. It's rather convenient, with the inheritance ready to be doled out. I don't know exactly what my father gave her in the divorce settlement. He refused to talk about it. The family businesses were out of reach; the prenup made sure of that. But I know she was taken care of." He sighs. "He may not have been the most loving man, or able to give her everything she wanted, but he did love her in his way, and she broke his heart. He never remarried after that."

I reach for him, to straighten his tie, but really just to touch him. "She didn't just break *his* heart, did she?"

His throat bobs with a hard swallow.

"I don't mean to push, Henry, but it's time you faced her and let go of all this anger you've kept bottled up for her. I think it'll go a long way in you moving on from the pain she's caused you."

He regards me for a moment, his gaze unreadable. "Maybe you're right."

I offer him the smallest smile. Inside, my relief is exploding that he might listen to me.

He tugs at my dress, still in my hands. "I really need to get back to work, given I'm losing most of tomorrow, too."

Right. Tomorrow is the funeral.

I pull on my bra and dress quickly. I reach for my panties but Henry seizes them. He bunches them up in his fist, and then sticks them in his pocket.

I giggle. "What are you doing?"

"Reminding myself what's important."

"My *underwear* is important?"

"No. You. You're important," he murmurs, smoothing my

hair off my face. “Giving you what you need is important. Keeping you happy.”

My heart swells. “I’m happy as long as you’re in my life, Henry.” *I love you.* It’s on the tip of my tongue and I’m so damn scared to say it.

“I’ll see you tonight.” He hits the button to unlock the door.

The doorman must have been waiting for the sound because he immediately reaches for the handle.

I stand on the sidewalk for a moment to watch the limo pull away, ignoring the knowing looks.

My heart brims with adoration for that man.

CHAPTER 3

"When was the last time you were at a funeral reception?" I murmur, taking in the Manhattan Wolf's sprawling ballroom and the bustling crowd gathered from a small dais off to the side.

"Last January. My grandmother's. They held it in a church basement." Miles's nose scrunches up. "It smelled like mothballs and cat piss."

I giggle. "Let me guess, they had long tables along the walls, with platters of egg and tuna sandwiches."

"And cucumber. With the crusts cut off. I actually like those ones."

"Yup. Sounds like every funeral reception *I've* ever been to."

But here, tuxedo-clad servers weave through the crowd, carrying delectable canapés and crystal flutes of champagne in a setting that can only be described as lavish. I guess it's only fitting for a man of William Wolf's stature.

Miles makes a sound of agreement through a mouthful of quiche, his brown eyes searching for Henry, who's by the shrimp ice sculpture, speaking to several older men.

"Thanks, by the way. I got a whole hour last night with him. *Almost* uninterrupted. And he was in a half-decent mood."

I smile, even as my cheeks flame. "That's more than I got with him last night." I drifted off on the sectional couch, watching the sky as a spectacular storm rolled through, and then found myself lying in bed next to him when I awoke, unaware of when exactly he came home and moved me.

"But you're definitely getting *something*, aren't you?"

I spin around to find Belinda standing behind me, her arms folded over her ample chest. As usual, the Wolf cove general manager is dressed both provocatively and inappropriately, in a fitted black dress that's buttoned down the front and looking ready to burst from her curves.

It was only a matter of time. I avoided her sharp, knowing gaze earlier as I walked alongside Henry in the funeral procession, at his insistence. But I knew I wouldn't be able to avoid her forever.

"Give us a minute, Miles?" she says, adjusting her stylish horn-rimmed glasses.

With a nervous glance at me, he ducks away, likely sensing the tension swirling around her like a cyclone. She was the first to accuse Henry of employing me for the sole purpose of having an assistant to screw while in Alaska, even though she couldn't see the attraction. But she also couldn't see any other reason for my being there. I didn't meet Wolf Hotel's hiring standards.

He vehemently denied anything besides a professional relationship between us. He had to—his father was breathing down her neck to find out whether his son was keeping in line, given the mounting legal issues around Kiera.

And she bought it.

Belinda leans over the railing. "Innocent little farm girl, indeed."

"So when did you get in?" I ask lightly, trying to steer the conversation away from our deception.

"Henry says it started *after* you left Alaska?"

I feel her inquisitive eyes dissecting me as I try to grab Henry's attention. "So how's Wolf Cove doing?"

Her red-painted lips twist in thought as her gaze drifts to Henry. He's watching now, and he shoots Belinda a warning glare. I sense her changing her mind about whatever she was going to say. "It's fine. But I'm leaving, thank God."

"Really? They still have another month before they close down for the season."

"Everything's in place to run smoothly. I was only there for start-up. Henry wants me in Barcelona."

"To the Wolf that's at risk of shutting down?" Where Henry was supposed to go after France.

"That's the one. I'm flying out in a few days, after I get organized." She pauses. "Will you be going with Henry when he goes?"

Just the thought of Henry leaving again makes my spirits sink. "No. I need to get back home to help out with the farm and my family."

She frowns at a chipped nail. "That's too bad."

I can't tell if she's being sincere.

And I also can't help but look at those lips of hers and think about where they've been on Henry. He said it was only the one night. I don't doubt that she'd happily take another. What woman wouldn't? "Why do you say that?" I ask, unable to hide the wariness in my voice. Is she going to make another play for him?

"Because his mood swings have been horrendous lately and I've finally figured out why. He's much more tolerable—actually, pleasant—to work with when you're around him, and he's a fucking bear when you're not."

My face splits with a smile.

"You're not supposed to find that amusing."

"It's not that. It's just...." My words fade, because I don't want to get into a heart-to-heart with Belinda over Henry, but she has no idea what she's just confirmed for me—that Henry misses me. That our time apart isn't just hard on me.

For a man who isn't good with expressing emotions, actions do speak louder than words, and he expresses his hurt through anger.

Belinda studies me for a long moment. "How is your father doing?"

"Much better, thanks." We spend a few minutes talking about my father's tractor accident before the conversation dwindles and her gaze drifts over the sea of heads. When her face pinches up with distaste, I don't have to ask to know that she's spotted Scott Wolf.

And he's in deep conversation with his mother.

"Who's that woman he's speaking to?" Belinda asks, frowning curiously.

"Not sure," I lie, my gaze searching out Henry. Has he seen her? Does he know she's here? If he does, he's masking his feelings well.

"Someone should go and warn her that she's talking to a lecherous snake," Belinda mutters, looking ready to lean over the rail and spit.

She gave birth to that lecherous snake.

And they seem to be on much better terms than she and Henry are. She's smiling at Scott, and his hand is settled on her delicate arm in a familiar, affectionate way. In a way that makes me wonder when they actually reconnected. I have a feeling it didn't just happen yesterday.

But why is she here again? Henry made it clear yesterday that she's not welcome. How does she even have the nerve to show her face? I'm disgusted by her, but also curious to understand her more. And, while I'm at it, to make sure she knows how badly she hurt her son.

But it's not my place to do that. And, besides, Henry would kill me.

"Well, I've made my appearance," Belinda announces, cutting into my thoughts. "I hope I see you again soon." She hesitates. "And, whatever you're doing to Henry... keep doing it. I've been going whole days without him biting my head off about something. It's been nice." I smile as I watch her saunter away, her hips swaying.

That was my first encounter with someone from Wolf Cove who I lied to about my affair with Henry, and it wasn't so bad. Maybe it won't be so bad, when the staff finds out about Henry and me, as they no doubt will—and soon. My smile grows wider, as I think about what Autumn and Katie will say. And Tillie will be through-the-roof jealous.

I find Henry watching me, a curious frown on his face.

What's that smile about? he mouths.

You, I mouth back.

He chuckles and opens his mouth to respond when a man grabs his attention and pulls him into a conversation with several others.

I take the chance to search out Crystal again. She and Scott are still talking, but now his arm is around her shoulders and they're heading past the crowd of people, toward the terrace.

I can't help myself.

I leave the dais and trail them outside.

It's midafternoon and stifling hot, the only reprieve against the hot sun coming in the form of shaded alcoves and decorative ceiling fans that keep the air from turning stale.

A few guests mill around, laughing as they sip white wine and champagne, waving pamphlets in front of their faces to cool themselves.

I spot Scott's stocky body on the opposite side of the fountain that sits as a centerpiece in the court—a goddess at least fifteen feet high. Feigning interest in the statue, I edge over.

"...I have enough to last me another three months. Four, if I live like a pauper," I hear Crystal say, her tone full of despair. "I swear, William died just to punish me. I never should have agreed to that divorce settlement."

"He would have ruined you otherwise."

"Still... as long as he was alive, I was taken care of. Now? I'm going to be living on the streets."

"No you're not, Mom. Don't worry. I'm going to take care of you."

I frown. Scott is certainly closer to his mother than I expected. And more forgiving of her than Henry, it would seem.

"But what about the mine?" Crystal asks.

"I told you, don't worry about it. Nothing will come of that."

She sighs. "I don't know, Scott. I still think you should fight for the hotel."

"And spend all my money arguing against Henry's lawyers? No way."

"But you deserve your share."

"So did you, and look how he screwed you over."

"Maybe Henry would be more reasonable than William. I tried speaking to him, but he won't even look at me. He's as vengeful as his father was."

"You need to work on his little girlfriend. Get her on your side."

"The redhead. What was her name again?"

"Abbi."

The hairs on the back of my neck stand on end.

"Right. She seems like a sweet girl. Henry will crush her heart." She doesn't sound worried. More like, full of pity.

"Believe me, she's not as sweet or innocent as she lets on. And she must have a golden pussy—"

"Scott! Don't be crass."

He heaves a sigh. "Whatever. Forget about the hotel, Mom. If I'm right about the mine, Henry will end up the chump in all this." There's something in Scott's tone—a promise—that curls my senses.

"Why? What do you mean?"

"Listen, don't say a word to anyone, but there's a—"

"Abbi! There you are!"

I jump at the sound of Miles's voice and spin around to find him marching toward me.

He jabs a thumb toward the ballroom. "Henry's looking for you."

Holding my breath, I dare glance over, to find both Scott and Crystal staring at me. Shit.

"Tell him I'll be there in a sec." I dart for the women's restroom.

"I THINK YOUR HANDS ARE CLEAN."

I look up from the sink to see Crystal McGuire leaning against the stone wall, her arms crossed over her chest. She must have followed me in.

"I don't know what Henry has told you about me—"

"Nothing. He doesn't talk about you." I grab a towel from the basket and roughly dry my hands. Here I was, pushing Henry to give her a chance to talk, but he was right. She's not here to reconcile or apologize, or even to see how her son is doing. She's here for money.

I head for the exit, intent on getting away from this repulsive woman.

"I never wanted children."

Her voice—and her admission—stalls my feet.

She strolls over to the mirror and leans in to inspect her eyeliner. "I thought I had won the lottery when I attracted *the* William Wolf. Of course he wanted to carry on the Wolf name, so I knew I'd have to have at least one child, but I wasn't in a rush to give up my freedom, or to share what little attention he afforded me with anyone else." She pulls a lipstick from her purse. "William was never home. That's the thing with Wolf men. I don't know if you've noticed, but they're addicted to success and control. That's what the Wolf businesses give them. It's exciting at first, being around such powerful men. Believe me, I know. And the money, the way of life, almost made up for the loneliness. All the business trips and the late nights and missed birthdays."

She drags the dusty rose color over her lips. "The red lipstick on shirt collars, and beautiful women smiling secretively. He swore he never touched any of them, but I don't see how he could resist." Bitterness flashes in her eyes—the kind that's dulled over the years, but still flares every once in a while. "Scott was an accident. But when I told William that I was pregnant, he suddenly changed. He was around more, he became more affectionate with me. I wasn't just the token wife that he took to events, I was the mother of his child. I realized that I played an important role. I finally had some control over him. That's why I had Henry. To maintain that control."

I feel my face twist with shock at her candid—and disgusting—admission.

"Of course, I hoped that those maternal instincts would kick in at some point," she adds as an afterthought, and then sighs. "Anyway, it didn't last. Once the boys started growing,

William became solely focused on the family business again, and getting Scott and Henry ingrained in it. Scott didn't take as quickly, but Henry...." She shakes her head and chuckles. "He had an impressive collection of suits and ties by the time he was nine. All he ever wanted to do was please his father. He took to it like, well, a Wolf. He turned out just like his father, faults and all."

"You don't know him. You left him when he was eleven years old."

"You don't think Henry's cold? Hurtful?" Her blue eyes shift from her own reflection to mine. I see the challenge to deny it in them.

"When the person deserves it." I learned that the hard way. But I won't let this woman stand here and talk ill of a son she abandoned and hasn't talked to in twenty years. "He's also passionate and caring, and thoughtful. And honest. And he has more integrity than anyone I've ever met."

"And he'll never make you his priority. I hope you realize that now." She smooths another coat of lipstick over her lips. "Take it from me, you will find yourself gravely disappointed otherwise."

"I don't expect to be his priority. I just want to be in his life. I just want to be able to love him and have him love me. Something you're clearly incapable of, because it sounds like the only person you've ever made an effort to love is yourself. And maybe you're right and Henry is just like his father. But I'm *nothing* like you. I'm not with him for his money or his power. He could give it all away tomorrow and work on my farm, and I'd be just as happy." The moment I say it, as ridiculous as the notion of Henry sitting atop a tractor and baling hay is, I realize that it's true. "Or he could keep working day and night for Wolf. I'd never ask him not to, because I know how important his family's business is to him and I admire his passion for it. And I don't expect to be the most important thing in his life, or that he give me all of his time. I already know that I won't get that, and I'm okay with it. And I *can't wait* to have children." It's ironic, given pre-Henry, I was avoiding Mama's pushes for grandchildren. "Lots of children. Not because I want to control Henry with them, but so I can listen to them laugh and hold them when they cry, and love them. I want to make them feel like they're the most important people in the world, because they are. I will give everything, sacrifice everything for them, *and* for Henry because I'm so madly, *deeply* in love with him." I can't help myself. "But I don't know if I'll ever get to do any of those things with him, because he had an utterly selfish woman for a mother who has left him terrified of—"

"Abbi."

Henry's calm voice stops my tirade instantly. I spin around to find him standing at the door of the women's restroom, holding it shut behind him, his face full of shock.

Oh my God. How much did he hear?

His gaze shifts from me to his mother, who at least looks somewhat chastised.

"Henry—"

"I'll see you at home."

My stomach sinks. What did I just say? I don't even remember, and I have no idea what he heard. It couldn't have been good. But I know when to obey Henry's requests, and this is one of those times.

"I'm sorry—"

"Abbi," he warns.

I head for the door, stalling in front of him, reaching for his free hand with my trembling fingers. Did I just screw everything up between us?

Finally he meets my eyes. He must see the fear in them. "We'll talk at home," he says more softly.

That's the most comfort I'm going to get from him right

now. "You were right, by the way. She's looking for money from the Wolf estate. She lost your dad's support when he died."

His jaw clenches and he gives the slightest nod.

I rush out of there and straight for the limo, shaking the entire way.

CHAPTER 4

The bed sinks with Henry's weight as he slides under the sheets at 3:05 a.m.

Instantly, I reach for him, smoothing my hand over his biceps.

"Sorry, I tried to be quiet," he whispers.

"It's okay, I was awake. The thunder...," I murmur, using the nasty storm that's rolling through as my excuse. Really, I've been lying in the dark, waiting for Henry to come back from the office, where Miles confirmed he'd gone after the reception ended.

Lying here, imagining all the things I'd say to him when he finally came home, so he wouldn't end this—us.

Now I can't seem to find the words.

It's Henry who finally breaks the silence. "I heard them fighting one night, right before she left. He told her that it was over, that no Wolf would put up with a cheating wife. She was screaming at him, blaming him for her affair, telling him that it was his fault for not paying enough attention to her. That he was a cold, uncaring bastard who was impossible to love." Henry's hard swallow fills the air. "And apparently I'm just like him."

"She's wrong."

"Is she?"

"Yes." I shift closer and he fits an arm beneath me, pulls me against his bare chest. I listen to his heartbeat for a moment. "So... how much did you hear today?"

"Enough."

I hold my breath.

"You didn't need to defend me."

"Yes, I did. She's a horrible human being. She doesn't get to pretend to know you."

"Maybe she's right."

"She's not."

He plants a soft kiss on my forehead. "Either way, she's out of our lives. Let Scott take care of her. He's the one she's kept in touch with."

I release a shaky sigh of relief. Henry's not mad at me.

"So... you'd rather I be a farmer?" There's a hint of playfulness in his voice.

"Yes, I would actually." I trace his collarbone with my fingertips. "As long as you're topless and sweaty while riding around on the tractor."

"What would the good folk of Greenbank, Pennsylvania, say about that?"

"I'm sure the female population would be quite happy about it."

"And your mother?"

"She'd accuse you of trying to get in everyone's good graces while you sell the land out from under them to build condominiums."

His deep, throaty chuckle makes my heart swell. "Make sure you pass on my thanks for the flowers, by the way. That was kind of her."

"I will." I've been gone from home for almost two weeks and didn't leave on the best of terms, after Mama resorted to taking a handful of adrenaline pills and giving herself what appeared to be a heart attack to foil my plans to visit Henry in Alaska. We've shared the odd text, just to touch base and to let her know that Henry's father passed and I'd be in New York with him until further notice. And then there were the two voice mails—one to tell me that my father almost fell using his walker and how bad it would have been, and another to note that there would be a floral arrangement arriving at the funeral home from Mama and Daddy and the Enderbeys, and that I should look out for it because those big city florists can't be trusted.

Henry sighs, his arm curling around my body, pulling me closer to him. "Get some sleep."

I guess we're not going to talk about all the other things that were said—like how I'm madly in love with Henry and want children. Henry's children. Lots of them.

Does he even want children? Will he ever consider marrying me?

There's no mistaking how serious I am about him now. I proclaimed my feelings in the hotel bathroom, with him standing behind me, listening to every word.

His heavy sigh fills the dark room. "Yes."

I frown. "Yes, what?"

"Yes, I do want children."

"How did you—"

"Because I know you, Abbi. I can practically hear your thoughts."

"Oh." I let my hand trail from his chest to his abdomen, farther down, to grasp his flaccid dick.

My whole body shakes with his chuckle, followed by his groan. "I didn't mean right now."

I smile. "But definitely one day, right?" I run my thumb in circles over his tip. He begins to harden almost instantly.

"Yes, one day, with the right woman. I won't make the same mistake my father did."

Will I be that right woman? His words spark a memory from yesterday. "You told Scott that your dad knew about us?"

"I came clean before we left for France. Figured it was better he heard it from me than the media, should it for some reason become an interesting story."

"What did he say?" Henry had sworn that there was nothing going on between us. How would a man like William Wolf have taken being lied to, straight to his face?

Silence meets my question.

And wariness creeps in. "Henry?"

"He said that I must be pretty serious about you."

I bite my lip to stop myself from asking the question he *must* know I'm desperate to ask.

Suddenly I'm rolling onto my back, my grip of Henry lost as he fits himself between my legs, resting his elbows on either side of my pillow to cage me in with his arms.

I inhale that heavenly cologne as he fits his face into the crook of my neck to lay a trail of kisses along my jawline. "What do *you* think? Am I serious enough about you?" he whispers, gently grasping my earlobe with his teeth as he expertly finds my entrance without the use of his hands and pushes into me.

I moan, as much from the feel of him invading my body as from his words. I wrap my arms and legs around his body, trying to bring him as close to me as humanly possible as my emotions for this man overwhelm me.

I don't want to spend any more days without him.

I would die if anything ever happened to him.

Is it even healthy to feel this way about another human?

I can't say for sure, but it's the truth.

And I can't keep it in anymore. "I love you."

It's a whisper in the night, against the rhythmic thump of the headboard. And yet it's out there, and my chest suddenly constricts with fear that I've somehow misinterpreted his words.

Henry slows his thrusts to a pause, to peer down at me. I can just make out the handsome, hard curve of his jaw. His eyes are piercing, even in the darkness. "I can't remember the last time I used those words. With anyone."

I run my hands through his thick mane, pushing the strands that have fallen forward back off his face. "But you can feel them, right?"

His long lashes flutter with each blink. "Every damn day." He closes his mouth over mine, ending any chance for more words as he begins thrusting into me once again, this time with the strength and intoxicating beat that is Henry.

We climax together within minutes, shrouded in darkness, to the sound of rumbling thunder around us.

CHAPTER 5

Henry's already showered, dressed in a charcoal suit, and picking from a plate of fruit and crisp bacon delivered by the hotel when I emerge from the bedroom, a plush white robe wrapped around my naked, tired body.

"Margo's in New York. She wants to meet up with you. I gave her your number," he announces through a sip of coffee.

I stop dead. "Meet up? For what?" Paranoia creeps in instantly.

He smiles. "Relax. She tried those demos you left for her and she loved them. She wants to talk more about your plans."

"Oh." My pride swells. *The* supermodel Margo Lauren, who could probably afford to clean herself in gold-laced soap on a daily basis, loves *my* simple soaps, made in the back room of my parents' hundred-year-old barn? "So, what? Are we all going to do dinner or something?" Henry and me, Margo, and her perverted photographer boyfriend, who makes a living taking close-ups of women mid-orgasm and then hanging them in prestigious art galleries around the world.

"Sounds like she's thinking just the two of you, but I'll let you sort that out. I'll be tied up all day with work, and the lawyers in the afternoon, over my dad's will."

"Right. That's happening today." They don't waste any time. I pause. "So, how do you think that's going to go?"

He shrugs. "I've already got the hotel. Scott will get Wolf Gold and they'll liquidate and split the rest, likely. At this point I just want this done and over with, so we can all move on."

Move on with his billions of dollars.

I give my head a shake. How is this even real? How did I, a farm girl from Pennsylvania, end up with a man like this?

"I've gotta run." He leans in to plant a kiss on my lips, leaving the taste of coffee behind.

"Wait. When are you leaving for Barcelona?"

"I don't know yet. Likely in the next few days." His blue eyes search my face. "Why?"

Because I don't want you to go?

Because I want to go with you?

"I'm just figuring out when I'm heading back to Greenbank," I say instead. I've been gone for almost two weeks—a week longer than expected—and while everyone has been understanding, I do have responsibilities that I can't shirk forever.

"I'll sit down with Miles and figure out my schedule today."

"Okay. And I'll let you know what Margo wants to do after I talk to her."

He leans in to kiss me again, this time lingering long enough to occupy his hands with my robe tie, unraveling it. "Just don't let her seduce you again."

My eyes widen at the thought, earning his chuckle. He steps back and holds open my robe. The slow heated gaze he treats me to as his eyes roll over my breasts and farther down makes me think I might be able to keep him for another hour.

With a groan and one last, chaste kiss, he grabs his keys and phone and heads for the door, hollering over his shoulder, "Call you later."

I smile as he disappears, thinking back to those early days of Henry Wolf in my life, and to how far we've come.

"Abigail," Margo purrs, my full name that I hate sounding like chords of classical music on her French tongue. She stands from her seat at the upscale Manhattan café and reaches out to clasp my slightly trembling hands. I'm nervous to see her, I realize.

I know what comes next, and yet having her lean in to air kiss both my cheeks has my blood racing in a strange way, given our sordid history.

But I also catch a hint of my mint-and-lavender soap on her skin, which makes me beam.

"What are you doing in New York so soon?" We only just saw her last week.

She tucks her shiny raven hair back behind an ear as she settles into her seat once again. "I have a photo shoot for an ad," she says, waving it off as it's no big deal. Meanwhile, I passed a billboard of her in Times Square only ten minutes ago. "I took the liberty of ordering a Beaujolais for us. It's light. Good for earlier in the day." As if her words made him appear, the waiter—a rather handsome guy in his early twenties, I'm guessing—is suddenly by our side, holding the bottle of wine out for her approval.

"Perfect." I sigh. It's barely past noon and I haven't proven myself to be the best at handling my liquor.

This should be interesting.

"You must make me more of this soap!" she demands, ignoring Daniel as he empties the bottle into our glasses and his gaze drifts over her lengthy legs, bared by the deep part in her navy wrap dress. She's dripping with sexuality, even when she's not trying. "I want to send samples to my friend Jaden at Nordstrom. She's the buyer for the soaps category. And to Devon. She's the Beauty Care VP at Macy's. Oh! And...." She rambles on, naming all these influential people at these huge stores, leaving my mind swirling.

"So?" She leans in to study me intently through her piercing green eyes. "When can you bring me something?"

Suddenly I'm hit with a flash of those same eyes peering up at me another time, in the grotto of her chateau, when her face was between my legs.

My cheeks flush. It's the first time I've felt even a hint of awkwardness since seeing her. Our conversation has remained friendly and genuine, and completely casual. It's as if what happened between her and Henry and me was natural. For her, it probably was. In any case, I feel oddly closer to her, as if I've known her for years.

"I'd have to go back to Pennsylvania to make some more." And I'll have to call my account manager at Nailed It Branding, the company Henry hired behind my back to turn my hokey hobby into a real product line, to let her know the packaging is perfect and I need more. "A few weeks?"

"*Non!* Sooner, you *must*, Abigail." She reaches over to grasp my hand in hers, her long fingers sliding between mine for a long moment before releasing me. "I am here for a week before I go back to France. I must hand-deliver those packages. It will be more personal and urgent that way, *oui?*"

Uh... oui? "Well... I'm going home as soon as Henry leaves for Barcelona." Which could be any day, I accept with a heavy heart. "I can let you know by tomorrow?"

"Bon!" She claps her hands together. "What are you doing for the rest of the day?"

"I don't know." I check my phone to see that it's almost three. No texts from Henry yet, but that's not unusual when he gets wrapped up in work. Plus, he has that meeting with the estate lawyer sometime this afternoon.

"Then let us go. Daniel?" She guzzles back her wine and holds her credit card in the air. Daniel arrives almost instantly to collect it.

"Where were you thinking?"

"My photo shoot." She stands gracefully and collects her purse. "I was supposed to be there an hour ago." She sees the panic on my face and laughs, then shrugs. "You Americans love your schedules. The French? It's more a guideline."

I doubt whoever is paying for the shoot would feel as laissez-faire about it, but I guess when you're Margo Lauren, you can get away with a lot.

I grab my purse and trail her out, enjoying the midday wine buzz coursing through my limbs.

Ronan: *Cat's out of the bag about you and Wolf. Just a heads-up.*

I smile at the text on my phone, even as a wave of nervousness crashes into me. I haven't heard from Ronan in weeks.

Abbi: *What are people saying? Have they figured it out?*

Do they know that Henry broke his own rules? That we were together while I was his assistant?

Ronan: *No. Doesn't sound like it. Expect to hear from Autumn and Katie soon.*

I let out a sigh of relief. Not that it matters anymore, but I hate lying to everyone and I'll have to if they ask.

Ronan: *They're jealous AF is all. No big deal.*

Everything to Ronan and Connor is "no big deal."

Three dots pop up with another incoming text.

Ronan: I made Connor stay quiet. I'll make sure he stays that way.

About us. About the things we've done together. I can just imagine adding those rumors to the mix.

Abbi: *Thank you. How are you?*

Ronan: *Same old.*

He caps that text off with a winky face and I roll my eyes. "Same old" for Ronan means something entirely different than it does for most people.

Ronan: *And you? What are you up to?*

I chuckle.

Abbi: *I don't think you'd believe me if I told you*

Ronan: *Maybe you can hitch a ride the next time he comes to Alaska. We miss you around here.*

Abbi: *I miss you guys, too.*

I smile at the thought of going back to Alaska.

"Have you ever been to one of these before?" Margo's voice pulls me away from my text conversation with Ronan.

I look up. "Uh... no," I stammer, averting my gaze as the red silk dress drops to the floor, leaving Margo standing naked before me. I've seen this woman naked way too many times. She of course is not bothered at all by it, waiting for her stylists to bring her another dress. "Not like this, anyway." Henry had one done while we were in Alaska, but it was just a guy with a camera. Nothing like this, with lights and umbrellas and a team of professionals.

It's easy to see why Margo is in such high demand. She strolled in front of that white backdrop like she owned the place and began posing with the expertise of a woman who was born to do this.

"Erique!" she calls out as she steps into another dress, this one sheer white.

The director, whose name is actually Eric—but Margo turns everyone's names into French version—trots over, getting an eyeful of her perky breasts before she's fully covered. "I want the photographer to take a few pictures of Abigail."

"What?" I blurt, at the same time as Eric opens his mouth, no doubt to tell her that she can't just demand those kinds of things.

She glides over to him to smooth her palms over his t-shirt clad chest. He's in his midthirties, balding, and, I would think, has no hope of ever appealing to Margo, who tends to sleep with highly attractive people. "She is an entrepreneur with a promising product line and she is Henry Wolf's woman. You are going to be seeing and hearing a lot about her in coming months. You want to be taking these photos."

His eyebrows rise as he takes a second look at me. After a moment, he says, "I could probably get another half hour out of the studio before they force us out."

She smiles triumphantly at him. "Bonnie? Morgan?"

Her two assistants—the twentysomething-year-old girls who came to Henry's penthouse to dress me, that first day I met Margo—come to either side of me, awaiting orders.

Margo's assessing gaze drifts over my frame, currently clad in a figure-hugging navy-and-white maxi dress. A sly smile curves her red-painted lips. "Let's go with sexy but sweet."

I tuck my phone into my purse, all thoughts of Ronan and Wolf Cove forgotten.

"LEFT. More... more... hold! Now reach up with your right hand and toy with the end of your hair. Perfect." Click after click sounds as the photographer snaps a multitude of pictures and I keep my eyes locked on a vacant corner in the distance, trying not to feel the fool.

And appreciating Hachiro much more for taking that picture of me when I wasn't paying attention. Candid photos are definitely my thing.

This?

I hate this.

Yet here I am, in a short cobalt blue silk dress that Margo insists complements my hair color, posing in front of a highly skilled team who normally works with supermodels.

"She needs more lipstick," someone calls out. Morgan immediately runs over to dab my lips with the rose color they painted on.

"I look like I'm about to spill out of this thing," I mutter, peering down. The strapless dress hugs my torso like a corset and poufs out at the waist in the shape of a bell.

"That's the whole point," she whispers with a wink. She and Bonnie spent a good fifteen minutes with their hands on my breasts today, taping and adjusting them just right. I'm well past the point of modesty with them.

"Okay, turn to face us," Eric calls out. "Give us something more sexy... more provocative...."

I stare blankly, first at him, then at Margo.

"A moment." Margo saunters toward me, her movements naturally sleek and enticing. In my five-inch heels and her in bare feet, I meet her at eye level for once.

"I don't know how the hell to do provocative!" I push through gritted teeth, trying to keep my smile, now oozing with nervousness.

"Come now, Abigail. You can do this without even trying," she murmurs, grasping my hair to bring some of it forward, her fingers sliding down the length of the strands, skimming my collarbone, and farther down, to the tops of my breasts. "Just think of Henry. Think of him as he walks into a room, of how your heart begins to flutter at the sight of him, how your blood begins to race. How you can't wait for his hands to roam your body. His hands... and his mouth." She reaches down to place her hands on my inner thighs. "Stand like this," she murmurs, pushing my legs apart. I adjust my stance. She leans in to whisper in my ear, her fingers grazing higher up my thigh playfully. "And if it's too hard to imagine without him here, then imagine *my* mouth." She pulls back to look at me knowingly, somehow drawing me back to that very private moment the three of us shared.

My body flushes with heat. What is it about her that's so enchanting?

Margo steps away to take her place behind the camera, a satisfied smile curling his lips. "She is ready."

Eric lets out a deep exhale, muttering something that sounds like, "So am I."

"Okay?" the photographer asks.

I let out a shaky breath and close my eyes. And think of Henry. "Yup."

CHAPTER 6

Henry is home when I arrive at seven. He's occupied with a phone conversation, his back to me as he stands before the wall-to-ceiling window, looking down at the city below. I quietly admire the view for a moment, of his sculpted shoulders and the way his black dress pants hug his ass. He's tossed his jacket and tie on the couch, and the cuffs of his crisp white dress shirt are unfastened.

He ends his call around the time my fingertips begin itching to touch him. I kick off my heels and saunter forward. "The cat's out of the bag in Wolf Cove," I say, repeating Ronan's words. I've received texts from all of my old cabin mates, including a barely concealed scathing one from Tillie, asking me when exactly it started. "I haven't responded yet…." My voice drifts as Henry turns to face me, and I see the split on his bottom lip and the bruising on his jaw. His shirt is speckled with blood. "What the hell happened to you?" I rush to him, instinctively reaching for his wounds.

He grabs my wrist before I make contact. "It looks worse than it is. I'm fine."

"But... who—"

"Scott."

I groan—because *of course* his brother would hit him—and head to the kitchen to wrap a few ice cubes in a towel. On the way back, I pour a drink of Scotch for him. "Sit down."

"Yes, ma'am," Henry mocks. He flops into the couch, accepting the ice and the drink with a mumble of thanks. He's much more calm than I'd expect him to be.

His questioning gaze drifts over my expertly painted face and then to the cobalt blue dress that Margo insisted I wear home for Henry. "Looks like you had a better day than me."

I roll my eyes. "Margo took me to one of her magazine shoots, and the next thing I know, I'm in this and told to look 'provocative' for the camera. I doubt they got a single decent shot."

"I'll bet they got *plenty* of decent shots." His eyes rest on my ample cleavage, which drew looks and poorly concealed grins from the doormen on my way in.

"Stop changing the subject. What happened today?"

He settles back into the cushions and takes a sip of his drink. And winces. "We met the estate lawyers today, to read my dad's will. There were some surprises."

"But I thought it was going to be straightforward."

"So did I." Henry pauses, studying the drink in his fingers for a long moment. "My dad left me everything."

My mouth drops open.

"Well, not *everything*. He gave Scott the house in Cape Cod. But he left his last shares of Wolf Hotels to me, and Wolf Gold, plus all of his investments and the rest of his assets."

"Wow. That's... a lot." Henry's in shock, I realize.

"You have no idea."

"I *really* have no idea," I agree. "So that's why Scott hit you."

"Basically. And then he said he's going to sue the hell out of me. Can't say I blame him, to be honest."

"But that's not your fault! You didn't write your dad's damn will!"

His head falls back, showing off that jagged Adam's apple that I like running my tongue along when I'm riding him.

"Did your dad give any explanation?"

"He did. He wrote a letter, stating his reasons, that the lawyer read out loud." Henry takes another sip of his drink, winces again. "Scott isn't his son."

My mouth drops open a second time.

"She'd had an affair early on and got pregnant. She told my father that the baby was his and he was none the wiser. Then I came along a couple years later, and he had two Wolf sons, as far as he was concerned."

I quickly play back the conversation from yesterday. "She said Scott was an accident."

Henry snorts. "I'd say so."

"When did your dad find out?"

Anger flashes in Henry's eyes. "When he caught her fucking their accountant and stealing money from one of the charity accounts. A charity for sick children."

I feel my face twist with disgust. "*What*?"

"Yeah. It's all in the letter. That's when all kinds of truths came out and he started wondering about Scott. He looks nothing like a Wolf. So he kicked her out and we were sent off to boarding school. My dad agreed not to pursue legal action as long as she left. He didn't want it getting out in the press. And he agreed to raise Scott as his own, to call him a Wolf. He figured Scott shouldn't be punished for what my mother did." Realization dawns on Henry's face. "It's all beginning to make sense now.... Why my grandparents gave *me* all of their land; why my dad insisted that I run Wolf Hotels. Why he didn't wait to give me the hotel, but he held on to controlling shares of the mine. It wasn't just because I'm the more capable one or because I was the one who truly appreciates Alaska. It's because I'm a true Wolf and Scott isn't."

"So he was never going to give Scott the mine?"

"I think my dad always had his reservations, but no, Wolf Gold was going to go to Scott, until Scott pulled that bullshit with Kiera. It was proof that he's just like our mother. He doesn't care about the Wolf legacy. He just cares about Scott." He heaves a sigh. "That, together with what's in there made him change his mind." He nods toward the thick stack of folders spread out on the coffee table. "My dad ordered an internal audit of the mine operations. He told Scott it was to look for efficiencies, but it was really to see if Scott was running it well. They must have dug a lot deeper than Scott realized they would, because they uncovered budget cuts and safety protocol skips that Scott pushed for. Things that could get people killed. *Will* get people killed eventually."

"Oh my God! Why would he do that?"

"I don't know. But there's money being funneled out somewhere and he's put the family name and the entire business in jeopardy."

My stomach twists with shock. I knew Scott was disgusting, but to actually risk innocent people's lives like that? "When did that audit come in?"

"A week before he died. He met with the lawyers and changed the will that very same day. Wrote the letter right then and there, just in case something happened to him." Henry shakes his head. "That guy really did cover his bases."

"And he didn't waste any time." Though I already knew that about him. When William Wolf found out how Scott helped try to pin rape on Henry, he immediately moved up the transfer of ownership. It was as much a statement to Scott—that he would never get the Wolf Hotel that he so desperately wanted—as it was to prove his confidence in Henry, that he knew Henry's intentions for the family business would always be true.

Henry... his only true son.

I rub a soothing hand over Henry's thigh. "And you didn't know about any of this?"

"No. My dad called me while we were in France to tell me he needed a face-to-face with me, that there were going to be some big changes coming soon. But he didn't tell me what, exactly. And then he died the next day."

"Scott still thought he was getting the mine." He said as much to Crystal. "He must not have known any of this."

"He had no fucking clue. Of course he's claiming that he's a legitimate Wolf and it's all a lie. But my dad had the DNA tests run without Scott knowing."

I shake my head. "And here I thought dealing with my family was hard."

"Told you." He holds his glass of Scotch out for me.

I wave it away, my eye catching on a small, ornately carved wooden box sitting on the coffee table next to the audit. "This is pretty."

"It was my grandmother's."

I hesitate. "Can I open it?"

There's a pause. "Sure."

Inside is a medley of jewelry.

"She could afford the biggest diamonds in the world, but she didn't care for them. Or jewelry to begin with. But she loved pearls."

"I see that." I hold up an elaborate silver and pearl brooch to inspect it more closely.

Henry watches me closely. "You like that one?"

"I do. It's beautiful."

"I gave her that for Christmas one year. It ended up being my last holiday with her." There's a hint of sadness in his voice.

"You have good taste." I set it back in the box and pull out a ring.

"That was her engagement ring."

I hold it up to the light. It's simple in design. The gold band is thin and smooth, with several well-placed claws reaching up to secure a small white pearl at the center. Surrounding it is a cluster of tiny diamonds. Just enough to give it some sparkle. "It's so... understated and yet classy."

"That was her." I feel Henry's eyes studying me as I admire the ring, imagining the kind of woman she must have been. She was really the only mother figure he ever had, and it sounds like he was close to her.

"I think I would have liked her."

"I think so, too," he says quietly. "My grandfather pulled that pearl right out of an oyster. And then he went down into the mine and mined the gold for the band."

"He did not."

"Did, too."

"That's... really romantic." But I shouldn't be too surprised. I've seen the wood cabin that Henry's grandfather built with his own two hands in Wolf Cove, not far from the hotel. That Henry and his grandparents spent their summers in.

Henry takes a long sip of his Scotch. "And now I have that fucking gold mine, full of traps and God knows what else to solve for. How the hell am I supposed to do that while I'm running the hotel? I can't be in all these places at once." He pinches the bridge of his nose, the tension radiating off him. I've never seen Henry overwhelmed before. Even when Wolf Cove was opening and the pressure was high, he remained steely.

Or maybe he's just opening up to show me what was hiding under that tough exterior all along.

"How'd your grandfather do it? And your dad?"

"There were always two generations of Wolfs to manage things. And the hotel chain was half the size that it is now. And they had a guy they trusted for the mine. He worked there for almost fifty years before he died."

"Sounds like you need to find people you trust, too."

"I don't trust anyone."

I stifle my eye roll as I pull my legs up onto the couch, getting comfortable. "You trust Belinda. You're sending her to Barcelona."

"Yeah, she knows what she's doing," he admits, reluctantly.

"I'll bet there's at least *a few* more of her working for Wolf. People you pay a lot of money to, so they can do things like... oh, I don't know... run hotels."

He mock frowns. "Are you telling me how to run a multi-billion-dollar company, Abigail Mitchell?"

"*Me?*" I press my hands to my chest. "I would never even attempt to do that. I'm just here to look pretty."

His gaze drifts over me. "You do look pretty, tonight. In fact, stunning."

"Thank you." I smile and then lean in to plant a kiss on the tip of his nose, afraid to press against his injured lip. "Margo wanted us to meet her and friends tonight. But we don't have to go anywhere if you don't want to—"

"I don't want to," he says without missing a beat.

"Okay."

"I just... I don't know what the fuck to do, Abbi. Even though I can't stand that bastard, at least I could rely on him. I thought I could. Now? I'm it. I'm the last legitimate Wolf."

"Well, for now, maybe. But once you have kids...." My words drift as his eyebrows spike. Probably not the time to bring that up. I settle my hand around the back of his neck, and let my thumb draw along it. "Don't worry. You'll figure it out. You're just shocked and overwhelmed right now. Everyone's allowed that for a night."

He sighs.

"So what do you want to do?"

"*Not* think." He reaches for the TV remote, his calloused hand smoothing over my bare knee as he hits the power button. "Watch the ball game, call for pizza, and fuck you right here, on this couch."

His words are an instant promise that I feel between my thighs. I can't help but shift my legs apart. "In that order?" I ask innocently, watching his gaze drop and become heated with intent.

He slips his hand beneath the hem of my dress and between my legs, all the way to hook under my panties. I gasp as his fingers sink deep into me with one push.

"No, definitely not in that order." He turns the TV off.

"I'm leaving for Barcelona," Henry announces the moment I step into the closet—an entire room, really, with more suits hanging on racks than I've seen in any department store.

"So soon?" I watch him throw open his suitcase and my disappointment swells. I knew this was coming, but after yesterday's shock, I figured he'd be sticking around for a while.

"The sooner I get Belinda up to speed with the new management team in place, the sooner I can get back."

"But what about Wolf Gold?"

As if mention of the mines reminds him of Scott's actions, he reaches for his lip. Aside from the thin cut and some discoloring, it's barely noticeable this morning. "I've already shared the internal audit with the legal team who has power of attorney, and they agree the issues need to be handled urgently. They're shutting down the mine." Henry eyes the racks of custom suits before carefully plucking one out. "Navy?"

"No. That's black. This one's navy." I point to another. "But that's a lot of people out of work."

"That's a lot of people who won't die in the next few weeks. At least, not while in my mine," he counters, grabbing three more suits and carrying them out to toss on the unmade bed, where a garment bag waits. "It's the right thing to do. It gives us a chance to address the biggest safety issues as quickly as possible."

Gone is the overwhelmed and vulnerable Henry of last night. This Henry is the powerful tycoon whose father left him in charge for good reason.

I sigh, unable to hide my frustration as I pull out several pairs of socks and briefs from the drawer for him. "Okay. I guess I'll see what kind of flight Miles can book for me, back to Greenbank."

"You need to get those samples to Margo."

"Right." I updated him on the day with Margo while lying in bed last night. He seemed more excited about it than I am. "For the record, I think she's nuts." Now that I've had some time, I'm able to think more rationally. "Why would Nordstrom or Macy's want to carry *my* product line?"

"If anyone knows that industry, it's Margo. Trust her." He grabs stacks of t-shirts and a few casual outfits and sets them into his suitcase without thought, like he's done this a thousand times—which he probably has.

"But what if her tastes are skewed because of her... feelings or attraction, or whatever it is she has for me."

Henry smirks. "If there's one thing I love about Margo,

it's her ability to separate her sexual proclivities from her business conquests."

"So her helping me has nothing to do with you?" The way she spoke about Henry yesterday, of using thoughts of him to pose in a provocative way, it was as if she was pulling from personal experience. Which maybe she is, because they have slept together. Between that and the fact that she wants to partner with him for the chateau she owns in France, to turn it into a boutique Wolf Hotel location, she has plenty of reason to try to impress me as incentive for him.

"You trust me, right?"

"Right."

"And I trust Margo. If she's helping you, it's because she believes in your product line and she thinks you have something people will want. And because she likes you." Tossing his toiletries kit in, he tugs on the zipper of his suitcase. "She is one of the most honest and transparent people you will ever meet. Take her advice and her help, and run with it. She'll get you set up. Call me before you make any big decisions and don't sign anything without passing it through my legal team, but otherwise you're in good hands. She'll get your business off the ground better than I could."

"I doubt that."

"You've got big things coming your way, Abbi. I promise."

Bigger than Henry Wolf? I think not.

"Why does it matter so much to you, anyway?"

He sighs, almost with exasperation. "I've already told you why. Because I want you to have something in your life that's yours, that you can feel proud of."

I wander over to my suitcase, lying open on the floor in the corner and overflowing with a heap of clothes. I groan. "How much would I have to pay Raj to do my laundry while I'm here?" The male housekeeper comes three times a week to clean the penthouse and take care of Henry's household chores when he's in town.

"I'll add it to his list of responsibilities." Henry smirks, eyeing the mess. He knows how much I hate any sort of housekeeping.

"I might need to borrow a suitcase from you, just to get all this home. I didn't realize how much clothing I bought."

"They're in the hallway closet." Henry is halfway out the bedroom door when he stops, frowns. "Why don't you just leave it here? There should be some room on the left side of my closet."

"Really?"

"Yeah. You shouldn't be living out of a suitcase when you're in New York, anyway." He regards me carefully. "Leave whatever you want. Toothbrush, razor... whatever."

He vanishes out of the bedroom as my stomach flips with both nervousness and excitement.

Henry checks his watch, though the clock on the stove beside him has the correct time. Henry's a watch guy.

And a prompt guy.

"I'll call you when I land." He grabs his phone and MacBook. His luggage has already been taken down by a bellhop.

"Wait!" I round the island to rope my arms around his waist.

"We've already done this."

I peer up at him. "And now we're doing it again."

His jaw tightens. "You know I hate long goodbyes."

"And I hate saying goodbye to you, period."

"Well, unless you're coming to Spain with me, we can't avoid it, now can we?"

"I wish I could, but I can't. You know that. Not until my father's healed enough to get around on his own."

"I know it. But I don't like it," he says in that typically cool tone of his. It's his way of countering his emotions, I realize now.

I reach up to adjust a strand of his wavy chestnut brown hair. The perfect Henry Wolf has to spend a good fifteen minutes styling it to be that way. The tousled look he wakes up with? It's equally sexy, but no one gets to see it except for me. "As soon as my daddy's back on his feet, I'm all yours. I promise."

His lips twist. "Whenever I want?"

I lift onto my tiptoes to run my nose just under his jawline, a weak spot for him. "Whenever you want."

"Wherever I want?"

I let my lips part to taste his skin ever so lightly. "Wherever you want."

"Aren't you supposed to be going back to school?" he asks smoothly, as if this isn't affecting him at all. But his quickening breaths betray him.

"I'm a college dropout, remember?" I have one year at Northgate Christian College in Chicago to go. At first I was deferring it because of Daddy's accident. Now? If I'm being honest, it has more to do with Henry. I know that's wrong and stupid, that my education is important. I just can't see myself trudging through the snowbanks with a backpack of books, or giving all my focus to my studies when this man is around to distract me.

He chuckles. "I thought you were looking into correspondence?"

"I have. I'm starting two courses next week. Jed's taking them with me. We can study together."

"Great." Henry glowers. "Make sure Fuckface doesn't get any ideas."

"Don't forget that Fuckface is the reason I was able to go to France with you."

"Because your mother wouldn't let me hire help for the farm."

"And she never will. Besides, Jed realizes that we're better off as friends." I press myself against him, and feel that he's fully hard. "He knows how I feel about you."

Henry closes his eyes and demands softly, "Say it."

I haven't said those words since the other night. But my courage swells with his invitation. I stretch onto my tiptoes, my lips reaching for his ear to whisper, "I'm madly in love with you, Henry Wolf. I can't stop thinking about you. Wanting you. Needing you. Every part of you."

His responding exhale is long and heavy.

I reach down to fumble with his belt and zipper.

"Abbi, my plane is waiting," he reminds me in a pained voice.

"I'll be quick, I promise," I murmur, dropping to my knees, taking his pants and briefs with me to expose his swollen length. It's in this act, when my fingers dig into his bare hips and my mouth has full control over his pleasure, that Henry is the most vulnerable.

I run my tongue along the smooth underside of him from root to tip, eliciting a deep groan. I tease him for another few long moments, swirling the tip of my tongue around his sensitive tip, tasting the saltiness that begins to bead, before he groans a second time. "Stop teasing me," he hisses, gripping the back of my head roughly—but not painfully—in one hand, his eyes blazing.

With a smile, I open wide and he thrusts his hips, filling my mouth. I can tell it's not going to take long as I suck hard and he swells even more, until my mouth is stretched as far as it can go and my teeth graze lightly against his skin.

The bright kitchen fills with his cries as he releases into

my mouth. "Goddammit, Abbi," he curses between pants. "I need you with me."

I smile, climbing to my feet once again, the taste of him on my tongue. "Soon," I murmur, gently tucking him back into his briefs and doing up his pants for him. I cup his now sensitive area through his pants and give it a rub, earning his sharp hiss. "Until then, think about that. And don't be mean to Belinda. You need people like her working for you."

He leans down to press his forehead against mine. He opens his mouth and I hold my breath, sure I can sense the words on the tip of his tongue, desperate to hear them.

"I'll call you when I land." With a gentle kiss on my lips, he peels away and heads out the door.

CHAPTER 7

The silver Dodge Ram that Henry bought me is sitting beside the barn when the airport limo pulls into the driveway to drop me off. Jed stands next to it, shirtless and deeply tanned, smoothing a soapy sponge over the hood.

I thank the driver and, leaving my suitcase on the grass, I make my way over. "Looks like you took good care of it."

"Of course I did. I want you to keep letting me drive it." He flashes me a grin as he scrubs the grill. "It got pretty dusty out here on these roads. Lots of dead bugs."

I giggle. "Trust me. This is nothing compared to the trucks in Alaska." The truck I used to drive around in with Connor and Ronan had a permanent, thick layer of corpses on its hood.

Thoughts of that bring me to thoughts of those two guys, and how much I miss working—and laughing—with them every day.

"So?" Jed tosses the sponge into the bucket. "How was France? I mean, I know the trip was cut short and all, but you must have had a great time." He may have finally relented to the idea that we're better off as just friends, but I know Jed well enough to know it still irks him that I'm with Henry. Or, maybe more specifically, that he will never be able to compete against a guy like Henry and win.

I smile. "It was incredible. If you ever have a chance to go, you should."

"Yeah... one day, maybe." His hands run through his shaggy blond hair. Not for the first time do I notice how much more muscular he is. The old me would have been drooling over him. Now? Not a skipped heartbeat, not a flicker of desire.

"How have things been around here?"

"Same old. Busy." He throws a hand toward our original barn, to the new shiny silver metal roof that I fought with Mama to pay for. "They just finished putting that in two days ago. Looks good. Solid."

"And just in time. I have a lot of work to do." I tell him about Margo and her ideas.

Jed's mouth is hanging open by the time I'm done. "*Margo Lauren?* You, like, actually *know* her?"

"I do." *You can't even imagine how well.*

"Dang. This new life of yours is something else."

"Tell me about it."

"If you had any idea how many times I've jerked off to her picture—"

"Jed!"

He gives me a sheepish smile and shrug. "What? You don't think when she's standing there in her panties and bra posing that she's not aware what guys are gonna be doing to the end product?"

"Oh, she's aware. I'm sure she'd gladly watch," I mutter under my breath, but not quiet enough.

Jed's eyebrows spike.

"Where's Mama and Daddy?" I ask, changing the subject.

"They went into the city. Your dad's getting the rest of his casts off today."

"Really?" Has it been that long since the accident already?

Jed reaches for the hose. "Yup. Slowly but surely, he's on the mend. The golf cart you had delivered will be super helpful for him to get around. I think he's going nuts from being cooped up with Bernadette."

I frown. "What golf cart?"

"The one over there." He points to the side of the house, where a shiny new black cart is parked.

"I didn't...," I begin to say, but my words drift off as I clue in. Henry. He is, as always, five steps ahead of me. And Jed's no doubt right—Daddy needs his independence back before Mama drives him to drink.

Jed begins spraying the soap off the truck.

"Okay, well, I'll be in the barn if you need me." I hope I have enough supplies. My herb garden is severely lacking. I may have to run into town to purchase some of the annuals that I didn't plant this year, having been in Alaska.

"So, can I still drive this while you're home?"

"Depends how nice you are to me," I holler over my shoulder, heading for the house to drop off my things.

I shriek as a spray of cold water from the hose hits my back.

THE FAMILIAR, musty smell of my little workshop in the barn brings me an odd sense of comfort as I wander around, surveying my supplies and making a list of ingredients to rush order. Margo demanded a dozen sample kits, minimum. The packaging should be arriving tomorrow by courier, so at least I'll have that. It'll take a few more days to get up and running.

The soft whirring sound is the only warning I have before I look up to find the golf cart in the middle of the barn, my dad in the driver seat and grinning like a fool. "I thought I heard someone tinkering in here."

"Daddy!" I dart around the table and rush to him, trying to be gentle as I wrap my arms around him in a hug.

He squeezes me back, some of that strength I've always associated with him back. "I've missed you, girl."

"I missed you, too. What did the doctor say?"

He spends a few minutes giving me the rundown—the lung that collapsed is at about 75 percent, and he'll need the walking cast for his left leg for another two months, but things are looking up. Then, he slides his hands around the steering wheel of the golf cart. "This was some surprise to come home to," he begins, in that tone I know too well. It comes with gentle scolding. "These aren't cheap, Abigail."

I offer him a tight smile. "But you need it. It's giving you some of your independence back, right?"

"No doubt about that." His gaze lifts to survey the new roof. "I haven't actually seen this place up close until now. Looks good. And it was needed, so I appreciate it. But you need to stop spending all your money on me. This cart was too much."

I can't take credit for this and I don't want to. "Actually, it was as much a surprise to me. Henry arranged for this. I didn't know he was doing it."

"I wondered about that." He heaves a sigh. "How is he doing?"

"He's... Henry. He's on his way to Barcelona now, and likely Alaska after that to sort out problems with the gold mine."

"He's a hardworking man, that's for sure." He hesitates. "Maybe too hardworking?"

"Maybe," I agree with a sad smile. "But he's a hardworking man who I love."

"Yes. I'm well aware." He peers around the kitchen. "So, what are you up to here?"

I fill Daddy in, just as I did Jed earlier.

"So you're actually *friends* with Margo Lauren now?"

"Yeah. Why? *You* know who she is?"

"*Everyone* knows who she is, thanks to your mother's fretting." He gives me a look and I roll my eyes. "Come on, hop in. She's waiting for you on the porch."

I oblige, settling in next to him on the cushioned bench. He presses on the pedal and the cart lurches forward.

"It's sure got some kick to it for an electric thing," he murmurs as we sail out of the barn and down the path toward the house. Sure enough, Mama's there, in a flowing blue floral dress, her short curly brown hair looking freshly cut. "Maybe let's not tell her exactly where the cart came from?"

"As if she doesn't already have her suspicions."

He chuckles. "Oh, no doubt she does."

"How's she doing anyway?"

"Better, though she was cranky as all hell for about a week, going through caffeine withdrawals. But she's over that now and your aunt May has been coming by, making sure she's cooking healthier and getting out for two walks every day. She's lost about twenty pounds already."

"That's great!" She's got a long way to go as far as weight is concerned to be healthier, but it's a good start. "And how is she... otherwise?"

"Oh... she's coming around, very slowly. I wouldn't expect her to welcome Henry with open arms quite yet, but I think she's finally realizing that the only thing she's going to succeed at with all this nonsense is driving you away from us."

"She could never do that."

"I sure hope not."

I pat his hand with reassurance as we coast up to the house.

"Just remember, it's always coming from a place of love," he mumbles as the cart comes to a stop.

Mama sets the watering can down and eases her way down the rickety steps. Her breaths are still labored, but I can see a subtle change in her. The bags under her eyes aren't so pronounced, her face isn't quite as swollen. "You heard the doctor, Roger! Your lung is only at 75 percent! What are you doin', whippin' around in that thing at warp speed!"

I lean in to kiss him on the cheek and whisper, "Just remember, it's always coming from a place of love." I climb out of the cart. "Hi, Mama!" I offer with as conciliatory a voice as I can.

"Hello, baby girl. Come here." She ropes her arms around me, squeezing me tight against her, as if nothing out of the ordinary has happened between us. "You know, getting him that thing so he could go gallivanting around wasn't the best idea."

"I'm sure he needs the freedom."

As if to prove his point, he backs up and takes off, hollering over his shoulder, "Going to pick some corn for dinner!"

"You're gonna roll that thing! And then what!" Mama screams after him.

"I'll make sure he doesn't, Bernadette!" Jed runs across the field and Daddy slows down just long enough for him to jump in.

She shakes her head. "See what I have to put up with? That man's tryin' to give me a heart attack!"

I bite my tongue before I remind her that *she* nearly gave

herself a heart attack. Or at least, something that looked like one. "So, how are things around here?"

"Oh, where do I start...."

I follow Mama up the steps and into the kitchen as she prattles on about everyone and everything, as if I've been gone for two years and not two weeks. So and so is pregnant, so and so is splitting up. "Oh!" Mama exclaims, and then hesitates, as if afraid to tell me. "Celeste said that Jed has been talking to Laura Lox a lot lately."

"Really. That's good. I remember her being nice." She was a couple years younger than us in school.

"I suppose so." Mama sniffs her displeasure as she begins rinsing a head of lettuce in the sink. The truth is, Laura Lox could be an anointed saint and Mama probably wouldn't approve.

"Henry wanted me to pass along his thanks for the flowers."

There's an exceptionally long pause, as if Mama is deliberating how to respond. "Yes, well... it's the least we could do after all he's done for this family." She begins shredding the lettuce into a bowl, her back to me.

I smile to myself.

Yes, it's definitely a start.

CHAPTER 8

"Can you have the samples ready by tomorrow?"

I do a quick scan of all the molds I've filled over the last three days. "I think so."

"Perfect! I'll come and get them."

"What?" I frown. "No, I'm in Pennsylvania. It's too far from New York."

"*Oui.* I will come there." Margo's smooth voice fills my ear.

"I can just courier it to you."

"No, I want to see your shop. I want to see where the masterful Abigail creates her pièce de résistance. It *must* be special."

My eyes roam the dusty little room in the hundred-year-old barn that stores our equipment, and then down over myself, at the stained and torn apron that protects my sweats. "I promise you, it's not all that impressive or masterful."

"Impossible. Send me your address."

"But—"

"I will fly out first thing in the morning."

Shit. She's serious. And relentless. Crap. "What time?"

"Let's say eleven." Her musical laughter fills my ear. "But you know me."

"Yeah… that could work." Daddy has physiotherapy in the city tomorrow, and then plans to see some cousins for dinner on the way back. Mama will be with him.

That would be best.

"How's Barcelona?"

"Busy and hot, but productive. To be honest, I've been on the phone for most of the day, dealing with the press around the gold mine shutdown. The media's having a field day."

"Yeah, I read about it." Everyone seems interested in what's to become of the Wolf fortune. Apparently it's the first time the Wolf gold mine has shut down since it opened, and on the heels of William Wolf's death, there are plenty of rumors about why. "Has Scott said anything?"

"Not yet. I'm guessing his lawyers have told him to shut up. The idiot probably doesn't realize that he could go to jail for some of the shit he pulled. He should be thanking me for taking over, but…."

I close my eyes and let myself get lost in the deep melodic sound of Henry's voice, imagining that we're having this conversation while lying in his bed in New York, my cheek resting against his bare chest.

"Your dad made the right choice."

He sighs. "I know. Still, I can't help but feel a bit bad for the guy, losing his father who he found out isn't really his father, and then being all but cut out of the will."

"Because he tried to ruin your life." And made sure my heart got crushed in the process. I scowl. I don't want to think about Scott Wolf anymore. "How's everyone doing over there?"

"Miles looks like hasn't slept in four days." He chuckles darkly. "And Belinda is demanding a salary increase."

"She probably deserves it."

"Are you telling me how to run my business again?" I hear the amusement in his voice. "Speaking of businesses, I hear Margo's on her way out."

"Yeah, she's insisting."

"Are you ready?"

I eye the dozen Farm Girl branded lavender paper gift bags, filled with freshly made samples and lined up on the table in front of me. They're such an odd contradiction to the worn wood and rusted metal everywhere else in the barn. "I finished the samples for her, if that's what you mean." But ready to have Margo here, in Greenbank Pennsylvania, on my family farm, unintentionally dripping sexuality with her every step, her every word, her every touch?

I've barely slept all night, worrying about it. At least Mama isn't here. I told them over dinner that Margo Lauren "might" be coming for a visit "soon" and Mama's jaw just about hit the floor. I'm pretty sure the word "jezebel" was about to fill the kitchen, but then I quickly explained why—that she loved my soaps and wanted to help me sell them at a major retailer—and Mama's tune changed somewhat, though still with heavy traces of disapproval. "Make sure she doesn't try to steal your company like she tried to steal your man," Mama said.

"Okay, Mama," I said politely, fighting the eye roll.

Thankfully, they left for the city an hour ago, with no idea that "soon" meant today.

"Trust her. She knows what she's doing. You can use the article in your website."

I frown. "Wait. What article?"

"The one her friend is going to write." A pause. "What exactly did Margo tell you?"

"That she wanted to come see where I work?" Wariness creeps down my spine. "Why?"

Henry chuckles. "Margo's bringing Ryan McCleary to write a piece about you for *Ares*. It's an indie business magazine with a huge reach."

"What? Do you mean like a journalist?"

"You could call him that. And likely a photographer. Being featured in there will put your name on the map."

"Oh my God. You're kidding, right?"

"No."

I let out a small cry of panic. I cleaned the space up, figuring Margo would take a quick stroll and then be done with it. It's nowhere near ready for a photographer, though. And me.... It's 10:00 a.m. and I haven't even showered, and Margo is surprising me with some magazine writer!

"Nailed It is already working on your website for you, right?" Henry asks, switching topics as my mind is still tangled up in this latest surprise.

"Uh...." When Zaheera mentioned creating a website for me last week, I laughed and told her that the people who buy my soap in Greenbank aren't going to look me up on a website.

"Abbi."

"Soon! They'll start soon."

"And make sure they've already started the copyrighting process."

"Copyrighting?"

"They can send it directly to my lawyers. And they should already have started on the regulatory testing process."

"Regulatory testing?"

"That's going to take a while, so don't waste another day. Ryan's likely going to ask you about me, but don't give him too much. This article is about you and your venture."

"Okay. Slow down!" My head is about to explode. "This

place is a disaster! I am a disaster! I can't have some guy from a magazine here to take pictures! And answering questions? What kind of questions? Why the hell did she tell *you* about this and not *me*?"

"Probably because of the way you're panicking right now. Relax. You can do this. It's not a big deal."

"Says the guy who just said this was a huge opportunity for me." My stomach is in knots. As much as I don't want to end my call with Henry, I need to get moving if I have a hope in hell of being ready.

"I have full confidence in you, Abbi. The article will be great. Margo will make sure of it."

I heave a sigh. "I've gotta go. Have you figured out when you'll be back in New York?"

"For the Wolf charity golf tournament next week."

"Really?" Despite my anxiety, excitement sparks. That's sooner than I had expected.

"Yeah. My dad always represented the company, but now... I need to." He pauses. "I need you there with me."

"Of course. Yes, whatever you need. Except I don't golf."

"You don't have to." I hear the amusement in his voice.

"Okay. I've gotta go now. I miss you." I hesitate. "I love you."

There's a long pause, and when he speaks, his tone is softer. "Call me later."

I spend another twenty minutes tidying things and cleaning the old woodstove before rushing out the barn door toward home.

And plow right into Jed.

"Whoa! Slow down."

"I can't! Margo's going to be here in an hour and I still have to shower." I frown as I take him in. "What the hell happened to you?" When I saw Jed at eight this morning and told him that Margo was coming, he was wearing his usual dirty worn jeans and t-shirt. But he's since showered and traded them in for a white button-down and tie, and dark wash jeans.

And he's had his hair trimmed. It's still shaggy, but now it looks more stylish.

He grins sheepishly. "It's not every day a supermodel shows up in Greenbank."

"So now what? You're going to bale hay like *that*?"

He shrugs. "I'll figure something out."

I roll my eyes. "Well, at least *you're* ready for her," I mutter, running toward home.

"THIS FARM IS as precious as I imagined!" Margo smiles at me as she climbs out of the driver seat of a silver Jaguar. She's wearing a relatively modest plum-colored maxi dress that's so long, the bottom brushes the dirt driveway, quickly coating the hem in dust. She doesn't seem at all fazed by it as she heads straight for me to take my hands and offer me her signature two-cheek kiss. "It's so good to see you again."

The passenger door opens and a handsome man climbs out. He's tall—well over six feet—and, though on the thin side, defined with muscle.

"Abigail, meet my friend Ryan."

He rounds the front of the car with a bit of a hop to his step, rushing over to extend his hand. "Hi, Abigail. I've heard so much about you from Margo. It's a pleasure to finally meet you. I'm looking forward to writing this article." In his bright hazel eyes, I see only eagerness.

"Welcome!" I spear Margo with a look.

"Would you mind terribly if I stole a moment alone with Abigail?" She bats her long lashes up at Ryan.

He smiles down at her, his desire for her blatant. “I’ll call to see how far away Ethan and the others are.”

Margo loops her arm through mine. “We will begin walking and meet you at the barn.”

“What others?” I hiss.

“This way, yes?” she asks, leading me down the path. “Ethan, the photographer; Jolene, who will help spruce up the set. And, of course, Morgan and Bonnie. They will make your already beautiful face shine.”

“I’m going to kill you and bury your body in the fields.”

She laughs my threat off with that musical charm.

“What did you tell Ryan about me? I’m not even a legit business!” Though apparently Zaheera has already begun setting Farm Girl Incorporated up, and the regulatory and copyright processes are well underway. I just found that out ten minutes ago, after calling to tell her I need that website after all.

She giggles, lifting the hem of her dress up a touch as we make our way along the grass, still damp from a morning rain, revealing rose-gold beaded sandals and clear-polished toes. “Do not worry about Ryan. He is eager to help in any way he can.”

“Why?”

“Because he is madly in love with me.” She says it so simply.

“So you’re using him.”

“Yes! And he knows it. But he also knows that I firmly believe in this product of yours.”

I sigh, unsure of how I feel about this entire arrangement.

She squeezes my arm with affection. “Relax, Abigail. This industry is all about friends and favors. I have many friends, and they owe me many favors. I’m simply collecting on them.” Her pretty face scrunches up as she peers into the distance, to where Jed is slowly rolling past in the tractor on his way out to fill up the empty wagon attached behind. "Who is that man?"

"That's Jed. My ex-boyfriend."

"You mentioned him once. He hurt you badly, yes?"

"He did. But it turned out to be the best thing he could ever have done, because then I met Henry."

"Then he did you a big favor." She smiles. And then frowns. "Do all American farmers wear ties while working the fields?"

I groan.

"Wow. You're good," I murmur, as Ethan leans in to show me a sampling of the pictures I just spent two hours posing for. I actually look... professional.

He grins. "What can I say? The camera loves you."

I hesitate, unsure if it's considered rude to ask. "Would it be possible to use any of these pictures for my website?"

"Of course it would be," Margo interrupts with a grin. "You must use them. They are spectacular. Everything about this is spectacular." Her excited eyes roll over the small room that the spunky blonde set designer, Jolene, transformed in twenty minutes, with the help of a box of supplies and some lighting. The previously bare metal-top table is now decorated with strategically placed cobalt-blue jugs filled with lavender and mint, and woven baskets of plump lemons. Fresh, brightly colored tea towels and a copper kettle give life to the worn old woodstove in the corner. Even the barn wood walls look more festive, with colorful plates hung in a line.

"I'd love to get a few more pictures of Abbi around the farm, if you don't mind," Ethan asks.

"I love that idea. Girls, you can finish up here?" Margo

says, leading us out to the sound of the tractor rumbling. Jed is passing the barn with a trailer loaded with hay.

I roll my eyes at the sight of his unbuttoned shirt, tie hanging loosely over his sweaty chest.

"On here, yes?" Margo asks, marching out in front of the tractor. She holds a hand up, signaling for Jed to stop.

I know Jed well enough that I can tell he's sweating buckets of nerves as he climbs down, even though he's trying to play it cool. He tosses his work gloves to his seat and brushes a hand through his hair, sending it into disarray. "Hey. I'm Jed."

"*Oui!* The ex-boyfriend."

He looks nervously at me, his face beginning to turn red. "I'm not sure what you've heard but—"

"Only good things." Margo winks. She runs through quick introductions. "Would you mind if we borrow this for a moment?"

"Of course not! Go right ahead. And I can take you out for a ride later, if you want."

I stifle my laugh. "Where do you want me?"

"How about in the seat, first. Do you need help getting up?" Ethan holds out hand.

"I think I can manage." I climb up with ease, trying not to flash the guys in this short floral skirt they put me in.

"Definitely a country girl." Ryan's grinning. He waggles his pen between me and Jed, asking Jed, "So, you two dated? Did I hear that right?"

"Yeah. For like eight years, I think. Right, Abbi? Since we were thirteen."

"High school sweethearts. Cool."

"Yeah. We were gonna get married."

"Really." Ryan's eyebrows pop with curiosity. "So why'd you break up? Did it have anything to do with Henry Wolf?"

"No. We were already broken up when I went to Alaska," I

cut in, hoping to end that conversation. "What do you guys want me to do up here?"

I spend the next five minutes doing whatever Ethan suggests—"put your right hand on the steering wheel," "Now your left hand," "Now lean back and put your legs up on the dash, crossing at the ankles," while watching Ryan jot notes down that I'm trying not to stress about. At least he's not getting too much out of Jed, who has eased his way over to Margo to try and impress her.

"How about on the hay bales now?" Ethan asks.

"Sure." I hop down from the ladder and climb onto the wagon, this time sure I've inadvertently flashed someone. I settle onto the lowest row, trying to ignore how the fresh cut hay scratches my bare thighs. "This good?"

"Wait, let me help you." Margo turns to Jed. "Would you please help me climb up?"

"Uh... sure. Yeah. Okay." Jed, flustered about where to put his hands on her, finally settles on her tiny waist. He effortlessly hoists her up onto the wagon.

"Merci."

"Yeah... I mean *merci*. I mean...," he babbles, grinning like a fool.

But Margo has already dismissed him, focusing her attention on me. She pokes and prods and adjusts me as if I'm a mannequin, stepping out of the way long enough for Ethan to snap a few shots.

"I think we're good!"

"Wait! One with me now, please." She cozies up beside me on the bale, resting her chin on my shoulder playfully.

"That's perfect," Ethan croons, checking his screen. "Yes, awesome."

"And now one for me." She pulls out her phone and holds it up in front of us, capturing both our faces in screen, along with the view of the bales in the background. "Smile!" Her long, delicate thumbs play with the settings. "There. See? Beautiful!"

"Wow. How did you do that? It looks like a professional shot."

"Hey!" Ethan chirps, but then he grins.

Margo's thumbs fly over her keypad.

I frown. "What are you typing? Are you posting that?"

"*Oui.* On Instagram." She holds it up for me to see her comment: *A beautiful day on a farm with my beautiful farm girl.*

"Oh my God!" I exclaim. "Fourteen million people are going to see this?"

"And I tagged you. See?" She clicks on something and suddenly an @farmgirl profile pops up, with a picture of me from the day of that photoshoot, in my royal blue dress and my breasts spilling out.

My mouth drops open.

She giggles with glee. "Surprise! I asked Henry to make sure your branding company has your social media up. We need to begin building your platform."

"Oh my God! You are worse than he is!"

Her giggles turn into wicked laughter as she reaches for Jed to help her down. He stumbles in his dive to get to her. "Come. We are done work for the day. I brought us a picnic."

I sigh, the whirlwind that is Margo leaving me unsettled, yet again. "Let me guess. There's wine."

"I SHOULD GET BACK TO WORK," Jed says. But he doesn't move.

I don't blame him. We've been settled on these blankets beneath the shade of the big oak tree for the better part of an hour, nibbling on the array of cheeses and bread and other snacks that Margo brought with her. The last thing I want to do is move.

Margo must sense my thoughts. "It is beautiful here."

"It is." Especially now, with the farm fields ready to be harvested.

"Well, I think I have everything I need," Ryan murmurs, scribbling a few last words down on his pad of paper before tucking it into his messenger bag. He peppered me with questions throughout our meal, and I think I handled them well enough. The few times that the conversation swerved toward Henry, I managed to steer it back quickly, giving him nothing more than vague answers.

Jed's phone rings. He checks his screen and then winces. "Ah, shit. I forgot I promised my dad I'd help him with something. I've gotta go." Climbing to his feet, he looks down at Margo, his face filled with pain at the prospect of leaving her beauty.

She stands and takes his hands. "It was lovely meeting you, Jed. Thank you for joining us this afternoon." She leans in to give him her signature two-cheek kiss, leaving him staring at her dumbly for a good five seconds before shaking his head and trotting off.

You won't be needing any magazine pictures to help you tonight, will you, Jed?

"And then there were three," Ryan says. Ethan and the others left a while ago.

"You can swim in there?" Margo asks, gazing down at the lake below us.

"We do all the time. In the summer, anyway." The days are still hot but the nights have really cooled down.

With a long, leisurely stretch over her head, Margo begins walking toward the water. Halfway down the embankment, the view hidden from the farm, she pushes the straps of her dress off her shoulders. It cascades to the soft grass below, giving Ryan and me a full view of her naked form.

Here we go again.

She peers over her shoulder at us, a coy smile touching her lips. “Who will swim with me?”

Ryan’s eyes blaze with heat. He turns to me.

“I have to call Henry back, but be my guest.”

He smiles sheepishly. “I didn’t bring my bathing suit either.”

“I figured as much.”

“You don’t mind?”

“I’ve gotten used to Margo’s... style.”

He doesn’t waste another second, charging down the hill, peeling off his clothes and casting them aside as he goes.

And I immediately text Henry.

Abbi: *I think I know what you mean now when you said Margo would make sure Ryan writes a favorable article.*

Ten seconds later, my phone starts ringing with a Face-Time request.

I smile at the sight of Henry’s striking face as it fills the screen. It looks like he’s in his hotel room.

“What is she doing?” I can’t tell if he’s angry.

“Remember that lake on my property? The one I was swimming in that time you surprised me here?”

His eyebrows raise. “Yeah....”

I turn the phone toward the lake, so Henry can see Margo slowly wading in from the shallow side, seemingly unperturbed by the temperature of the water. Meanwhile, Ryan is down to his underwear, hopping from foot to foot to peel his socks off.

I turn the phone back to face me, keeping my eyes locked on Henry so he knows I’m not watching as Ryan yanks his briefs off.

“And she invited you to join them?”

“She asked if I wanted to go swimming. I politely declined so that I could call you. Do you want me to leave?”

"No." Henry shakes his head, but there's at least amusement in his face. "How did today go?"

I lean back against the tree trunk. "Fantastic, actually." I give him the rundown of the day, trying to ignore the sounds of Margo's musical laughter and their playful splashes. "I think I have this whole 'running a company' thing down. I don't know what you're so stressed about, with your hotels and your gold mine," I tease.

He smirks. "I want to see those pictures they took. Immediately."

"I don't know about *immediately,* but I'm sure Margo can get them within the next day or two." Ethan said he'd work on editing them tonight. "Oh, and by the way, no more conspiring with Margo over creating social media accounts." I give him my most severe glare to let him know I'm not kidding.

He matches it. "If you didn't move at the pace of an injured snail, I wouldn't have to."

"Not everyone moves at your pace."

Henry studies my face. "You look beautiful today."

"Thank you." More softly, I add, "I miss you."

"Yes. Why aren't you here with me, again?"

I roll my eyes. "How's Belinda?"

"Demanding that Miles gets you on a plane for here tonight."

I giggle. "Are you done working for the day?"

"I am." He takes a sip of his Scotch and then asks so smoothly, "Are they fucking yet?"

My lower belly tightens, and I can't tell if it's from his words or that tone. "I'd have to look."

His brow arches. "Yes, I'm aware of that."

With soft sigh, I glance over to the lake. Margo and Ryan have ended their playful game of foreplay and are now facing each other in depths that just barely covers Margo's breasts, kissing intensely, their hands' activity invisible below the water. "Not yet, but I'm guessing it won't be long."

"Where are you, exactly?"

"Up on the hill, under the oak tree."

"Show me."

I use the phone to display the view around me.

"And where's your family?"

"Gone."

"And Fuckface?"

"Jerking off to thoughts of Margo at home."

His lips twist in thought. "And what are you wearing?"

I feel my excitement begin to burn between my legs as I tip the phone to show him the flirty white blouse and short floral skirt that they styled me in.

When I tip the screen back, I find a smile of satisfaction waiting for me. "What's that smile for?"

"Take off your panties," he demands softly.

"Right *here*?"

"Will anyone be able to see you?"

"No." I'm turned away from them, and the grass is long enough.

"Well then... It's been too long. I'm waiting."

With a sigh of both trepidation and excitement, I set the phone down and, glancing once to make sure Ryan's attention is focused intently on Margo, I peel my white panties off and set them in the grass next to me.

I look down at Henry's waiting face. "Okay."

His quirked brow tells me what I already know—that my words are not enough.

Blood begins rushing between my legs as I hold my phone down there, giving Henry the view he wants.

"Push your skirt back."

"What if they figure out what I'm doing," I whisper.

"Do you really think they're paying attention to anyone else right now?"

Margo is pulling herself onto the wooden floating dock, her naked body dripping with water as she sits, waiting for Ryan to follow. She hasn't glanced up here once, as if whether I'm watching or not is of no consequence to her.

Ryan does glance up once, to catch me looking, and then he pulls himself up alongside her. He begins stroking his length furtively as he settles onto his back. The water must be cold.

"Abbi." Henry's voice breaks my intent focus.

"No. They're not paying any attention."

"Good. Then open up for me."

I follow the order, bending my legs and pulling my skirt up until I can feel the warm September breeze against my sensitive flesh. And then I hold the phone down.

"Touch yourself."

I hold my breath—I'm always so self-conscious at the start, and that's behind the safety of a door—and reach down.

"Do it how I like it," he murmurs, and I hear a zipper unfasten on his end.

I run my fingertips through my slit several times, feeling myself grow more wet by the second, and then I push the folds back.

"You have no idea how much I can't wait to fuck that again."

"This?" I whisper, pushing a finger inside. "Show me how much."

The screen angle adjusts, and I watch Henry stroking his ramrod cock. I only get a glimpse and then the camera is back on his face. I can't help the sound of disapproval.

"What are they doing now?"

"She's straddling him." Margo has climbed onto Ryan, facing me, her hands woven through her hair, her perfect body tensing as her pelvis grinds against his cock at a steady rhythm, ripples of water being sent in every direction around them as the dock bobs. Ryan's hands skate over her svelte body, one reaching up to grasp her perky breasts while the other settles on her clit.

With slow, precise strokes, I rub myself to the same beat that Margo fucks Ryan.

"You're getting really wet, Abbi," Henry notes between pants.

A few moments later, Ryan's grunts carry up the hill.

"He just came," I whisper.

"Did she?"

"I don't think so." I watch as she unceremoniously slides off him and shimmies upward. He grips the backs of her thighs and opens his mouth as she settles onto his face. "No, definitely not."

Suddenly, Margo looks up, stalling my fingers.

"Keep going," Henry commands.

Her eyes settle intently on my thighs. She may not be able to see but she knows what I'm doing.

That alone is enough for me. The familiar tingle begins to move down my spine and my legs fall farther apart of their own accord.

Henry's breathing quickens. He's jerking himself forcefully, also seconds away from coming.

Reaching down to grasp the top of Ryan's hair, Margo begins grinding on his face, her free hand smoothing over first one breast, then the other. Her lips part and one moan after another begins rolling out, pushing me over the edge fast and hard. I have to bite my lip to keep from crying out as my body rides the waves rushing through me.

Henry comes seconds later, shifting the screen down in time to let me watch him spill his seed everywhere.

I quickly slide on my panties, assuming Ryan and Margo

will be making their way up here momentarily. But when I dare look down again, Margo has stretched out languidly on the dock and has settled her mouth over Ryan's cock.

She spends the next ten minutes sucking him off while I answer Henry's questions about the interview.

Wondering how the hell these kinds of things keep happening to me.

"THANKS so much for giving me the opportunity, Abbi." Ryan sets the dozen Farm Girl sample bags I prepared into the back seat of the Jag.

The opportunity to what? Interview me? Or to fuck Margo?

I force a wide smile. "Of course. I hope the article is worthwhile for you."

"It's a great story. And Margo loves your products."

"So do you. Remember? You complimented me on the smell of my skin." She grins.

Ryan has the decency to blush. "Right. Well... thanks again."

Margo tosses the keys to him. "You drive. I am tired."

"Sweet. Don't have to ask me twice." He rounds the car and jumps in to the driver side. The engine starts with a purr.

Margo turns to smile devilishly at me. "Today was fun, *oui?*"

I heave a sigh, and then laugh. "It was *something,* all right."

Grasping my biceps, she leans in to place kisses on both my cheeks, before leaning in to murmur in my ear, "He will write a magnificent article for you."

"You don't have to screw guys on my account, Margo."

She winks. "That was for me." With one last kiss, this one

flat on my lips, she slides into the passenger seat. They pull away shortly, honking the horn several times on the way.

And I'm left shaking my head. Thank God Jed left when he did. Though he has stopped running to Mama about these kinds of things. If she knew what'd happened here today, she'd have Reverend Enderbey in to perform an exorcism on the land.

CHAPTER 9

I tap my foot impatiently on the tarmac, watching the Wolf private jet as it glides off the runway and turns toward me. Henry's flight from Barcelona was delayed by three hours due to poor weather. I should have just flown to New York and met him there, instead of having them stop at this small airport outside Pittsburgh to pick me up, but Henry insisted.

The plane's engines are barely shut off when the exit door pops open. Jack Rodan, one of Henry's regular pilots, pulls the stairs down. I assume that means it's safe to approach, and so I do, not waiting for the attendant to give me the okay.

One by one, they all file out—first Miles, who's practically running to get away, then a flight attendant I don't recognize but whose face is filled with trepidation, then Jack and a slender graying man who must be the other pilot.

Henry's voice carries all the way down. He's yelling at someone.

I hesitate at the bottom of the steps, looking to Miles. "Who's he talking to?"

"He's on the phone. Something to do with Scott." Miles

gives me knowing look. He must have some idea about what's going on. "He said to send you up right away, though."

Jack takes my suitcase out of my hand. "We'll be back in the air to New York as soon as he lets us back on."

I climb the steps, my excitement over spending a few days with Henry now marred with worry.

Henry's back is to me when I step inside the plane. His phone is pressed to his ear, his other hand settled on top of his head. "I don't give a fuck! No! You and I both know there was nothing wrong with his mind in the week leading up to his death.... No...."

I toss my purse onto the seat, earning a glance from over his shoulder.

I smile warmly at him.

He turns away. "There's no way I'm going against my dad's wishes. You've seen the audit.... Are you fucking kidding me?" He roars. "Downing is one of the most reputable audit companies! I don't have time for this bullshit. Shut it down, now!" He ends the call, then whips his phone at one of the white leather reclining chairs. "Son of a bitch!"

Knowing better than to ask him what's wrong, I quietly make my way to him and reach around his body. Every muscle in him is tense, and his chest is heaving. I press my face into his back and smooth a hand over hard the ridges of his abdomen, hoping that might calm him down.

"Jesus, Abbi. I'm really not in the mood," he mutters.

"Shhh... I know. I just missed touching you," I whisper softly, my other hand going to his chest, pulling him closer into me. I inhale deeply, his scent alone stirring my blood.

Several silent, tense beats pass.

And then suddenly I'm being pressed up against the wall and Henry's mouth is on mine, his lips forcing mine open, his tongue plunging inside, barely giving me a chance to breathe.

"Henry!" I gasp, breaking free, only to have his mouth move to devour my neck while his fervent hands unfasten the buttons of my blouse in seconds, then my bra. His stubble scrapes across my skin as he takes in a breast, even as his hands yank on my belt.

"Henry!" I glance over at the gaping doorway. "They're coming back any second!"

"Why the fuck would you wear tight jeans to see me?" He curses, ignoring my worry. He yanks them down over my hips roughly, pushing them all the way down to my knees, taking my panties with them.

"Henry!"

He grabs me by the waist and carries me around the corner to a tiny service area, hidden from view of the plane's entrance.

The miniscule metal counter is cold against my bare flesh as he hoists me onto it. He yanks off my shoes and then my jeans past my ankles, throwing them to the floor. "Dresses, Abbi. Skirts. Make it easy for me."

With a sharp tug, the tiny service area curtain closes. He hastily unbuckles his belt and zipper.

"I thought you weren't in the mood," I mock, looking down to see his hard length jutting out.

He hooks his arms under my knees and hoists my legs back, testing my flexibility as he opens me up to him. "I changed my mind."

I cry out with his first hard thrust into me, the intensity almost too much.

"It's been weeks, Abbi." Another hard thrust, and I bite my lip to keep everyone from hearing me. He's tense and angry —not at me, I accept—and he needs a release.

And, I'll admit, this ruthless side of Henry every once in a while is a turn-on. So I brace myself on the narrow counter, and I watch as over and over again Henry drills into me, my body growing more wet with each thrust.

"I had you in France, whenever and however I wanted you, and then in New York, and then nothing for almost three goddamn weeks! I don't like it," he growls as his hips hit my thighs over and over, our skin slapping against each other's. "I'm done with this long-distance shit. I'm done with phone calls and texting, and watching you touch yourself over a fucking tiny screen." He releases my legs and slides his hands around my hips to grip my ass, changing the angle. I moan as he gets deeper inside me, his eyes glued to where we're joined, not relenting the pace as he begins hitting that spot that only he seems to know how to hit. "We need to figure out another plan, because I can't take this anymore."

"Sure. Whatever," I pant, the back of my head smacking against a tiny cabinet, the pressure building deep inside. I won't even need to touch myself to come this time around, if he keeps at this pace.

Ten brutally hard and fast thrusts later, I'm coming on him, trying not to make too much noise. Almost immediately after, Henry's teeth grit together tightly and his thrusts slow. I feel him pulsing inside me.

And then our ragged breaths are the only sound on the plane.

"God, I hope no one came up those stairs," I mutter, the embarrassment of Jack and Miles hearing any of that burning my cheeks.

"I told them not to step foot on here until I signalled that they could, or they'd be looking for new jobs," Henry mutters, leaning in, his forehead pressed against mine.

I rub my hands up and down his biceps. "Do you feel better now?" There's certainly less tension in his arms.

"For the moment."

"Do you want to talk about it?"

With a heavy sigh, he slides out of me and tucks himself back into his pants. “Scott is arguing that my father might have been mentally unstable, and that the audit was false and that I had something to do with fabricating it. He says he has proof.” He shakes his head. “I don’t even want the goddamn mine, but there’s no way I’m letting him have it.”

I brush a wayward strand of hair back off his face, and then another. “I’m sorry.”

His gaze rolls over my naked body, still perched on the counter, my legs splayed. I don’t think I have the strength to move right now. He cups my heavy breasts in an almost reverent manner, tenderly smoothing his thumbs over my nipples. “I’ve missed you.”

“I noticed.” The fact that he’s freely admitting to it feels monumental. I hesitate. “Did you mean all that before? About being done with the phoning and texting and—”

“Ignore me. I’ll be fine.”

“Are you sure?” The last thing I want is for Henry to decide this isn’t worth it anymore. That he’d rather find a woman who’s free to follow him around the world. To be there whenever, wherever he needs her.

“Yes. It was in the heat of the moment. I normally have more control than that.”

Control over what?

His words? Or his emotions?

I swallow away my relief. “Just remember, this isn’t forever. Daddy’s doing really well and summer harvest is coming to an end soon. So if you want me there... I’ll be there. Soon.”

He chews his lip in thought. “Did you get any grief for coming out to see me?”

“No, oddly enough. Mama’s been a lot better lately. I think she might be coming around.” Between my dad’s physiotherapy appointments, and harassing him about speeding around in the golf cart, and complaining about everyone not "mindin' their business" and telling her what to eat and drink and when to go for walks, she seems too preoccupied for thoughts of all the sinful things Henry might be doing to me to fester in her brain.

Of course she turned sulky when I told her I was heading to New York for a few days. She felt the need to vent to Aunt May in the kitchen that same night, loud enough for me to hear from my bedroom. And Aunt May—God love her—put her stubborn sister in her place quickly, reminding her that I love Henry and nothing Mama says or does will stop me from running to him, but the things she says and does will make me run from her.

Mama's mood was improved the next morning, even if it was only a brave front on her part.

With a sigh, he grasps my hips and pulls me down. My legs feel like Jell-O. "Come on. Let's get home."

"So what exactly do you need me to do?" I ask as I settle into the golf cart.

Henry slides into the driver side. "Amuse me." He's in a better mood this morning than on the plane yesterday, though I did hear him raising his voice with someone over the phone while I was eating breakfast.

The golf cart lurches forward and I grasp at my hat before it flies away. It's one of those floppy wide-brimmed sunhats that I'd never choose for myself. I asked Margo what one wears to a golf tournament when they're not playing, and the next day a package arrived at my house in Greenbank with this inside. She insisted it would look "incroyable" on me, and I trust her judgment far more than my own. As far as style goes, anyway.

We speed along the paved path of the elite golf club, an hour's drive from the city.

"Do you golf a lot?" I ask, mesmerized by the rolling hills and perfectly manicured grass, a bright green usually reserved for early spring months.

"Not if I can help it. It's never been my thing." Henry looks as enticing as ever in a fitted black golf shirt and dark gray pants that hug his ass.

"What does it involve exactly?"

He throws a surprised look my way. "You've *really* never golfed?"

"Does mini putt at the church's charity picnic count?"

He makes a sharp right. "Concept is basically the same. We go from hole to hole, trying to sink our ball with as few swings as possible." He smirks. "But there aren't any clown heads or train sets to aim for."

Up ahead of us, seven men loiter on the embankment.

"Is that your team?"

"Along with the caddies, yes." The young blond guy who swooped in to grab Henry's clubs from the trunk of our car is busy organizing his bag.

I frown, eying the empty golf carts. "Where are the other.... I mean, did anyone else bring their wife or girlfriend... or *whatever* here?" How does Henry classify me, exactly? We've never talked labels, and the last time we had the relationship talk, it was, "let's see where things go."

"I'm sure they're getting drunk in the clubhouse. The girlfriends are taking advantage of the spa and conspiring about how to swindle a marriage proposal. The wives are bragging about all the money they're spending and the pool boys and landscapers they're fucking behind their rich, ambivalent husbands' backs. I can drive you back to the club house if you'd rather—"

"Nope. I'm good here."

The corners of his mouth twitch. "You sure?"

"As charming as they sound... yes, I think I'll stay with you."

I note everyone is dressed in similar fashion to Henry, in pants and collared shirts and special shoes. I adjust my seat, tucking my skirt beneath myself. "Am I dressed appropriately?"

"You're with me. You can wear whatever the fuck you want." He told me to choose something comfortable but nice enough for dinner in the reception hall, so I went with the modest emerald green sundress that Margo sent along with the hat, and strappy flat sandals. "But, yes. You look fine." His eyes settle first on my chest, then farther down, to my lap. "How are you feeling today?"

"Still a little sore," I admit.

"Hmmm... I'm sorry about that."

"Are you?"

"Depends." His lips twitch. "Will I be able to fuck you tonight?"

I keep my voice light and indifferent, even as I feel his words right between my legs. "Probably not until tomorrow. Or even the next day. I guess we'll see how I feel."

His jaw tightens and I start to laugh.

"Do you really want to play this game, Abbi?"

"Maybe."

He reaches over to slip his hand beneath my skirt, settling it between my thighs, inches away from my panties. "You'll break *long* before I do."

"I think you're wrong."

He drags his thumb back and forth against my skin, oh so close, and I instinctively open my thighs wider, inviting him in. "I think I know you pretty well."

"Care to bet on that?"

"Winner decides on the prize?"

I hesitate. Agreeing to that last time is how I ended up with Margo. But this time, I can win. "Deal."

With a sigh, he slips his hand out and sets it on the steering wheel once again.

I distract myself with the men ahead. "So who are you playing with?"

"The guy on the left is George T. Rowling. He owns Dillon & Wells."

"The bank?"

"That would be the one. And the guy in the red-striped shirt is Rick Newman. His family owns the firm that manages most of my investments."

"So, another rich guy."

He smirks. "They're *all* rich guys. And important business partners for me, especially now, with the mine. Which is another reason why I had to come to this tournament."

"And that last guy?" The tall, wiry man who watches us quietly. He must be in his forties, his dark hair graying at the temples. There's no hint of a smile.

"That's Dyson, a Wolf lawyer."

I feel my brows lift. I saw plenty of confidential mails between Dyson and Henry, back when I was Henry's assistant and Henry was dealing with "the Kiera mess."

"Does he know we're together?"

Henry pulls the cart up behind the others and hops out. "If he doesn't, I'm guessing he's figured it out now. Why?"

"Just wondering what he thinks about it." Henry's romantic involvements with his staff were termed "indiscretions." Does Dyson consider me nothing but an indiscretion?

"He gets paid to cover my ass, not to have an opinion about my love life."

Henry's love life. That he didn't say "about who I'm fucking" makes my heart swell.

He pauses. "What's that smile for?"

"Nothing."

His narrowed gaze tells me he knows where my head's at. He opens his mouth and I hold my breath.

"There are drink carts at almost every hole, and food stations along the way. And you can't ask for better weather than this." He glances up at the blue skies, not a cloud in sight. It's going to be a nice day—eighty degrees Fahrenheit, according to the weather channel. "I'll introduce you when we move to the next hole. Unless you really want to come up there and listen to a bunch of guys talk business."

"I'm good right here." I hold up the paperback I tucked into my purse. "Mama insisted I read it."

"What's it about?" He smirks. "How to become a nun?"

"Funny, but no, she would *never* suggest that. She's desperate for grandchildren. No, it's some crime thriller she picked up."

"Well, enjoy it. And don't get too drunk." With a fast, hard kiss against my lips, he marches through the grass toward the group. I watch him exchange handshakes with the men. This is the business-savvy schmoozing version of Henry that I've seen before. He doesn't kiss ass, he doesn't fake laugh. He carries himself in a cool, calm way that seems to earn the respect of everyone around him.

After five minutes of chatter, someone flips a coin and Dyson slaps Henry on the shoulder. Henry hollers something at the caddy. The blond guy moves fast, grabbing a club from the bag and running to hand it to him.

Henry may hate golf but I watch him tee the ball and swing like a man who looks like he was born to do this. He sends the ball sailing into the air. I squint, trying to see where it lands. I can't see it.

Henry and Dyson seem happy with the shot though, high-fiving each other.

"Would you like a mimosa, ma'am?"

I'm startled by the server who snuck up, a young blonde around my age standing next to me, holding a platter of orange-colored drinks in champagne glasses.

"Uh...." I glance at my watch. It's only 10:00 a.m.

"It's five o'clock somewhere!" she chirps with a broad smile.

My curiosity outweighs my need to not look like a clueless fool. "So, where exactly are they aiming, anyway?"

She points into the distance. "See that white flag *way* over there, near that pond?"

"Yeah...," I say warily. That has to be some five hundred yards away.

"That's what they're aiming for. And they have seventeen more holes after this one."

I glance back in time to see the banker swing—not nearly as elegantly as Henry, though that might have to do with his protruding belly. This time I see the ball land, halfway to the flag.

"Seventeen more holes," I repeat with a heavy sigh. This is going to take *forever.*

"So... that mimosa?" She shifts the tray closer to me, tempting me.

I shrug. "Why not?"

"YOU MIGHT BE BETTER off selling it. Or taking it public," I hear Rick say to Henry as they approach the carts. "I know you don't like the idea of that but—"

"No. I *hate* the idea of that," Henry corrects. "It's the cornerstone of my family's legacy."

"But is the cost and the risk really worth it anymore?"

"Isn't that what you're here to tell me?"

Rick chuckles. "Just give me the green light and I'll get my consulting firm on it."

"Give me a few weeks to sort out the immediate issues. I can't sell a mine that's plagued with traps and currently—down." He hesitates over that last word as his gaze lands on me, on my tongue as I take a long swipe of my vanilla ice cream cone.

Rick pats Henry on the shoulder and then, throwing a wink my way, heads for his golf cart.

Henry climbs in. "Any good?"

"Delicious. You should grab one." Each hole has held a food truck with a new surprise—beef sliders, shrimp cocktail, chicken tacos—but the soft-serve ice cream at hole seven has been my favorite so far.

"Watching you eat one is more fun."

"Really? Why is that?" I make a point of flattening my tongue and running it up one side, like I've done countless times to him.

His gaze lingers on my mouth for two... three... four beats. "Because I like it when you get yourself worked up."

"*Myself* worked up? And what about you?" My gaze drifts down to his groin, looking for the telltale bulge. He's acting cool, but it's there.

"How many of those orange drinks have you had?"

"Just a few."

"Uh-huh." With one hand on the steering wheel and his other arm slung over the back of our seat, he leans in and takes a long swipe of the cone with his tongue.

I can't help the sharp breath. Just the thought of that tongue between my legs has me clenching my thighs together in anticipation.

The cart lurches forward with his knowing chuckle.

An older man in a forest-green collared shirt with the club emblem on the breast approaches the team as they make their way back to their carts after playing the ninth hole. They share a few words that I can't hear, and then everyone checks their watches.

"...we should change the odds to make it more fair," George is saying to Henry as they reach the cart.

"You're the one who set the odds."

"Yeah, back when you said you hadn't touched a club for five years and I assumed you'd be rusty!" The boisterous banker barks.

Henry smiles wickedly. "You should know better than to bet against a Wolf by now."

"You're tougher than your old man ever was." He turns to me and says, "I need you up there, distracting him for me, okay?"

I grin. "He's pretty hard to distract when he's focused."

"Tell me about it." He climbs into his cart and, with a lazy wave, pulls away.

"What's that about?" I ask curiously.

"Just a side bet we've got going on."

"For how much?"

Henry sucks back half a bottle of water, his throat bobbing with each swallow. A thin sheen of sweat coats his forehead. "Fifty G's."

"As in fifty thousand dollars?" I shake my head. I don't know why I'm still surprised by how these guys throw their money around.

"Relax. It all goes to charity. Loser pays out of their personal account, in addition to whatever their company is already sponsoring."

I guess that's at least noble. "And I take it you're winning?"

"Of course I'm winning." He settles into his seat. "You having fun?"

"Hmm... let's see... amazing food, delicious cocktails, and a really hot guy...." I shrug. "It's all right."

He chuckles, eyeing the paperback sitting on the dashboard. "And a good book?"

Ugh. I should have hidden that. "It was okay."

He frowns. "Really? Your nose was in it every time I turned around."

"The writing is good."

"What was it about?" he asks through another sip of water.

"Murder. Hey, shouldn't we be going to the next hole?"

He watches me for a moment. "You're being evasive."

"No, I'm not."

"Yeah you are. Over *a book*. Why?" He doesn't wait for my answer, picking up the paperback from the dash to read the back. "A woman is accused of murdering her wealthy hotel chain-owning husband?" His brow furrows. "Your mother suggested you read this?"

"I guess she thought I'd like it?" I don't know what the hell she was thinking.

He takes another sip of water, this one long and thoughtful. "So how does it end?"

"They drop all the charges."

"And who murdered him?"

I sigh. "She did. She gets away with it and takes all his money." *Dammit, Mama. You just can't help yourself!*

Henry doesn't say anything for a long moment. And then he starts chuckling. "She's coming around, huh?"

"In her own way."

His chuckles turn to deep belly laughter, and soon I'm laughing along with him. Because what else can we do?

He heaves a sigh. "Mark my words, I will find a way to make that woman like me."

"Yeah, I might have to bet against a Wolf on that one."

"Yeah, me too." He hits the power button. "We're breaking for lunch now."

"Lunch? You're kidding me, right?" I hold up the dish I just emptied with chocolate mousse in it. "I haven't stopped eating. I'm going to explode."

"We don't have to go if you don't want—"

"I don't."

He smirks. "Fine. We have thirty minutes. I can take you on a quick tour."

"I'd love that." A half hour alone with Henry. "Your arms are getting red, by the way. Did you put on sunscreen?"

"No, I forgot." Henry frowns disbelievingly at his arms, tanned a healthy golden color.

"There's some in there." I nod toward the small canvas tournament bag that sits in the small console.

"Oh, good." He reaches in. "I forgot that they include..." His voice drifts as his hand stills. "...women's panties in the tournament bag."

I cover my giggle by sucking back the last of my Long Island iced tea. I've been pacing myself pretty well. This last one though, has me hovering at that thin line I don't want to cross at a charity golf tournament.

Then again, I might already have crossed that line, covertly sliding my panties off when no one was looking.

I roughly clear my throat. "Maybe they figured they'd include some of Henry Wolf's favorite things in the bag this year."

Henry's gaze drifts to my lap and sits there for a long moment. And then, with nothing more than a tiny smile in warning, he grabs hold of my waist and hoists me onto his lap. "You said you wanted to drive, right?" He throws the cart into motion.

"Slow down!" I squeal, as we sail along the path, whipping past other players. With Henry's hands on the steering wheel and controlling the speed, I'm not actually driving. The only purpose this serves is to let me feel his erection growing with each bump and jolt, his arms encircling my waist, holding me tight against him.

He makes a left turn onto a narrower path that leads toward a picturesque wooded area, and slows down.

"What is that over there?" I point to a clearing in the middle of the woods with a pergola on one end.

"They host a lot of wedding ceremonies here. That's one of the locations. It's popular, especially in the fall."

"Wow. That would be nice." I picture rows of white chairs and well-dressed guests, colorful bouquets of flowers and a bride on the small dais, all surrounded by crisp leaves in hues of orange, red, and gold.

"It has nothing on Wolf Cove," he murmurs as we pass.

"You don't have to tell me that." I sigh, sinking back into his chest. "You weren't there for the wedding in the ballroom at the end of June. It was stunning. Though, honestly, I think I'd want to have my ceremony on the ferry, sailing around the bay, with the trees in the background and those little white twinkle lights strung up all over...." Unease creeps into my body as I realize I sound like I've given a wedding in Alaska a lot of thought. And it wouldn't be hard to figure out who I'm imagining for the groom.

Smooth, Abbi. First he catches me telling his mother that I want to have his children, and now I'm telling him all about the wedding I've planned for us. And we've been together, on and off, for what... four months?

Henry admitted to wanting children with the "right woman." I'd have to assume he also means to marry "the right woman." But he's never said anything to hint that he thinks *I'm* the right woman.

But things are just feeling so much... more, lately. I can't help but start to hope for a real future with Henry. Am I a fool?

I bite my tongue to keep from saying anything else stupid and simply enjoy the feel of Henry as we keep going down the shady path. Soon the trees open up to a grassy area, to a small lake up ahead. The path continues around the right side of the lake, where several people meander, talking and laughing and tossing bread to the family of ducks.

But Henry takes the cart off the path and heads left toward the bull rushes and large canopy of trees. I don't bother asking if we're allowed out here, because Henry does what he wants.

He stops the cart beneath a massive oak, in a secluded area. "How's this?" He leans in. His mouth grazes my earlobe as he whispers, "Private enough for whatever you have planned for me?"

Butterflies erupt in my chest, all worries of scaring Henry off by talk of marriage temporarily vanishing. "I don't know what you're talking about."

"No?" he asks lightly, both of his hands settling on my knees. They begin a painstakingly slow climb beneath my skirt and up the length of my thighs, only to stop just short of the apex. Heat begins to pool in anticipation. But the seconds pass and he doesn't dare make a move.

"You've clearly misunderstood my intentions," I say sweetly, punctuating the last word by grinding into his lap, savoring the feel of his hard length against my backside.

His deep, dark chuckle vibrates through my limbs. "So you *didn't* take something off while I was playing my round and leave it in that bag?"

I look down at my dress and mock frown. "I don't see

anything missing." I'm surprised by how even my voice is. I shouldn't be teasing him like this, though. I doubt he's above undoing his pants and taking me right here.

And I doubt I'd be above letting him. He's turned me into a sexual fiend.

"Well played, Miss Mitchell." He grips my inner thighs tightly. His soft, raspy breaths are tickling my ear, driving me crazy.

My back is still to him when I slip my leg over to straddle his thighs, opening myself up for his hands. "So you're saying the game is over and I've won?"

His hands slip away from where they were settled. He grasps my waist and shifts me back to my seat. Climbing out, he makes a point of facing me to adjust himself, the bulge in his pants unmistakable. "Nice try."

He walks toward the water's edge. "I used to come out to this spot when I was young." Reaching down to collect a stone, he expertly whips it at the lake. It skips over the surface five times before sinking. "Until my dad realized how good I was at golf and started making me play."

I feel a touch light-headed when I climb out of the cart. I'm not sure if it's the day of booze and sun, or that all my blood is pooling in my lower belly. I'm aching for release as I settle onto the back of the cart. "So, what *aren't* you good at?"

"Nothing."

I roll my eyes. "Come on. There has to be something. Tell me."

His lips twist with amusement. "Maybe one thing."

"And what's that?"

He tosses another stone over the water. Six skips this time. "Relationships, according to every woman who's ever tried to pin me down."

"I think you're doing okay." Though his words give me pause. Is that a warning to me not to try?

"Do you, really?" He settles his hands on his hips, his back to me as he peers out over the water. "I have a home, but I'm hardly there. You see me a day or two at a time, and have to drop everything in order to do it. I work from the moment my eyes open until they close, and that will never change, Abbi. I am who I am. I enjoy who I am, and my life."

"I know that. I'm okay with it."

"You may think that now. But one day you won't be."

"You can't know that."

"I'm never wrong."

"You are about this," I say defiantly, as much to quiet him as that insecure little voice that always lingers. What if he's right?

Is this the start of him breaking up with me? Is this the turning point, when he realizes we've gotten too serious and it's time to move on?

Silence lingers for a moment. "My mother couldn't handle it."

"I'm not her, Henry. She is a horrible, selfish woman who thought she could change him. She wanted to control him. I don't want to change or control you. I love you just the way you are." My panic begins to rise.

"I know you're not her, Abbi," he says softly. "You could stand to be a bit more selfish. People walk all over you because of it. *I* walk all over you because of it."

"No, you don't—"

"I wanted you in Barcelona. I wanted to phone and demand that you fly out to be with me, to sleep beside me at night. I was going to guilt you into dropping your family and your life and come to me, even though I knew what a difficulty that would be for you. That is the definition of selfishness."

"But you didn't do it."

"No, I didn't," he admits. "But I wanted to."

"And I would have come, happily. Because *I* wanted to sleep beside you at night."

"Is that the life you want, though? Chasing me around the world to get time with me?"

"As long as I knew you wanted me there."

He half turns, just enough to show me his handsome profile as he studies the rocky ground beside him. "I'm not used to feeling this way. Of wanting someone this much. You've brought something to my life that I didn't even realize was missing."

I fight the urge to run to him, to throw myself at him. "I've never felt like this, either. And as long as you never stop looking at me the way you do, that will never end."

He peers over his shoulder to study me. A light breeze rustles his chestnut brown hair as his gaze drifts down the length of my body, slowing at my breasts and not stopping until it reaches my crossed feet. "And how exactly do I look at you?"

"Like I'm enough for you."

"You *are* enough for me."

"Just me? Just like this?"

A knowing look touches his face. He understands what I'm saying. No risqué stuff, no Margo. "That's never been about me. You're a lot younger. You were still a virgin when I met you. I wanted to make sure *you* didn't have regrets."

"I have no regrets. I know what I want." I uncross my ankles and part my legs. His eyes follow the movement, settling between my thighs as I slowly draw my dress up between pinched fingers. Warm air kisses my sensitive flesh.

"My, have you gotten bold, Abigail," he whispers. The bulge in his pants that had diminished somewhat is suddenly prominent again. "At the children's charity tournament will be a first for me." With intent eyes, he marches for me, his fingers fumbling with his belt.

The telltale whirl of an approaching golf cart stalls his hands.

I have just enough time to push my skirt down and adjust my legs back to a sedate position before a cart rounds the bend.

"Fuck," Henry mutters, covertly fastening his belt and adjusting himself behind the cover of the tree.

"Wolf! Someone said they saw you come this way," the lean graying man driving calls out with an easy smile.

"Frank. How are you?" Henry's typical mask of calm has taken over.

"Good, good. The tournament is a great time, as usual. And this weather! Did you order it?" He gestures to the sky with his palms up. "But listen, I wanted to bend your ear for a few minutes. Get your advice." He nods to me. "Hope you don't mind us interrupting, miss."

"Not at all." I smile. "But he might not be in the best mood. I just won a *huge* bet against him."

Henry gnashes his teeth through his smile. "What do you need, Frank?"

"I wanted to get your take on Sanderson Monroe...." The men begin discussing Henry's experience with an architectural company that built one of the Wolf Hotels. Frank is considering hiring them for his next condominium development.

I tune them out, closing my eyes and tipping my head back to enjoy the warmth of the midday sun. Soon, the leaves will begin changing, the days will grow short.

And Henry will have to leave again.

But before long, I will be with him.

CHAPTER 10

"I'm getting the signal." Henry gives his mouth a wipe with his napkin and then reaches under the table to lightly squeeze my knee. "You good?"

"Yes. Of course. I'll just be thinking about how best to collect my winnings." I smile sweetly at him.

He leans in to whisper against my ear, "Just remember, I have much darker proclivities than you do and *many* ways to exact revenge."

A shiver runs through my body.

Smoothly standing from his seat at the dinner table, he heads for the dais at the front of the golf club's ballroom, where a microphone waits for him to give his thank-you speech. Behind him is a wall of windows with a panoramic view of the rolling green hills and a setting sun.

I watch his even, sleek steps with a smile. He didn't play nearly as well on the back nine. He still beat George, of course, but George made several comments about how distracted he seemed.

"So, where did you two meet?" Anastasia asks, her elbows on the table, her owlish gray eyes shifting from her overt admiration for Henry's hard ass to my face. I'd put her in her early thirties—twenty-five years younger than George, I heard him telling someone. She's his third wife.

Also, I'm pretty sure she's drunk.

"At work. I was his assistant."

"Really...." Her perfectly shaped blonde eyebrows rise as she gives me a once-over. "I didn't take him for the type to date the help." There's nothing polite about that look or her words, but Henry already warned me that she can be belligerent once she passes the three-glass mark.

He also warned me that she'd hit on him at some point in the night. Likely right in front of her husband.

I force a wide smile. "We didn't start dating until after I quit."

"And what are you doin' now that you've left Wolf, hon?" Shelly asks with her southern croon. She's Dyson's age-appropriate wife from Tennessee, and I could kiss her for steering the conversation away. Henry said she was a sweet lady and would help serve as a good buffer.

I tell Shelly—and by default, Anastasia, and Rick's wife, Tami—about my dad's injury and the farm. "So I'm going to finish my last year by correspondence and help out where I can there. And I'm starting my own little soaps company. It's nothing big, but Henry's helping me with the business side. I have no idea how to do any of that, and he's so good with it. He really wants me to do it." I'm babbling, but Shelly only smiles encouragingly.

"Wolf is going into the soap business now?" Anastasia mumbles through another sip of champagne.

"Farm Girl Co. That's a great name," Tami says politely, ignoring her. "Tell me more about it."

I spend the next five minutes explaining how I started, and what Nailed It has done for me so far. I even show her a few professionally staged pictures of the packaging that

Zaheera sent over. I let Margo's name slip, because I figure she wouldn't mind.

"I take it Henry's backing you?" Tami asks, her sharp green eyes narrowed as if keenly interested. She's an attractive woman in her late thirties, by my guess, with shoulder-length brown hair and creamy skin.

"Oh, no. I mean, we haven't talked about it but I want to do this on my own. Or at least try. He's already done more than enough."

"Well, it sounds like you have a great product." She reaches into her purse and hands me a card. "I own a kick-starter company. We're always looking for great new ideas to invest in. Give me a call."

"Oh, wow. Okay... thank you." I'm not entirely sure what a kickstarter company is, but I'm not about to make myself look stupid by asking.

I tuck the card into my purse as a server comes around to clear our plates. A second swoops in immediately after with a carafe of coffee.

"Here, Anastasia. I'll bet you could use one of these," Shelly says, shifting her champagne out of reach.

Anastasia grumbles something but doesn't argue, her fingers twirling absently in her hair, her big eyes locked on Henry, who's speaking to a man. He's moments away from giving his thank-you speech. "Gosh, I never realized how much Henry looks like his father. His brother sure got the short end of that stick."

That's because he doesn't have William Wolf's DNA.

I wonder how long before people find out.

"Where is his brother, anyway?"

"I guess he couldn't make it," I answer politely, occupying myself by pouring cream into my coffee, pretending the topic of Scott isn't a sore one.

"Hmm…." Her fingers keeping twirling through her hair. "I never did find out what that huge fight was about."

I frown. "What huge fight?"

"The one Scott and William had right here, in the dining room. Over there." She says it like it's so obvious, pointing to an area by the window. "I don't know what William said to Scott, but whoa, was Scott ever pissed. He must feel the ass, though, if he didn't apologize."

Unease begins slipping down my back. "When was this fight?"

"The morning before he died! Are you not listening!"

I ignore her rudeness. "Scott and William were here the *morning* before William died, and they had a huge fight?"

"Yes!" she exclaims, irritated. She reaches past her coffee for her champagne.

"Good evening, everyone." Henry's smooth, deep voice radiates from the speaker system, ending my chance to ask anymore.

I listen to the ten-minute speech that he so eloquently gives, thanking everyone for attending and their generous contributions to the children's hospital charity fund. He earns shock and applause when he shares the staggering fundraising total. He even slides in several effortless jokes that have everyone laughing and the woman in the room swooning.

While I'm brimming with pride that the man up there is mine, my mind keeps going back to Anastasia's claims of this huge fight between Scott and William the morning before William died. Scott told Henry that he hadn't seen or spoken to his father in the week leading up to his death.

Is Henry mistaken? No… Henry's never mistaken, even when he's drunk.

So Scott lied to him.

Why? What was this fight about?

Did Scott know about William's intentions to cut him out of the will after all?

"AND HE SAID THAT. You heard him say that?" Henry looms over the pint-sized server.

"Yes. I mean, I think so. I mean...." The poor girl trembles as her gaze drifts from an intimidating Henry, to Dyson, to the dining staff manager, then to me who's loitering in the back of this staff hallway beside the dining hall. "The older man, Mr. Wolf... I mean, your father, told the younger guy that he didn't deserve to be called a Wolf and that he'd make sure he couldn't do any more damage."

I wasn't planning on mentioning anything to Henry until we got home. But when he finished his speech and came down to the table, he could see the worry etched into my face and demanded to know what had happened, who had upset me, what had been said. So I had to tell him.

I watched his eyes as pieces fell into place, and I knew what he was thinking before he stormed out of the dining hall to find the server who'd been working that day, Dyson in quick pursuit of us.

Henry turns his menacing glare toward Dyson now. "He knew about the audit." They share a knowing look. "I want that son of a bitch investigated. I want to know where he was the night my father died. And if he had *anything* to do with—"

"I'm on it," Dyson cuts him off, pulling his phone out. He points to the frightened server. "You, come with me." To the dining manager, he demands, "I want the schedule of everyone working that night. I need...." He rattles off a dozen instructions. He may be a lawyer, but I can see why Henry goes to him with messes. "Go home and don't talk to anyone about this. And stay the hell away from your brother, Henry," he warns in a stern voice.

"He's no brother of mine," Henry growls, pacing like a caged animal. "I'm going to kill that mother—" His words are muffled by the sound of dishes crashing into the wall as he sends a dish trolley flying.

"Take him out through the back door and get his car around," Dyson tells the manager. "He doesn't need to be near anyone right now."

I struggle to keep up as we weave through an enormous kitchen in the midst of cleanup and then down a maze of employee hallways. Henry's black Porsche sails up as the exterior doors are opening for us. The valet hops out, his curious eyes on us as Henry passes him without a word and climbs into the driver side. If this place is anything like Wolf Cove, rumors of this will be swirling into every nook and cranny by midnight.

I offer the young guy a smile of thanks as he shuts the door behind me. I barely have my seatbelt on before the engine is revving and we're speeding away from the golf club, the blue skies and talk of deep feelings squashed by the dark night and even darker suspicions.

THE TIRES of the Porsche come to a screeching halt in the valet area of an unfamiliar high-rise.

"Where are we?"

"Stay here," Henry demands, climbing out with purpose.

While I'm relieved to be back in Manhattan and in one piece—Henry tested his car's capabilities by racing all the way home—my frazzled senses are telling me he shouldn't be doing whatever he's about to do. That's why I follow him out.

"Good evening, Mr. Wolf! I'll buzz your brother to let

him know you're on your way up. Would you like us to park your car?"

Buzz your brother.

Oh my God, this is Scott's house.

"Henry, no!" I run to intercept him.

"Abigail," he warns in a low tone, his jaw hard, looking ready to shove me out of the way.

To the doorman holding open the door, I say, "Do *not* tell Scott that we're here. Do *not* park the car."

He looks from Henry to me, uncertainty written all over his face.

"Can you please give us a moment?" I ask, overly calm, to counter my rising panic.

"Sure thing, miss." With a slight frown, he shuffles to the other side of the door.

"Henry, you heard Dyson," I warn calmly.

"I don't give a fuck about what Dyson said. Get out of my way." He reaches for the door handle behind me, intent on pushing me aside to get through.

I step into him, grabbing his forearm, corded with tense muscles. "And what are you going to accomplish by going in there right now?"

"What am I going to accomplish?" He's crowding me, and I'm forced to take a step back, My back hits the glass. "I'm going to find out if that bastard somehow slipped my father a pill that he knew would kill him!" In his eyes, I see the pain that he didn't reveal earlier at the golf club.

"And *then* what? You two can't be in a room together for more than five minutes under normal circumstances. What's going to happen this time around?" By the steely look on Henry's face, by the tension radiating from his body, by the tight fists hanging at his sides, *nothing good* will come of it. I drop my voice to a whisper. "You just said you were going to kill him in front of four people, plus whoever else heard. You can't go in there, and you're smart enough to know you can't, so stop being stupid and let Dyson and the police do their jobs! Do not throw your entire life away because of what he might have done!"

My words must finally sink in.

"God damn it!" he bursts, marching back to his car. He stalls in front of it to cover his face with his hands. Hands that are shaking.

I give him a gentle push toward the passenger side. "Get in. I'll drive us home, if you'll just tell me where to go."

"Go to bed."

"You first," I mumble into Henry's chest, fighting my exhaustion. The nights are much too cool to be lying on this lounge chair on Henry's rooftop deck at 2:00 a.m., but that's where he is, so that's where I'm staying, curled up into his body, my arms wrapped around his torso, welcoming the heat that radiates from his body.

"I'm not going to Scott's. I'm not going to ruin my life."

"Good."

"But I might have, had you not stopped me."

"It's a good thing you keep me around then." I don't think my words even make much sense anymore.

Gentle fingers stroke my hair back, over and over again, lulling me. My eyelids are too heavy to open. "Thank you for standing up to me. For caring enough."

In my thoughts, I smile, but answering will take too much effort so I don't even bother.

Henry shifts, and then I feel myself being lifted and carried into warmth, and settled into Henry's soft, king-sized bed. My ears catch the sound of a zipper pulling and then Henry's hands are on my body, sliding my dress off and then removing my bra and the panties I put back on before dinner.

"Abbi," Henry whispers into the dark, pressing his warm body against mine, pulling the silky white sheets over us.

I drift off to the feel of his soft lips pressed against mine, the sound of his voice murmuring something I don't quite catch.

CHAPTER 11

I lean against the doorframe of the bathroom. "Was that Dyson, earlier?" I woke up to the sound of Henry's deep voice carrying from the living room.

"Yes." Henry drags the razorblade across his foamed cheek. It leaves a fresh, clean line of smooth skin. "The police are involved now."

"Good." I wrap my arms around my chest, hugging Henry's t-shirt that I slipped on to my body, reveling in the smell of it. It smells like him. "What do you think they're going to do?"

"Pull the video surveillance from my dad's place and Scott's, for starters." With smooth precision, he shaves the stubble across his throat. "And likely from the club. Try and get more details about that fight."

"That won't prove anything though, will it?"

"It'll prove motive. They'll also question Becky more thoroughly than they did that night."

"Do you really think she could have given the pills to him?"

"Maybe. Though she doesn't seem the type."

I think back to the blubbering blonde at the funeral. If she has a murderous bone in her body, she hid it well.

Finished with shaving, Henry rinses his razor in the sink and sets it on its stand before turning to face me, giving me a full view of his chest and abs. He must have worked out this morning before I got up; his body looks tighter. "What exactly did you hear him say, the day of the funeral?"

"I can't remember *exactly*, but your mom did ask about the mine. She sounded worried and he told her not to be. That nothing would happen, or something like that."

Henry's jaw tenses as he ponders that. "My dad obviously told him his intentions to take Wolf Gold away from him, but he was legitimately shocked when the will was read."

"He could have been faking."

"I know Scott. That reaction was genuine. Which means my dad must have told him he was going to do it, not that he already had." Henry sighs. "My dad... he enjoyed delivering threats. Scott must have assumed that's what that day was about—threatening him. And that my dad hadn't actually done anything with the will yet."

I think back to the phone conversation I overheard between Henry and William, when I was still Henry's assistant and Henry was facing criminal charges and a lawsuit over Kiera. William threatened to give the hotel to Scott and banish Henry to the gold mines. He was certainly good at delivering that threat.

"Did he say anything else?" Henry asks.

I think back. "Your mom was pushing him to go after the hotel, but it sounded like there was something in the mine that he wanted. Something that would...." My words drift.

"Something that would what?" Henry presses.

I hesitate. "Would make you look like a chump."

"What the fuck are you up to, Scott," he mumbles, his

arms folding over his chest, his gaze piercing the Berber rug with thought.

Despite the topic, I can't help but admire his body, desperately willing the towel that's wrapped around his waist to slip off and let me see more of it.

Unfortunately it stays firmly in place.

"I'm heading into the office."

"And you're leaving for Spain tomorrow?" I ask, trying to keep the disappointment from my voice.

"What?" He frowns. "No. I'm not going anywhere while this investigation is going on."

"Really?" I tamper my excitement. It's not right to be excited. I head into his dressing room to fish out socks and briefs for him, but really to hide my smile.

His footfalls sound against the carpet behind me. "I can't be on the other side of the world. I need to be right here, breathing down the detectives' necks to get answers."

"Makes sense."

There's a long pause. "Will you stay with me?"

I look over my shoulder at his waiting gaze. "If that's what you want." Mama's not going to be happy, but Henry needs me. Besides, I have a bone to pick with her over that book. Wait until Daddy and Aunt May hear about that.

A slight sigh—maybe of relief?—escapes him. "I'll leave you the passcodes to my home computer so you can get work done. I think Zaheera is waiting for some answers from you about the website?"

I glare at him. "How do you know about what she's waiting on me for?" I told her I'd get back to her three days ago with the preliminary design feedback, but then I got caught up in coming to New York.

"Because I'm blind copied on all your emails."

"What?" I let out a sigh of frustration. "I told you to stop interfering!"

"And I have." He closes the distance to collect his socks and briefs from my hands. "But I won't stop making sure they bust their asses for you. Or give you advice when I think you need it. Unless you don't want my advice." There's only soft sincerity in his voice.

"No, it's okay. I do." I'd be an idiot not to want to learn from Henry, and to have his protection. Speaking of which.... "Hey, what do you know about Tami Newman's kickstarter company?"

"I know that Tami Newman has a kickstarter company. Why?" He slips his towel off and hangs it on the towel rack by the entrance to the bathroom, and my eyes linger on his perfect bare backside, distracted.

"Uh... because we were talking about my company last night at dinner and she gave me her card. She told me to call her—"

"No."

My eyebrows pop at the sudden severity in his voice "No?"

"No. You are not having Tami Newman or anyone else back you. That means giving up control and you're not doing that." He pulls up his briefs, sliding his hand down the front to adjust himself. "Besides, you already have the start-up money."

I should have known. "Henry—"

"I'm not arguing about this, Abigail." He picks through a rack of dress shirts. "You have me to help you. You don't need anyone else."

"But then it's just you backing me instead of someone else. How is that different?"

"Because I'm not staking any claims, and not expecting any cut of the profit. It's 100 percent yours."

"But the money is—"

"An interest-free loan with no strings attached. You can

pay it back when you earn out. Or not, I don't care." He turns to settle his intense gaze on me. "You count on me to give you everything you need, because I can and I want to. I take care of you." A little more softly, he adds, "And you take care of me. That's how we will work. Okay?"

"Okay." I swallow against any lingering objections and wander over to pluck a pale blue shirt for him. "I like this one."

"Yeah?"

"Yeah. It makes your eyes pop."

He sighs, and smooths my hair back off my face. "I know you're not with me for my money, Abbi."

"I'm not with you for your money," I confirm, leaning into him, reveling in the heat from his skin, to lay a trail of kisses along his collarbone. On impulse, I slip a hand down into the front of his briefs. "I'm with you for this."

His deep chuckle warms me from the inside out.

"I NEED MORE!" Margo exclaims, so loudly that I have to hold the phone away from my ear. "I am hosting a party next weekend and there will be many influential people there. I want to give them to everyone as gifts."

"Um... okay." Margo's enthusiasm is palpable. Excitement courses through my limbs. "How many were you thinking? Another dozen or so?"

"Two hundred."

I burst out laughing. "Margo, I can't make enough for two *hundred people* for next weekend! I need ingredients and supplies and... I'm just one person! Plus, I'm in New York, at Henry's."

"Why. Is his kitchen not big enough?"

"No, it *is*," I concede, as my eyes roam over the cupboards. The kitchen island alone is twice the size of the tack room.

"Then you must make them! And then you will fly to L.A. and attend my party. Henry will come, too."

Just jump in a plane and fly to L.A. for the weekend. How has this become my life? "That sounds amazing, Margo. But I don't know if that will happen right now. Henry has... a lot going on." Not that I don't trust Margo with the truth, but it's not my place to tell anyone of our suspicions about Scott. "He might not be able to leave New York for a while."

"We shall see." She says it lightly, as if she's already sure the answer will be a favorable one. I'm guessing she's going to phone him as soon as she gets off the phone with me. "But you will make the soaps, yes?"

I sigh. My gut says this is a huge opportunity. If Henry were a part of this conversation, he'd tell me to commit. And it's not like I have much else to do, with Henry gone all day. But it means buying pans and ingredients, and getting packaging. Not that it's very complicated packaging, but still, it required a printer. "Let me talk to Zaheera first, before I say yes."

"*Bon!* This will be *magnifique*!"

RAJ's deep brown eyes are wide as he stands on the opposite side of the monstrous kitchen island and takes in the heaps of dirty pots and pans, and the rows of freshly poured molds.

"I swear. I'll clean it all up!" I cross my fingers across my chest where my heart is, and hold my breath that Henry's housekeeper doesn't quit on the spot. I've met him a handful of times already, so he's likely figured out that Henry and I are in a relationship, but we've never actually talked.

"No, miss. It's no problem. I was just surprised to see

anyone cooking in here. But it's... it's...." He struggles to find words while staying professional. Finally he sheds the cordial persona. "What the hell are you making in here?"

I chuckle. "Soap."

"Soap?"

"Yes. Soap." I hold out one of the wrappers that Zaheera sent over.

"Farm Girl Co," he reads out loud.

"It's my company." It sounds odd to say that.

Raj leans in to smell the row of lemon bars I just finished. "That is... lovely."

"Thank you. It's one of my favorites. Anyway, a friend asked me to make some for her. I normally work from my kitchen back home but Henry said I could use his." He demanded that I use it after I suggested that I could go back to Greenbank for a few days. He also demanded that I rush order as many supplies as I need and charge it to his credit card.

Raj's gaze roams the table. "So these are *all* for your friend?"

"For her party. She needs two hundred by next Friday. I know," I quickly add when Raj's eyes widen again. "I'm crazy for agreeing. But I did, so now I have to get these done, even if it means not sleeping."

"Then I shall let you get to it." He nods toward his arms, loaded with Henry's dry cleaning. "And I must get to my work."

"Oh, by the way, I ran a load of towels and things through the wash already. They should be almost dry now."

A small but genuine smile touches his normally serious face. "Mr. Wolf mentioned that a lady friend would be staying here when he is in town. You are not at all what I expected."

"You're not the first person to say that."

"That is not a bad thing." His gaze takes in the stack of pots in the sink. "Allow me to put some of the laundry away, and then I will come and help wash some of these dishes for you." He disappears down the hall.

I heave a sigh, taking in the mess. When Margo said she wanted soap for two hundred people, she actually meant three different scented soaps for each person. Six hundred bars. I thought Zaheera was going to tell me to go to hell when I asked for the packaging, but the courier arrived forty-eight hours later with boxes of it.

I've been working tirelessly for days, since the first shipment of supplies showed up at Henry's doorstep.

I only have seventy-five more to go. And then there's putting them together, of course. But I should be able to get it done in time to courier to her.

My phone rings and my heart skips two beats as it always does when I see Henry's name on the screen. "Hey," I croon softly, unable to hide my goofy grin, even if he can't see it. "You know, I blame you for introducing me to that crazy Frenchwoman," I joke, stirring the pot of melted glycerin.

"Are you almost finished?"

"Soon. You know, I could get used to working in this kitchen."

"Not if you're going to be selling your products commercially."

I roll my eyes. "So you saw that email, too." He runs a multibillion-dollar business, but of course he manages to keep up with the messages from Zaheera about my rinky-dink business. The latest included a list of regulation-approved production kitchens, because apparently if I want to sell my products to anyone beyond church ladies and visitors at our Greenbank farmers' market stand, they have to be made under certain conditions. "All of those places are around New Jersey."

"Which is close to Manhattan, Abbi," he says calmly.

"I don't live in Manhattan, Henry."

There's a long pause, and I hear muffled voices in the background, as if Henry's put his hand over the receiver.

"So, what's happening on your end, anyway?" Henry doesn't often call me during the day, too wrapped up in meetings and problems. "Are you still going to be home for seven?" I glance at the clock to see that it's five minutes to. Dinner should be here any minute.

"No. I'm meeting with the estate lawyers again." There's an edge to his tone that I hadn't caught before.

My hand stills from stirring. "What's going on?"

"Becky broke under questioning. She admitted to drugging my father."

"Oh my God! You're kidding me!" *Becky* killed William Wolf? "Did she know about his heart condition?"

"No. But Scott did, and guess who Becky's been fucking for the past few weeks, while she was also fucking my father?"

I feel my face twist up with disgust.

"And guess who came home from the golf club the day he found out he was going to lose Wolf Gold and called up Becky to tell her he wanted to marry her?"

"No...."

"And guess who convinced Becky to slip three crushed pills into my father's drink without him knowing that same night, so that his last night with her before she left him would be beyond memorable?" Henry's tone is laced with bitterness. "After my dad died, she called Scott in a panic and he told her that if she said a word about the pills, he'd say she stole them from him and she'd go to jail for murder."

"*From* him? Does that mean—"

"Scott's dick hasn't been working for a while now. He's

definitely not a Wolf." Henry snorts, a poor guise for the emotions that must be rolling through him right now.

This is too much. I have to lean on the counter for support. We were right. "So... what happens now?"

"The police have issued a warrant for his arrest. They haven't been able to find him, though."

Oh my God. "Stay far away from him, Henry. I don't trust him not to hurt you, too."

"Relax. Dyson has four security guards standing outside my door. Of course, that's more about keeping me from hunting down Scott to kill him than him coming after me."

I'll have to thank Dyson for having that foresight. "Okay. Well... we can talk more tonight. I'm so sorry, Henry."

His sigh caresses my ear. "Right now I just want to get home to you."

"Hurry," I say softly, my body aching to lie next to his. "I ordered pasta for us, so it'll be easy to reheat when you come home."

"I'll call you when I know what's going on." The line goes dead. I instantly miss him.

With a sigh, I try to turn my attention back to the melted pot of glycerin.

From the corner of my eye, I notice a figure. I let out a yelp of surprise when I turn to see Scott standing near the kitchen entrance, his arms folded over his chest, quietly watching me.

"I doubt this kitchen has ever been used before." Scott saunters in, his gaze taking in the island.

"How did you get in here?"

"I'm Henry's *brother*, remember?" Scott smiles, but it looks like a sneer. "Was that him you were just talking to?"

"Yes." I glance to my phone, sitting a few feet away.

Scott reaches out to stick a finger into the top of a semisolid lavender bar, leaving an indent. "You couldn't just leave it alone, could you?"

"I don't know what you're talking about."

"Oh, I think you do." He has the same icy tone that Henry sometimes does. It's ten times more sinister coming from Scott though, especially now that I know what he's capable of. And his eyes are glossy. I can't tell if it's from alcohol or drugs, but Scott is definitely on something. "I think you've been telling him things. Things about what you might have overheard." Like a predator edging in, he moves slowly around the island, toward me.

I instinctively step back, putting distance between us. "I'd be more worried about what Becky is telling the police right now. They're looking for you." I try to sound confident, but my voice holds a tremble.

"So I've heard. It sounds like Henry's going to get what he's always wanted, which is me gone."

"He didn't do this. You did."

Scott gives the pot of glycerin a stir. "You know, it seems like ever since you stepped into my brother's life, I've been getting fucked over."

"I've had nothing to do with any of that." I covertly reach for my phone. Could I get to the bathroom in time? I can call security.

"Do you know what it feels like to have someone fuck with your life?"

"Actually, I do. Remember? You fucked with my life, back when you made me think Henry was sleeping with that news reporter. You broke Henry and me up."

"If you hadn't been lying in the first place, none of it would have mattered." Another step forward. "I can't stop wondering what it is about you that has my brother so sunk." A wicked smile curls his lips as his cold gaze slithers down my body. "I think I should find out."

I bolt for the bathroom as a bloodcurdling scream escapes my lungs.

I make it four steps before his stocky body plows into me and I'm tackled to the floor, the wind knocked out of me. He covers my mouth with his hand before I can regain my breath and scream again. My heartbeat pounds in my ears.

"That callous bastard has already taken *everything* from me," Scott hisses into my ear. "So I figured I'd take something of his. Something important."

I squirm under his weight, fighting to break free. But he's far too heavy and strong.

"What exactly do you do for him, anyway?" Adrenaline courses through my limbs as his free hand slips under my t-shirt to roughly cup my breast. "I'll bet he likes these. Fuck, no wonder." His fingers dig under the lace of my bra to grope my flesh

I pull my lips apart and bite down hard, sinking my teeth into his fleshy finger.

"You fucking bitch!" he howls as the taste of copper touches my tongue.

I manage one scream before he grabs the back of my head and slams my forehead against the hardwood. Agonizing pain explodes between my eyes and I struggle to regain clarity. I'm only vaguely aware of Scott tugging my leggings down. "I'm going to love telling that asshole how good it felt to shove my dick inside you. By the time I'm done, he'll never want to touch—"

There's a loud thump and then Scott suddenly grows still, his threats silenced.

A moment later, his body is rolling off me.

I scramble across the floor on all fours to get away from him, while struggling to pull my leggings up

"Miss Abbi?"

Raj stands over Scott, the handle of a heavy-bottomed pan gripped within his fist, fear and shock filling his face.

I let out a shaky cry of relief. I'd forgotten he was here.

We both stare at Scott's unmoving body, waiting for a twitch, a stir. Something to tell us we should run.

But after a minute of nothing, a new wariness settles in."Raj, how hard did you hit him?"

"Hard. Very very hard," he admits, his light Indian accent ringing with worry. He crouches down next to Scott, to press two fingertips to his throat where a pulse would be.

His caramel complexion pales.

CHAPTER 12

"…Don't believe it's a concussion, but if she starts vomiting, get her to the hospital immediately.

I close my eyes and revel in the feel of the ice pack against the sizeable lump on my forehead as Henry speaks to the doctor just outside the bedroom door.

"Don't let her sleep too long. An hour at a time at most for tonight. Just as a precaution."

As if I'm going to be able to sleep tonight, I want to holler.

By the time Henry raced into the penthouse with Dyson in tow, after getting a courtesy call from the head of security about "an altercation" involving his brother, this place was crawling with police and paramedics. Henry's normally cool and collected façade was replaced by pale-faced panic. He saw me and looked ready to vomit.

Hours of chaos later, the penthouse is finally quiet once again.

Scott was pronounced dead at the hospital.

As much as I couldn't stand the guy, as much as he deserved a harsh punishment for all the harm he caused Henry, the memory of his dead body sprawled out on the hardwood is firmly emblazoned in my mind, making me tremble each time it creeps into the forefront.

Soft footfalls approach, and a moment later the bed sinks under Henry's weight. His warm hand settles on my shoulder to caress it. "How are you feeling?"

"Like my head was smashed into the hardwood floor." It's a dull ache now, but it's terrible all the same. At least I didn't need stitches.

"Let me see?" Ever so gently, he lifts the ice pack from my forehead. His handsome face winces. "Fuck. I'm so sorry—"

"This isn't your fault."

"Like hell it isn't." He settles the ice pack back in place and then he's on his feet again, and pacing, his hands on his hips. "Scott knew I pushed for the investigation, so he went after you to hurt me. He figured you'd be here and I wouldn't be."

"But he didn't figure on Raj being here, thank God." I sigh. "Either way, it's over with, and I'm fine."

"Are you really?" Henry's eyes drift downward knowingly, to my thin cotton t-shirt. He heard me give the police my statement. He knows exactly where Scott touched me.

I fight the urge to shudder. "It's no big deal. He didn't get too far."

Silence hangs in the bedroom.

Finally, Henry asks, "Do you want me to call your family?"

"God, no." The very idea of my mother's voice in my ear right now makes me wince. "They can't find out about this."

"It's going to be impossible to—"

"They can't know that he tried to—" My voice catches on the word. Mama will never accept Henry if she hears what his brother—blood-related or not—almost succeeded at doing to me.

"Fine. I'll see what I can do to keep it out of the news. Just...." Henry sighs heavily, and his hands push through his thick mane of dark hair. "Tell me what to do to fix this, Abbi, so you don't...." His words stop as he clenches his jaw.

"Don't what?"

It's a moment before he answers. "So you don't decide this isn't worth it anymore."

"What are you talking about?" I attempt to sit up, but the pain in my hip and shoulder from where I hit the hardwood floor when Scott took me down is too much, and I finally give up on that idea. "What isn't worth it?"

"This." He gestures between us.

I study his face and, for the first time, see the fear in it. Still, I feel like laughing at the idea. "Why would I *ever* do that?"

"Oh, I don't know, Abbi!" He throws his hands in the air. "Maybe because my brother just tried to rape you! Maybe because my brother conspired to kill my father! Why the fuck would you want anything to do with me after this?"

"You aren't Scott. You didn't do anything to deserve what happened today, any more than I did."

"I wouldn't be so sure." There's something in his tone....

I frown. "Why would you think that?"

With a second heavy sigh, he sits down beside me again, his gaze on the soft ice pack that's molded to my hip, helping to soothe the bruising. "Scott used to be married."

"Right." I remember Tillie saying something about it.

"And he'd probably still be married, if it weren't for me."

My mouth drops open. "You slept with your brother's wife!"

"No! I mean, she probably would have been willing if I'd expressed interest, but...." When Henry sees my disapproving glare, he quickly continues. "He was cheating on her. He thought he was being covert about it, but I found out. I could have left it alone, but instead I made sure compromising pictures landed in her hands. Pictures that she could use to nullify the prenup they signed when they got married. Because of me, he had to pay out a shit ton of money. He accused me of stabbing him in the back. That was six years ago. We'd never been on good terms, but that's when things *really* turned sour between us."

"So you protected the poor woman from her cheating husband. I don't think you did anything wrong."

Henry's face turns sheepish. "Yeah... except she wasn't a poor woman. She was a bitch. I hated her. I didn't do it to protect her. I did it to fuck him over because he was a bastard and he made Belinda's life hell after she turned his advances down."

I'll never understand their relationship, but now's not the time to try. "Regardless, none of what's happened is anyone's fault but Scott's." And he has paid the ultimate price for it.

Once again, heavy silence lingers in the bedroom. From downstairs, the clang of pots and pans carries.

"Raj. He's cleaning up," Henry says by way of explanation.

"Seriously? You didn't tell him to go home?" The poor man killed someone while on shift tonight!

"He said he didn't want to go home to an empty house yet. He begged me to let him stay and clean up."

I sigh. "Is he going to be okay? I mean, legally?"

"Dyson's talking to the DA but he's pretty sure they'll rule it was in defense and completely unintended. Either way, I'll make sure he has the best lawyers money has to buy."

"He definitely deserves a huge raise," I joke. "I doubt 'clubbing employer's rapist brother to death with pot' is in his job description." The man was shaking while being questioned by the police.

Henry says nothing though, his piercing stare shifting from my face to my body and back again. His fists are balled up in his lap and his jaw is rigid.

"What is it?"

"I fucking *hate* that his hands were on you," he admits through gritted teeth. "It's making me sick."

My stomach tightens. "That's what he wanted. He wanted to...." My words drift. I don't want to repeat his exact words again. Once to the police was enough. "He said you wouldn't want to touch me again. Is that true? That you don't want to touch me?"

Henry's heavy gaze lifts to meet my eyes. "No. That's not true," he says evenly.

I swallow my doubt. "Then do it. Touch me. Please. I need to erase those other memories."

He opens his mouth, but hesitates. "Are you sure?"

"Yes. I need you to touch me."

Henry doesn't waste any more time, slipping his hand beneath my t-shirt, grazing over my abdomen on the way up to settle on my breast. "This one, right?"

I swallow. "Yes."

Where Scott's fingers were like thorns, Henry's are like the ocean, a soft caress over my skin. He quickly abandons the idea of sliding aside the lace cup for altogether unfastening my bra. Cool air kisses my sensitive skin as he lifts my t-shirt up and exposes my breasts.

Leaning in, he takes my left nipple into his mouth. I stroke my fingers through his soft hair and watch quietly as he spends the next few moments focused there, his hand and tongue reverent in their ministrations.

"What about here?" His mouth shifts to my bruised shoulder, pushing aside the cotton sleeve and the ice pack to feather my skin with kisses. "Does that help?"

"Yes." My chest swells with love for this man, and the rare doting side he's showing me. It almost makes everything I went through tonight worthwhile, just to see that he's capable of this kind of tenderness.

Henry shifts and, hovering carefully over me so as not to

put weight anywhere, he presses his mouth against my lips. "No one—not Scott, not anyone else—could *ever* make me not desire you," he says in a low, even tone. "Do you understand that?"

"Yes."

"Do you believe me?"

I reach up to smooth my palm over his cheek, now prickly with evening stubble. "I believe you."

He sighs. "When they called me to tell me what had happened…." I feel his jaw clench beneath my touch. "I was so sure I would lose you."

"No."

"I can't lose you. Ever." Rare emotion pours from his voice.

"You won't. Ever."

Piercing blue eyes bore into me as a swirl of unreadable thoughts pass through them. His chest rises with a deep inhale. And then the ends of his mouth curve upward ever so slightly.

"What?"

"Nothing. It's just…." His fingers skate over my cheek, pushing a wayward strand of my hair back in their study of the shape. "Never in a million years did I expect to fall in love with that virgin farm girl from Greenbank, Pennsylvania, in the interview video."

My breath catches in my throat. Did I just hear that correctly?

Did Henry finally say….

"I'm in love with you, Abigail Mitchell."

My eyes brim with tears as I commit this moment—his words, the sound of his voice, the look in his eyes—to memory. "I love you, too. So much, it hurts."

He takes another deep breath, as if he's absorbing this

moment, too, and then his lips drift over mine. "Where exactly does that hurt you?" he whispers.

"Everywhere."

"*Every*where?"

"Yes. Right down into my soul."

"Here?" He lays kisses along my jawline, down toward my collarbone, his lips barely a whisper against my skin.

I shiver. "Yes."

"What about here?" He shifts down.

I sigh against the feel of Henry's tongue dragging over one nipple first, and then the other. His stubble scratches across my skin as he moves farther, over my stomach, to the elastic band of my leggings, leaving a wet trail of kisses, sending shivers everywhere. "Here?"

Anticipation stirs between my legs. "Definitely there."

He sits up. With a gentle hand, he moves away the ice pack that's comforting my bruised hip. His fingers curl beneath the top of my leggings. He pauses to peer questioningly at me.

"It's fine." I do my best to stifle my wince of pain as Henry slides my leggings down over my hips and farther, until he's slipping them off my ankles and tossing them to the floor.

My panties follow immediately after, giving Henry a better look at the angry purple bruising along my side. His jaw tenses.

"It's not your fault," I remind him, stroking his hair back.

He settles his forehead against my abdomen. "At least he can never hurt you again." His warm breath skates over my skin with his heavy sigh. Over my womb. Exactly where our baby would grow.

I play with the ends of his hair as I digest that crazy thought, wondering exactly how crazy it is anymore. Henry told me that he loves me. I know him enough to know that wasn't flippant or ill-considered. Henry wouldn't have said it if he wasn't absolutely sure.

Henry loves me.

I have to keep telling myself that, over and over again, until this dream feels like reality.

He readjusts the ice pack so my hip is once again covered. "Does it hurt to move your hip?"

"A little."

He settles a knowing gaze on me.

"A lot."

His hand slips gently under my thigh of my uninjured leg. "What about this side?"

"I think it's okay."

He watches my face as he carefully lifts that leg up and out, opening me up for him. "And this?"

Heat begins to pool at my core. "Yes. It's okay."

He hooks my leg over his shoulder. "Good?" With his face positioned between my legs, the promise of what's to come is quickly overshadowing everything else, including the painful throb in my forehead.

"Yes."

Henry studies me carefully for another long moment, as if waiting for my façade to break, for me to crumble. Finally buying my words, he leans forward.

I gasp with the first swipe of his tongue, flat against me.

He smirks, excitement dancing in those beautiful eyes of his. "I know how I'm going to wake you up every hour tonight."

"Murder, Abigail! Murder!"

I cringe against Mama's voice booming in my ear.

"Do you see now? Do you see what kind of family he has

been raised in? The kind that would kill their own kind for a few bucks!"

A gold mine, Mama. Hardly a few bucks.

"And do you realize what kind of relations this William Wolf had with a *twenty-five-year-old girl*, Abigail?"

I think everyone has figured out what kind of relations they had, Mama.

"He was old enough to be her father! Maybe even her grandfather! And have you done the math! She's only four years older than you!"

I take a sip of my coffee and quietly curse the news for releasing the sordid details behind William Wolf's death, because there's nothing else I can do while Mama rages.

"Did you know all this was goin' on, Abigail?"

"We suspected it a few days ago, so Henry got the police involved," I say calmly.

"And were you there when this murdering brother of his showed up at the penthouse?"

Her words bring a dull throb to my forehead and the sizeable bruise. The bump has gone down, but it still aches to the touch.

"I was, but I'm fine. I can't talk about what happened right now. Not while the investigation is still open." Henry was able to keep Scott's attack on me out of the papers. For now. I'm sure it'll eventually come out, but I'll happily avoid dealing with Mama cursing Henry for it until then.

"Well, your father and I expect you to come home, where you're surrounded by good people. Today, Abigail, where it's safe."

We're back to this. She still thinks she can control me. And she's invoking Daddy's name in this. I wonder if it's true, if his support of me being with Henry is wavering due to the latest news.

I sigh and look around Henry's spacious kitchen. Oddly

enough, this place is quickly beginning to feel more like home than the farm. "Mama, I am happy and safe here, with Henry. I will come back to Greenbank when he leaves on business again. I'm not going to fight about this with you, but I'm an adult, and I'm living my life. And no amount of huffing and puffing or sulkiness from you will change my mind, so please stop trying to tell me what to do." I say it as calmly but firmly as I can.

Henry's voice carries from somewhere within the penthouse, growing louder by the second. "I have to go now. I'm elbow-deep in making soaps for a friend, and they have to be finished this week. I'll talk to you later. Bye, Mama. Love you." I hang up before she has a chance to retort.

"...I need quarterly reports in by this afternoon, at the latest," Henry demands, strolling into the kitchen in a t-shirt and track pants, his hair still damp from his shower. Miles scrambles behind him, notebook and pen in hand to jot down notes. "And set up a call with Belinda. I want a status update from her by three, our time."

"Our time? But in Spain that's like—"

"It's fine. She's found a Spanish guy to fuck until the sun comes up."

Miles's eyes flash to me before focusing on his notepad again to make his notes, his cheeks turning bright red. I doubt he's a virgin, but he seems like the type of guy who would have texted a girl from class for three months about homework assignments before working up the nerve to ask her out for a coffee.

Henry grabs an apple from the bowl on the counter. "Abbi, why are you out of bed?"

"Because I need to finish these for Margo." I wave a hand over the cluttered countertop of molds and wrapping.

"No, you don't. Margo knows what happened to you and has insisted that you not do this."

"No! This is a good opportunity! I'm not letting Scott fuck that up for me!"

"Fine. Hire someone to finish. You need to take it easy." His eyes graze my forehead.

I roll my eyes. "I'm not hiring anyone to do this. And stop mothering me."

Henry's eyebrow arches knowingly. "Is that what you call what I've been doing to you? *Mothering* you?"

My cheeks flush as I watch him take a bite of apple with the mouth that's been attached to me—to my lips, to my breasts, between my legs—since Monday night, helping to ease my discomfort.

It's been absolute heaven, and ironically I owe it all to Scott.

"Miles, when do the engineers need me on site?" he asks, still staring at me.

The sudden switch of gears throws Miles off for a few beats. "Uh... Wednesday."

"Okay. Make the arrangements. And get an ETA on when they think the mine can be up and running. You can leave for the office now. Call me if anything important comes up, but I'll be taking the next few days off."

Miles's eyes widen with shock at that news, but he's smart enough to not comment. He nods to me on his way past as he scurries out of the kitchen.

I focus on the simmering pot on the stove and try not to sound disappointed—because I've had Henry to myself for longer than I could have hoped for—when I ask, "So, you're leaving on Friday?"

"I have to meet the engineers about the ski runs," he says over the running tap as he washes his hands.

Ski runs. There's only one place that I know of where he's putting in ski runs. My heart skips a beat. "Wait... do you mean Wolf Cove?"

"Why?" He looks over his shoulder at me. "Did you want to come with me?"

"Yes! Of course I do!" I've been dying to go back.

A knowing smirk touches his lips. "Shouldn't you check with your family first to—"

"No. They're fine. I mean, they'll be fine. Besides, I'm not stepping foot in Greenbank until my forehead has fully healed."

"And what about all this?" He nods to the island. "Didn't you just finish saying you have to do it?"

"Well, it has to be done by tomorrow night anyway, to make it in time for her party on Friday night." I heave a sigh, suddenly overwhelmed. How am I going to do all this *and* get ready for Alaska?

"Rethinking that hired help?"

"Maybe... but who? They need to know what they're doing. It can't just be anyone."

Henry's gaze follows mine. "It can't be that hard to wrap these."

"I guess not." I reach for a sheet of lavender paper and a matching soap bar. My fingers work quickly, folding the paper around the bar, and then securing it with twine. I've already wrapped a hundred of them. I could do these in my sleep. "The trick is not creasing the paper, and making sure the twine is centered. See?"

Henry reaches for a bar and sheet of paper and, at a much slower pace, follows the steps with precision.

"Of course you're a natural," I mutter. An idea hits me. "You know, if *you* helped me, we could easily get this all done by tomorrow."

"You're asking me to do manual labor?"

"I thought you liked manual labor. You know... swinging axes and helping sweet old ladies...," I tease.

He sighs heavily. And reaches for another bar and paper.

"I don't work for free, Abigail," he says smoothly, while wrapping it. "My rates are high."

I school my expression and say innocently, "But I don't have any money."

"Luckily for you, you have a *very* skilled mouth." His intense eyes settle on my lips. He hasn't let me use them on him since the attack.

I glance over my shoulder toward the penthouse foyer, where three workers hammer away, erecting a wall. Henry had the security guard who allowed Scott in fired immediately, but he's still not satisfied, so he's closing off the penthouse from the elevator and putting in a door with a state-of-the-art lock for additional security.

They can't hear us from way over here, but still….

I edge up behind Henry and reach around him to settle my hand on the front of his track pants to firmly cup his length. "If you do a good job with these, I'll see what I can do about that payment," I whisper.

"When have you *ever* known me to not do a good job." He's growing hard against my palm. I'll never get bored of the feel of that.

It's so tempting to slip my hand inside his track pants, to grasp his velvety smooth skin in my fist and stroke him languidly until he comes, but that will inevitably lead to losing hours of valuable working time. So I pull away and move back to the gas range to stir my pot of glycerin, trying to ignore the mild groan of discontent that comes from him.

"What's that grin for?"

I *am* grinning. Stupidly, no doubt. And I don't care. "For going back to Alaska with you."

CHAPTER 13

"Had one heck of a storm roll through here just this morning," John says as he steers us along Kachemak Bay. "Caused some real damage."

"Anything on the resort?" Henry asks.

"No, sir. Nothing that I've heard of, anyway. See? There are two or three big ones down there." He points a wrinkled finger to a cluster of fallen trees along the shoreline across from us. Branches with golden-yellow leaves stick out of the water.

Everywhere I look, fall colors stipple the forested hills, mixed in with lush evergreens. Above us the sky is a crisp blue and clear, promising a beautiful sunset for tonight if it holds. But the temperatures are much cooler than I expected and I find myself huddling within my jacket, a shiver coursing through me.

"I warned you, didn't I?" Henry wraps his arm around me and pulls me against his chest. I instantly feel warmer. "Next time don't argue with me about packing appropriately."

I tip my head back against his shoulder to make sure he sees my eye roll. "There's packing appropriately, and then there's buying an entire fall and winter wardrobe for a five-day trip." I went to arrange our suitcases yesterday morning and remembered that all of my warm clothes are in Greenbank. Two phone calls and a few hours later, a stylist showed up at Henry's with racks of clothing and boots for me.

Henry insisted I try it all on. And then he bought *everything* that fit me, despite my argument. There isn't enough room in his closet to hang my things anymore.

He leans in to press his mouth against my ear and whispers, "And isn't it ironic that you won't be wearing *any* of it once we get there."

Heat washes down through my belly and between my legs. I inhale the smell of his intoxicating cologne and let myself sink into his hard body, clad in that yellow-and-black checkered jacket and black vest ensemble that I love, his head covered in a beanie to ward off the chill. It's a look that was made for Henry as much as his tailored suits, and one that I missed more than I realized. When he got dressed before deboarding the plane at the Wolf airfield outside of Homer, I felt the overpowering urge to kick Jack out so I could unfasten Henry's pants right then and there and wrap my mouth around him.

"You growing this out again?" I reach up to touch his jaw, dragging my fingernails across the thin layer of scruff.

"Maybe." He smirks. "Why? Do you want me to?"

"Maybe. I liked the lumberjack look."

"You only saw it for a night, and you were shit-faced, Abbi."

"Exactly. So I need to see it again to be sure. Besides, I'm curious what it will feel like, against my lips."

His mouth finds mine, pressing a kiss against it. Then it moves to my ear. "Those lips? Or your other lips?"

Henry's phone rings, interrupting a conversation we probably shouldn't be having right here. He sighs and presses a kiss against my temple before pulling away and heading for the other side of the empty deck to answer the call in private.

"So...." The old ferry captain's kind eyes flicker between me and the route ahead. "It's not just idle rumor then, is it?"

I smile.

He returns it. "Things have certainly changed since the first time I took you across here."

"You remember that?" With all the trips and all the people, I find that hard to believe.

"Your plane arrived late and you looked lost. Yeah, I remember you all right." He hesitates, his gaze flickering to my forehead, to the bruise that's covered up with foundation but not completely hidden in certain light, and when my hair blows back off my face. He glances over his shoulder to see that Henry is deep in conversation. "I hope he's treatin' you right."

"Yes, Henry treats me *very* well." I chuckle at the insinuation, even though it's not funny at all. It's preposterous to think that Henry would ever physically hurt me, and I don't want that rumor starting. "His brother did this."

John makes a sound. He must have heard the news about Scott by now. Everyone else has. "Messy business it is, having that much money. People do all kinds of things to keep it."

"Not people. Scott Wolf."

"Oh, believe me, I know about that one," John murmurs. "I used to shuttle them back and forth from the old Wolf cabin when they were young boys. Scott never did sit right with me, even from the start. He was the mean, jealous sort. I remember this one time...." The wrinkles in his brow furrow deeply. "Yes, it would have been around this time, because I remember the leaves all changin' then, too. Henry had a new toy. Can't remember what it was exactly, but it was a big deal. A birthday present, maybe. Anyway, his older brother grabbed it right out of his hand and tossed it into the water.

Just to upset him. Henry cried the entire rest of the way back. 'Course, he was really young then." John's shoulders shake as he chuckles in that way most old men do. "Yes, I reckon he'd toss his brother into the water if he tried that now. Well, if Scott weren't in a morgue already."

That's exactly where Scott is, waiting for his mother to plan his burial because Henry is not about to.

"Wait a minute...." While I love hearing stories about a young Henry—even terrible ones like that—it sparks another thought.

When the hell is Henry's birthday?

"What is it, dear?"

"Nothing," I mutter, peering back at Henry as I slide out my phone. It would *totally* be like him to not say a word and let his birthday pass, leaving me none the wiser. I quickly punch out a text to Miles.

John watches me curiously for a moment. "Well, anyway, what I'll say is that I'm glad it's Henry and not his brother that ended up in charge of the family businesses. He'll do a good job. His grandfather would be so proud of the man he has become—"

"Motherfucker!" Henry exclaims loudly.

We both turn to see the look of disbelief filling his face.

"What's wrong?" I ask as John locks eyes with the water ahead of us, trying to be inconspicuous.

Henry slides his phone into his pocket, having ended his call. "I just found out what Scott was up to." He shakes his head as he approaches. "The bastard was digging through the old ore mine, looking for diamonds."

"Wait, you have an ore mine, *too*?"

He waves it off as inconsequential information. "We shut it down years ago. But some geologist convinced Scott that the fault line running under it is optimal for diamond formation. My dad heard it all before, and never bought into it. He figured that if they hadn't come across a single diamond in all the years of mining, that it was a bullshit theory. Scott knew my dad would never go for investing a dime in it, so was doing it behind our backs, skimming funds from operations to put toward this venture."

"Oh my God." It dawns on me. "*That's* what he was telling your mother that day." Or, about to tell her, before Miles interrupted them, looking for me. Scott was convinced that he was sitting on an untapped fortune in the mine. That's why he didn't care about the hotel chain. That's why he called Henry a chump.

"What a sneaky, enterprising fool." Henry chuckles, but it's a bitter sound. A sound he makes when he's trying to cover up the fact that he's troubled.

I settle my hand on his forearm to at the very least offer some comfort with my touch. "So, what are you going to do?"

"Nothing for now. Get the gold mine back up and running. I'll deal with the rest of it later." He sighs heavily and then nods to something behind me. "Look."

I turn in time to see Wolf Cove hotel come into view, the massive lodge no less impressive now than it was the first time I saw it in May. Back when I was heartbroken over Jed and trying to escape my life. And *so* innocent.

Before I realized that everything I could ever possibly want in life was waiting for me, in the form of this all-consuming man.

I smile.

John was right. My, how things have changed.

"Feels a bit like coming home, doesn't it?" I murmur.

"More than you know." Henry's eyes settle on my face.

JOHN BRINGS the ferry alongside the dock. Two bellhops stand like sentries in their plum-colored uniforms, patiently waiting for the owner of their hotel to arrive so they can shuttle our belongings to Penthouse One. I recognize the tall, thin one on the left. Simon, I think. The last time I saw him, he was bent over and heaving into a trash can outside the staff lodge, unable to handle the shots of tequila that Connor was forcing everyone to drink.

"Who is that woman?" I ask of the tall brunette in a black pantsuit standing next to him.

Henry leans against the rail, his gaze taking in the majestic resort. "Isabella. Belinda's replacement. She's an assistant general manager in Aspen. I brought her up to finish off the season."

She's definitely more professional-looking than Belinda. But equally stunning, I note, studying her high cheekbones and full lips. I can't help but wonder if Henry knows her as well as he knows Belinda.

"No."

"What?"

Henry gives me a look. "You're too easy for me to read, Abbi. And the answer is no. I haven't."

My face flushes. Sometimes I hate that Henry knows me so well. At least he seems amused by it.

I avert my gaze, scanning the gardens and walkways where hotel guests mill about. Far off to the left, I spot two male figures in the telltale Wolf Cove vests and work boots, shovels in hand. They've taken a break from planting a cedar tree to watch the ferry dock.

My chest swells with recognition as the blond throws a hand up in greeting.

I grin and wave back.

"Speaking of people we've fucked...." Henry's hard gaze

sizes Connor and Ronan up. "Did you tell them you were coming back?"

"No. I never told anyone. But I'm guessing everyone's going to know soon enough."

"I'm not comfortable with those two being near you, Abbi," he says evenly.

What's he getting at? "But they're my friends."

"They've fucked you."

"Well, only Ronan has."

I get a sharp glare in return. "You know what I mean. Those two would be all over you if given the chance."

"Maybe," I admit. But I'm not about to back down. "And Margo would fuck you if given the chance."

He snorts. "And *you*, if given the chance."

"Fair enough. But they're not getting a chance, because I'd never give it to them. They know how I feel about you."

"You've told them?"

"I don't need to." Ronan saw the pain in my eyes, every time the name Henry Wolf was spoken. He knew that it was Henry who left my heart shattered. "I know I can't ask you to like them, or my past with them. But you said you'd never use it against me."

His jaw tenses.

But I push on. "Trying to stop me from seeing them while I'm up here would be doing that. You and I weren't together and they made my summer... bearable." Enjoyable, even, though admitting that to Henry might not be a smart move.

He heaves a sigh. "You're with *me* now. And there's so much press around us. If I find out they've been running their mouth about what they did—"

"They won't."

"They're fucking deviants, Abbi. If you knew half the shit they've been up to—"

"I can only imagine. But Ronan's a private guy. He never

says a word about anyone he's been with, and he told me he'd make sure Connor wouldn't." At least he promised he would. Connor's a bit hard to control. If he *has* told people about what happened between us....

A wave of nervousness hits me as I take in the picturesque view again. This is *all* Henry's and it's only a sliver of his empire. I was emptying trash and cutting firewood the last time. Now I'm a guest in a hotel that charges twelve hundred dollars a night, and that's for the regular rooms. I'm in a penthouse, with the owner. I was so wrapped up in coming back to Wolf Cove that I didn't really think about what it'd be like to face people again.

Sure, they all know about Henry and me by now. But what is this going to feel like? What kinds of things have they been saying behind my back? My stomach turns queasy at the prospect of being the topic of conversation. "Is this going to be weird? Being back here, I mean."

"For you? Probably."

"Thanks," I mutter, earning his dark chuckle. "I'm glad you find this so amusing. You know, there was a time when you were vehemently opposed to the idea of anyone knowing about us," I remind him.

"Vehemently?"

"Vehemently."

"You're right. But that was back when you were my assistant." He resumes a standing position, to tower over me. "Do you want that job back?"

"Maybe."

His brow arches.

"I'd get to spend more time with you."

"And I'd get *very* little work done."

I mock-frown. "Yes, I do remember your work ethic needing improvement."

He smirks. "Besides, I think Miles would feel betrayed if you made me replace him with you."

Speaking of Miles....

I hang back as Henry heads toward where staff is working quickly to help port the ferry, and pull out my phone, hoping Miles was able to get into Henry's personal information.

"Son of a bitch!" I exclaim, earning several looks.

"Abbi?" Henry asks, a puzzled expression on his face.

I offer him a tight smile. "Stubbed my toe."

His eyes narrow at my black boots and the fact that there's nothing around to stub my toe on, but thankfully Isabella approaches him then, distracting him from pushing farther.

Henry's birthday is in *two days*. What the hell kind of birthday present can I possibly come up with in two days, way out here?

With a wave goodbye to John, I step off the ferry. Simon steals a curious glance my way. I give him a sheepish smile as I hand him my carry-on. We've crossed paths enough times. He must recognize me.

"Ready?" Henry reaches for me, settling a hand on the small of my back to lead me toward the path that will take us to our cabin. "Welcome back."

CHAPTER 14

I close my eyes and take a deep breath, inhaling the fresh, clean air, before opening them again to take in the scenic view of water and trees from our sizeable porch. It's exactly how I remember it, right down to the rows of boats and float planes parked at the docks below, waiting to whisk guests off on an array of fishing and sightseeing excursions.

It feels *so* good to be back.

And so strange.

I've experienced so much in this place. The walls of Penthouse One—Henry's suite while he was here—have seen him win my heart and then break it. They've seen me give my virginity to him, my full trust, and my unwavering love. They've heard our angry words, my tears.

The last time I stepped through that front door was the day I realized that Henry had lied to me about sleeping with that reporter. That it was me and only me who had cheated on him with Michael. That day, after weeks of careful mending by Ronan and Connor, my heart shattered all over again.

As much as I've missed Wolf Cove, being away made it easier for me to forget, I realize now.

"I'm sure Miles has already told you that we won't be needing a liaison," I hear Henry tell Isabella. "I do not permit staff to walk freely in here. We'll call in for room service, but we're not to be disturbed otherwise."

"He informed me of your preferences," Isabella answers in her faint accent. Spanish, I think. So far, she's much more docile than Belinda ever was, all "yes, Mr. Wolf," and "no, Mr. Wolf" and "whatever you would like, Mr. Wolf," while staring at him with her big chocolate-brown eyes.

What does she really think of his request though? My roommates were convinced that Henry had to be hiding deviant things in his room, because he didn't want regular attendance by staff. But Henry's not stupid or unaware of his appeal, having faced numerous situations with maids throwing themselves at him, crawling through his used sheets. After the things I heard come out of Tillie and Katie's mouths about him, I completely understand his need for boundaries.

"And make sure that whatever Abbi asks for, she gets immediately," Henry adds.

"The concierge will be happy to assist with her requests."

"Have Anderson and his people checked in yet?"

"Late last night. They're at the site location now and waiting for you. We have a vehicle ready to take you out. I've also made 7:00 p.m. dinner arrangements for your group tonight at Lux. Will Miss Mitchell be joining you?" She's so prim and proper, and molded. I almost miss Belinda's sharp tongue, the way she challenges Henry.

"I doubt it, but we'll call in if you need to make changes to numbers. Thank you, Isabella. I'll be at the gate in ten minutes."

Henry steps out onto the balcony a few moments later. I'm expecting him to tell me that he's running, but instead he sidles up behind me and hands me one of two glasses of champagne. "To being back in Alaska."

I hold up my glass. "To being back in Alaska."

He sighs heavily. With everything that's happened over the last few weeks, I don't know how Henry has remained so forward-focused. On the business, on us. Still, I see him drifting off in thought sometimes, his jaw hardening, sadness in his eyes. He hasn't forgotten what Scott robbed him of, what else Scott tried to take from him. And, though he'll never admit to it, Scott's death must have a significant impact on him.

I turn into him, to press my body against his from thigh to chest. "It's over. He can't hurt us or anyone else anymore."

He clinks my glass with his again. I take a sip as I peer back out over the water. The champagne is sweet and bubbly, and probably more expensive than I can imagine. "I thought I loved the summer here, but now I'm thinking fall is my favorite."

"Wait until you see it in the winter. We should have the runs ready within two years. Three at most."

"So much for a seasonal Wolf, hey?"

"My long-term vision was always year-round. I just couldn't sell it as that before I proved this could work."

"You know, I've never skied."

He shakes his head and mutters something under his breath that I don't catch before saying, "We'll go to Aspen over Christmas. I'll teach you."

Aspen for Christmas. Wolf Cove for winter in two to three years. He says it like it's the most natural thing, to be planning so far ahead. To assume that we'll be here, *together*.

A flash of me, lying naked with Henry among a heap of blankets next to a roaring fire, makes me smile. I smooth my hand over his abdomen, my fingers splaying over each ridge.

"I have to head out—"

"I know. The engineers. And you're already late, so go." Henry *hates* being late.

He leans in to press his lips against mine. "I'm going to be tied up until after dinner. I assume you don't want to join us in Lux to listen to engineers talk about—"

"Sounds thrilling. No, thank you."

He chuckles. "I figured as much."

I trail him back inside and past the small fire burning in the fireplace, my eyes roving over the interior. It's exactly how I remember it—a palette of creams and grays, and pure designer luxury. Only then I was a Wolf hotel employee, a secret lover. Now I'm a guest. Not just any guest. Henry Wolf's woman.

"You remember how to call the concierge desk?"

"Yeah. And if I don't, I know where to find the instructions." In the tiny liaison room, where I never really spent any time.

"There's plenty for you to do to keep yourself busy."

"A Kodiak bear excursion by plane?" I watched Henry leave on countless tours, always wishing I could tag along.

He chuckles. "Let's maybe save that one. I was thinking more like the spa."

"I do want Tris to do my color again," I murmur, running my fingers through my lackluster hair. No one has done it quite as well since.

"Then book it. Between that and a few spa treatments, you'll be occupied until I get back."

I know what he's trying to do. "I'm going to see my friends, too, Henry. *All* of them," I say carefully. I spent too many years listening to Mama's orders and doing what others wanted me to do. But Henry pushes for us to always be open and honest with each other. I'm not going to start doing things behind his back now.

Henry's feet slow to a halt. He sighs heavily. "Abbi, I'm not going to tell you that you *can't* see your friends."

"Good."

"Just be careful what you get yourself into. I'm who I am and I do have to maintain separation and respect from my employees, even if we're together."

I frown. "What are you saying? That they won't respect you because you're with me?" My chest stings with that prick.

He holds up a hand in warning, closing the distance between us. "That's not what I'm saying. I just don't want you anywhere near the kinds of things happening in that staff village. I've seen enough security footage to know what goes on there."

I fold my arms over my chest. "I doubt it's worse than the things happening in a certain chateau in France."

"That's a controlled environment. No one's recording it—"

I snort. "A lot of art gallery walls would beg to differ."

"That's... different. Here? People will be watching you. The wrong ones will be looking for stories and pictures of you to sell. They're not your friends, Abbi. I'm trying to protect you."

I fold my arms across my chest. "And what kind of stories and pictures do you think they're going to get while I'm sitting on a couch in the staff village?"

"Well, you do have a bad habit of getting caught in rooms where people are fucking," he says evenly.

"At least half of those situations have been because of you!" I say indignantly, even as my cheeks flush.

"Regardless, you're not a Wolf employee anymore. You're openly with *me* now, and I own *all* of this. You are in a different class from everyone here."

"If you're about to tell me that I'm above everyone here,

then stop. Just because you have a swimming pool's worth of money, doesn't mean you're better than the people who clean that pool. You know, you keep talking about needing your employees to respect you. You'd go a long way with earning their admiration by getting to know them. Letting them know you're not the stiff asshole they all think you are."

Henry's mouth hangs open for a beat, speechless. "Did you just school me on how to act around my employees?"

I set my chin. "I guess I did. And also, you'd probably like Ronan and Connor if you got to know them. Or at least Ronan." Connor can be a bit much for anyone.

Henry shakes his head. "Look, I just like my private life to stay private, when it comes to my employees."

"You're being ridiculous. I don't know how me going to say hello to a few people I used to work with turned into me getting caught up in some orgy. And relax, I'm not going to give them intimate details about us."

He smirks. "Even when they ask you how big my dick is."

"They're not going to ask me that!"

He gives me a knowing look.

"Okay, *some* of them might ask me that," I admit reluctantly. I've heard firsthand just how crass the female staff can be when Henry is the topic of conversation. "And I'm not going to answer them."

"You're terrible at deflecting."

"Fine. I'll tell everyone you're hung like a horse."

His eyebrows rise in shocked amusement.

"What? I spent some time on the McArthur ranch when I was younger. I've seen things."

"Now who's being ridiculous? Just... remember who I am around here."

"You're the big bad wolf. How could I forget?"

"See? You've just proven my point. I've got to go. And

have someone come out for a massage. I noticed you were tense earlier. I'm sure it could help. A female masseuse."

"Yes, sir."

His brow arches. "Sir?"

"Sorry. This whole exchange is bringing me back to the early days, when you were my tyrannical boss."

"You weren't mouthy back then." He reaches up to cup one side of my face and smooth the pad of his thumb over my bottom lip. "You were shy and nervous, and awkward." He slides his thumb into my mouth, grazing my teeth.

I softly bite down.

Heat flares in his eyes. "But I'm beginning to think you've always been a wolf, hiding in an innocent girl's clothing." His gaze dips downward, over my fitted light sweater and the deep V that plunges into my cleavage. "How's your hip?"

I smile coyly. "I guess you'll have to wait to find out."

Henry's jaw tightens. And then a wicked smile curls his lips. "No, I don't think I will."

Everything changes in a split second.

Suddenly, I find myself facedown and bent over the dining room table. "Arms up." I comply and Henry tugs my sweater up and over my head, leaving my bare torso against the cool wood. With a flick of his wrist, my bra is unfastened and peeled off me. Then he moves on to my lower half, dropping to his knees to peel my leggings, panties, and socks off in one go.

In less than thirty seconds, Henry has stripped me bare.

"I've always loved the mirrors in this place," he murmurs, fumbling with his belt.

I look straight ahead to find our reflection staring back at us, my mussed hair and cleavage, and Henry hovering behind me, his hard cock gripped in his hand. Heat pools between my legs.

"I thought you had to leave," I say innocently, spreading

my legs farther apart and arching my back to give him a better view. My lips apart as I feel the first slide of his finger through my core.

"I do. I promise, this won't take long." Pushing his jeans down to his thighs, he slips his hands between my legs to wrap around the front of my thighs.

I gasp in surprise as my feet leave the floor, as my hips lift and tilt toward him. I have a second's warning—the feel of his cock pressed against my entrance—before he's sinking deep into me, earning my guttural moan.

And then he's thrusting mercilessly, and I'm crying out, my body not fully prepared for this. But I did taunt him, I remind myself. I should know better.

My back and shoulders strain as I manage to adjust myself on the table and watch us in the mirror again, to see the tense look on Henry's face, the concentration as he focuses on where we're joined, his eyes searing as he pumps in and out of me

This is the Henry Wolf of the early days. The seemingly cold, volatile rich bastard who intimidated me like no one else, who took me where and when he wanted, with no apologies but full of passion.

Heat builds deep within my body as he hits that special spot with each thrust. If he keeps this up long enough, I won't even need to touch myself to orgasm. "Harder," I demand through soft, shallow pants.

His searing eyes lift to meet mine.

I cry out as his hips slam into me over and over again, my ass taking the brunt of the impact as that heat spreads through my veins, along my thighs, into my lower belly. My fingers claw against the table, the only purchase for my body where my breasts press against the wood, the rest of me in the air and at Henry's mercy.

He comes moments later, his head thrown back, his cries

slipping from his parted lips as I feel him pulsing deep inside me.

Those pulses have barely stopped when my feet are settling onto the floor and he's pulling out of me.

"Henry." I whisper his name, but it's more of a pleading moan, the ache between my legs unbearable.

"Come here." He guides my body, wired with tension, up and over to the other side of the table. He lifts me onto it, and hoists my legs up to spread me wide in front of the mirror. He kisses my temple and then checks the reflection. "Fuck, Abbi," he mutters, his eyes locking on the view—of heavy, full breasts, my swollen folds. His seed is running out of me. Reaching for my hand, he fits it between my legs.

"Watch me."

His jaw clenches. "If I stay and watch that, I'll be fucking you on this table again, and I'll never get to the engineers."

He makes a move to tuck himself into his pants.

And hisses, as I seize his semihard length with my free hand. "Watch," I demand more firmly, unwilling to let go. "It'll only take a minute." I draw my finger through my slick core and over my clit, making circles around it with his cum.

He sighs heavily, but then caves, casting his eyes downward. With an arm around my back and a hand settled on my knee, he watches me as I masturbate for him, the mirror reflecting the entire intimate act.

Not even thirty seconds later, heat floods my lower half and that slow build erupts in waves of ecstasy that engulf my entire body, pulsing through my core, causing my muscles to spasm.

"See? I told you. Not even a minute," I whisper, releasing him.

He leans in to kiss me in a way that only Henry can, deep enough to make my knees buckle if I were standing. It leaves me dizzy with lust and brimming with love.

"And I told you what would happen if I stayed and watched." He gently pushes me back against the table and starts peeling off his clothes.

I SPOT her cinnamon-colored pixie hair and I smile.

"Oh my God! Abbi!" Autumn squeals. She runs out from behind the concierge desk and tears across the cavernous lobby to throw her arms around my neck, earning several looks.

"It's so good to see you again." I left in such a hurry the last time because of my father's accident, I never got to say proper goodbyes.

"Tillie said she saw you out on the dock."

"We just got in about an hour ago."

"So, where is he?" Autumn whispers, searching the faces around us.

"Meeting with engineers."

She grabs my hand and drags me over to one of the benches. "Sit and spill."

I laugh nervously. "There's not much to say."

She settles wide, knowing eyes on me. "Your boyfriend is Henry Wolf and there's not much to say? Oh come on! Enough with the lame answers you've been giving me over text. Talk!"

It sounds strange, hearing her call him my boyfriend. A man like Henry Wolf just doesn't wear a label like "boyfriend" well. And he's so much more than that to me.

I shrug.

"So, when exactly did it start?"

Of all my roommates, Autumn was probably the nicest. But still, I'm not about to admit to being with Henry all that time when I was working for him. He and I agreed that the only person who had a right to know the truth was his father.

"After I left to go home," I lie, hoping she doesn't notice the way I shift my gaze.

She studies me for a moment. "He told you not to talk about it, didn't he?"

"We agreed that there is enough gossip circulating about his family that we don't need to add more to it." That sounds like the best answer.

"Oh my God, right? I read about that. Isn't that insane! Were you actually there when Scott died?"

I wasn't just there. I was trapped underneath him. I fight the urge to touch my forehead, the bruise suitably covered now.

If nothing else, at least Scott serves as good distraction from the topic of Henry and me.

"Yes."

She shakes her head. "It's just crazy. Both of them gone in weeks. Henry's all that's left."

"I know. It's still a shock. So, how's life here?" I don't want to talk about Scott anymore.

"Oh, you know. Everything's changed and yet not much has changed." Autumn fills me in on Wolf Cove's goings-on for the next ten minutes—Tillie moved cabins because she and Lorraine couldn't make peace after that fiasco with James, Ronan and Connor got busted by security for being ringleaders to a secret fuck club—where players went into a dark cabin and waited for an unidentified person to be led in to perform a sexual act on them—and somehow weren't fired, and Katie and Rachel have finally admitted to dating each other.

"Come to the staff lounge tonight!"

"We'll see how late Henry's tied up. I want to be home when he gets back."

"I'll bet you do. Oh, shit, that's my supervisor." Autumn smiles and waves at the stern-looking man hovering nearby. "He can fuck right off. Does he not realize I'm talking to the future Mrs. Wolf?" she mutters.

"Oh my God, stop. That's *so* far off from where we are." But my heart pitter-patters all the same.

Her eyes twinkle. "It's so good to see you, Abbi. I'm glad your dad is okay. And Henry Wolf!" She lets out a little girlish scream.

"It feels like a dream. I was so nervous coming back here," I admit. "I was afraid of how people might react."

"Oh, don't get me wrong, we're all jealous as fuck. But we're also happy for you. Except for Tillie. She's just jealous, no surprise." She rolls her eyes.

"Great. Can't wait to see her."

"Whatever. Come to the staff lounge tonight and you can rub it in her face."

"I'll try. Tris is going to do my hair and then I'm going to the spa for a facial." I've never had one, but the brochure promises a glowing complexion.

She tsks. "Rough life you lead, huh? Come visit us peasants when you have a chance." With a wink, she trots off, leaving me shaking my head.

Henry: *I'm going to be another two hours. We just sat down at Lux. Someone delayed me from my day earlier, and discussions went later than expected.*

Abbi: *Those must have been some intense discussions. I heard they serve only the best scotch at Rawleys.*

Henry: *I see your vast network of spies is serving you well.*

I respond with a smiley face so he knows I'm not bothered. Rachel texted me an hour ago from the upscale pub where she was serving Henry and his engineers drinks, wondering when I was going to come in. It's almost nine now. With the time difference, and the fact that I'm curled up on the couch with a soft blanket, it's not likely that I'm going anywhere tonight. I'm struggling to keep my eyes open.

Abbi:*I'll probably be asleep when you get in.*

Henry: *I'll wake you up.*

Thoughts of how he might do that make my body stir with anticipation. After days of undivided attention—his hands and mouth on me at every opportunity—I'm suffering from Henry withdrawal. I need to feel the press of his body against mine. I keep inhaling, hoping to catch that delicious scent that is all him—his cologne, his shampoo, the lingering soap on his skin. And my fingers itch to crawl along his curves, weave through his silky hair, again. It's enough to drive a person crazy.

Abbi:*Fine. I'll just be lying on this couch, naked, waiting for you.*

I'm actually not naked, but maybe that'll make him rush.

It's a few minutes, but another text comes in.

Henry: *I'll show you exactly how much I love you soon.*

A thrill courses through me. Will I ever get used to that? Will Henry telling me that he loves me ever *not* make my heart swell? God, I hope not, because this feeling is like nothing I've ever experienced before. If what I felt for Jed was actually love, then whatever I feel for Henry transcends love.

With a sigh, I set my phone on the coffee table and replace it for the remote control, flipping through the channels in search of a movie.

My phone chirps with another text, and I assume it's from Henry.

Connor: *Yo. Is the Wolf in the house?*

I was wondering how long before I heard from those two.

Abbi: *No. He's at Lux.*

Moments later, there's pounding on the front door. It doesn't take a genius to figure out who's on the other side.

Henry will not like this, I recognize with a sigh. I wander over, torn between excitement for seeing my friends and unexpected anxiety over facing the two men I shared such an illicit afternoon with, one I don't think I'll ever forget, no matter how many orgasms Henry brings me to.

As soon as I open the door, as soon as I see Connor's goofy smile and the cans of beer in their hands, all I remember is the comfort and care and friendship they provided me with during those many dark weeks, and how many times they made me smile and laugh. How desired they made me feel, when I believed that Henry no longer desired me at all.

"Red!" Connor exclaims.

"What are you two doing here?" I laugh, reaching for him.

His muscular arms immediately wrap around my body to hoist me in the air. He makes me feel like a child.

"Oh my God, did you get even bigger?" I squeeze his bulging biceps.

"Alaska" is all he says, as he grins down at me with that devilish smile.

Ronan hangs back, reserved and sly as usual. "Hey, Red."

"Hey." I reach for my dear friend. Of the two of them, Ronan is the one I share an inexplicable but special connection with, something I *never* expected when I first met the brooding tattooed guy with the buzz cut.

Ronan envelops me in his arms and pulls me against his hard chest. His smell is familiar. It brings me back to many nights, but mainly the night he curled up in my bunk with me and let me cry about Henry on his shoulder without saying a word. He's the only one who seemed to have figured out what was really going on between Henry and me, way back when. "It's good to see you again." He's always had a deep raspy voice, but now it's tempered by softness.

It's a few extra beats before I pull away from him, my emotions swirling unexpectedly. "How have things been?"

"Without you here? Boring as fuck." Connor's voice booms into the night. He gives me a knowing look. One that matches the look Ronan's also giving me.

"That's not what I've heard," I counter, though I'm blushing furiously, wondering exactly what mental images are flashing through their minds right now. I've done a lot of things with Henry that I can't believe, but that day? That was all my doing. "Fuck Club?"

"The first rule of Fuck Club is: you do not talk about Fuck Club!" Connor's grin grows wide. "Damn, that was fun while it lasted. So?" He throws his arms in the air. "You went to see Autumn but not us when you got in?"

"I know. I'm sorry. I was at the spa for a few hours and then I ordered dinner."

Connor's gaze shifts from me to the open door behind me. "Damn, so this is what the penthouses look like. Good for you, Red."

"It's definitely an upgrade from the staff cabins." I laugh, suddenly nervous. "I wish I could invite you guys in but you get it, right? With our history and all." Henry may have relented on the idea of me staying away from Ronan and Connor, but there is no way he would be okay coming home to find my two "fuck buddies" on either side of the couch with me. I can't blame him. If the situation was reversed, I might be uncomfortable too.

Connor's brows pop with surprise. "Exactly how much does he know about that?"

I smile sheepishly. "There are no secrets between us."

"Whoa." He looks to Ronan and scrunches his face up. "Seriously. How the hell have we *not* been canned yet?"

"Because of her." Ronan nods to me.

"Well, whatever. That's fine. We don't want to hang out in here anyway." Connor exchanges a look with Ronan.

"Don't, man," Ronan starts.

Suddenly, strong hands are seizing my thighs and I'm lifted off the ground. I find myself dangling over Connor's shoulder. He slaps my ass playfully.

"Oh my God! Connor!" I squeal.

"Dude, you are going to get us fired for this," Ronan warned as Connor starts heading down the path.

"Why? Because Red wants to hang out with her friends?"

"Because you're manhandling Wolf property, you jackass."

"She'll protect us, won't you, Red?"

"Put me down!"

"Sure thing. As soon as we reach the staff lodge. There's a lot of people who want to see you. We'll have you back before he knows you've been gone. Plus I think you owe us some rounds of shots for being such a sly chick. Seriously. Banging the Wolf? Good on you. Never saw that one coming, did we, Ronan?"

"Nope. No idea." I look up in time to catch Ronan's wink.

"I MIGHT ACTUALLY MISS THIS PLACE," Rachel admits just before downing her shot of Fireball, her gaze drifting to the rafters and peaked ceiling of the staff lounge. "The money has been unreal."

"Is that what you're going to miss most? The money?" Katie grins as she rubs Rachel's leg with her hand. All three of us are sitting on the couch near the roaring fire. The heat radiating from it is warming my left side to an almost uncomfortable level.

Rachel smiles as she meets her friend's knowing gaze, her

fingers playfully twirling through her bottle-blonde ponytail. "*Definitely* the friendships."

"Don't you mean the fuckships? Lord knows you've had enough of those," Tillie murmurs in her southern croon, holding her flask to her lips. My guess is it's filled with Jack Daniel's, her alcohol of choice. And she's clearly had plenty of it.

Rachel's head falls back as she laughs, unaffected by our old cabinmate's intended slight. "Especially those."

Everyone starts chuckling. Everyone except Tillie, who studies her nails with a scowl.

I lean in to whisper to Katie, "Autumn told me she moved out of your cabin?"

"Oh, yeah. As ugly as things got between her and Lorraine when you were around, after that joke the guys played on her, they got ten times worse."

I frown. "What joke?"

Katie's eyes widen. "Oh, they didn't tell you about their little fuck club?"

"I heard about it."

"Well, Connor was egging Tillie on, saying that she didn't have the nerve to let go like that, calling her a prude and all sorts of things. People started thinking they split because Tillie wasn't any good." Katie waggles her eyebrows. "So Tillie agreed. I guess she assumed she'd end up with either him or Ronan, or one of the other guys playing. She stripped down and waited on the bed, in the dark." Katie pauses for effect. "They sent Lorraine in there."

My eyes widen. "Wait. So Lorraine's not straight?"

"She is, but that was the thing with this club. Whatever you walked into... was what you walked into."

"Oh my God."

"Lorraine must have assumed it was me or Rachel that she was with—"

"Wait, so you and Rachel were a part of this club?"

Katie shrugs, and offers me a sly smile. "Anyway, you weren't allowed to say a word, that was a strict rule. But then Tillie came and, well, she *sounds* like Tillie."

I think back to her in the shower. Yeah, there's no mistaking that.

"So both of them flipped out. Tillie, especially. We thought we were going to wake up to Lorraine's throat slit one morning." Katie's pretty blue eyes narrow as she regards Tillie. "That is one mean-ass redhead."

I frown. "That was a bit of a jerk move by Connor and Ronan, though." I never thought my friends would stoop to that.

"That's the thing—they got bombed that night and forgot. Moe decided to take the lead and set it up. So, she's pissed about that, and that we took Lorraine's side in the first place, but come on! Tillie knew those two were together." Katie's pretty brow furrows. "It's really too bad. We had some good times in that cabin together. All this started because of a stupid guy."

I think back to that first night, when I walked into a cabin full of laughter and budding friendships. It's sad that it's fallen apart, but with this many people in close proximity for this long, it was inevitable that someone would fall out of sorts. I hesitate. "What has she said about me being with Henry?"

Katie's gives me a look. "Nothing worth repeating. She's still bitter that Connor liked you a million times more as a friend than he did her when they were dating. The only reason she's lingering now is because she's hoping for some juicy gossip about Wolf."

And she's not going to get that.

"*So?*" Katie leans in to bump shoulders with me, her big blue eyes curious. "What's it like? Does he have a huge dick?"

I burst out with a nervous giggle, even as my cheeks flame. Why is Henry *always* right? "I am not talking about that with you."

"He must be huge. And I'll bet it's as amazing as we've all imagined." She waggles her brow. "Is he into anything dirty?"

Probably not by your standards, Katie. I take a long sip of the beer Ronan supplied me with, and ignore the question.

"Oh come on! Tell us something about him!" she cries in mock anguish.

"Or don't, seeing as you broke my heart by running off to him before I had my chance with you," Connor announces as he rounds the couch with a platter of shots and lemon wedges.

"Oh please. Don't act like you didn't find a quick replacement." Tillie nods toward another group sitting in the corner.

It doesn't take long for me to pinpoint the girl she's referring to. The striking willowy one with a messy bun of raven hair, who's stealing frequent glances this way, her sharp almond-shaped eyes shifting between Connor and Ronan, who sits perched on the back of the couch next to me.

I catch Ronan's eyes.

Really? You two and her? I try to convey with my look, my curiosity getting the better of me.

He merely shrugs. And then the corners of his mouth curve up in one of his signature dark smiles.

I shake my head. "You've been really busy."

He hesitates and then leans down, using the couch behind my head to hold himself up. "None of them come close to being with you," he whispers into my ear.

I chuckle, even as I blush. "Yeah. Okay. You tell that to every girl." I'm not stupid.

"You know I don't." He pulls back enough to show me his

eyes, and the sincerity framed within those thick, dark lashes. "You were special. You were different."

My chest fills with an odd sense of adoration. "You were special to me, too. I've never had a friend like you. I'm guessing I never will again." Unless I count Margo, but that friendship is unique on a whole different level.

His gaze slowly skates over my features as he takes a deep breath. "Does he make you happy?"

"Yes."

His jaw tightens. "Does he satisfy you?"

"Yes."

"Are you sure? Because you were ready to—"

Katie's sharp elbow against my arm pulls my attention away. That's when I notice that it's grown quiet in the lodge, the buzz of voices dying down to leave nothing but the sound of music through the speakers.

Henry stands ten feet away, staring at me. His face is unreadable but menacing all the same.

I hear a soft "fuck" slip from Ronan's lips. Slowly he sits upright again, and sighs as if resigning himself for the shit storm to come.

Oh God. What did that look like?

A few more uncomfortable beats pass and then Henry holds up my phone that I left on the coffee table at the cabin. "You forgot this." His tone is friendly enough.

I peel myself off the couch to weave through the bodies to him, feeling so many eyes boring into us. I wrap my arms around his waist. "I'm sorry. I didn't realize it was so late. I just swung by to say hello."

"Swung? Or were carried...," he murmurs low enough for only me to hear, his piercing gaze taking in the situation—the faces, the beer in my hand, the platter of tequila shots—with a lightning quick pass before stalling on Ronan. And narrowing.

Ronan doesn't balk, meeting his glare.

"For old times' sake?" Connor holds up a shot of tequila for Henry. There are no old times. These two have never drank together. If Connor is at all nervous—about the fact that Henry knows our history and could fire his ass on the spot if he wanted to, or give him a good run for his money in a fight—he doesn't show it.

Henry settles that steely gaze on Connor for two... three... four beats before he accepts the shot. "I think Abbi needs one, too."

"No, I'm good, thanks—" I start to say, but Henry smoothly plucks another from the tray and holds it out to me.

"Oh, no. You're going to need it," Henry warns softly. His smile is downright wicked as he throws back his shot without salt or a lemon wedge.

Despite the looming tension, my thighs clench with anticipation. He's going to punish me for what he just saw, but in a way that I'll enjoy.

I pour back the shot, wincing against the vile taste as I suck on the slice of lemon.

Henry lifts a hand and snaps at the bartender. "Next round's on me."

Everyone cheers.

"What are you doing?" I hiss.

He gazes down at me. "Getting to know your friends. Isn't that what you want?"

I QUICKLY SCRUB soap over my hands, intent on getting back to Henry as quickly as possible, before he's mauled by one of the drunker female staff or Connor says something obnoxious that sends him over the edge. My body is buzzing from the alcohol after the four rounds Henry bought for everyone and insisted I partake in. I'm one shot away from stumbling home.

"Oh my God, Henry Wolf is so hot. How can you even handle having sex with him? I don't know if I could do it! I'd be too nervous!" A girl—Tina, I think she said her name was —slurs as she fluffs her long brown hair in the restroom mirror next to me.

She's not the first to say that to me tonight, even though I've been attached to Henry's side until just now. But the combination of alcohol and Henry Wolf make most women brazen.

I simply smile at the girl, just like I've simply smiled at the others.

The farmost stall door creaks open and Tillie strolls out. "Abbi!" She offers me a wide smile that doesn't reach her eyes. "Your hair wasn't that red when I saw you on the ferry earlier."

"Yeah. I got Tris to do it again. She's so good at it." I subconsciously reach for my shiny red locks. I used to envy Tillie for her fiery red hair, back when I believed Mama was right and I couldn't dye my hair for fear of it turning orange, or worse, green.

"My, haven't things gone your way. Started out as a maid and end up in the boss's bed." She rubs soap all over her hands while watching me with her sharp eyes.

"It was definitely unexpected," I admit with a polite smile.

Rinsing her hands, she quickly towel-dries them and then slides out a deep crimson lipstick. "I guess now we know why Wolf hired you."

That's definitely not an "I'm happy for you." If what Autumn and Katie say is true, then I can only imagine the kinds of things a jealous Tillie has been saying about me behind my back. And to think that the first night here, Tillie and I walked arm in arm down the path, laughing and joking. I was ready to label her my new best friend. I was also blazing drunk, but that's besides the point.

"I heard Wolf does have a thing for his assistants, though, so we shouldn't be too surprised." She smears the lipstick over her lips. "It's too bad you're not actually workin' for Wolf anymore. The last one got a huge severance package out of it, didn't she?"

So Tillie has somehow heard about Kiera. And she's digging for more information. Something to gossip about.

Not that it matters, but it's annoying.

"No idea what you're talking about." I turn to leave.

"I know you're naïve, but are you actually stupid enough to think this is going to last? 'Cause I'm sorry to say, it won't. Everyone knows it. Everyone's sayin' it. They're all smiles to your face but you know they've got a pool goin' to see how long before he dumps you and goes back to his supermodels."

Her words spear me right where she intended—my confidence. "Who? Who's betting in this pool?"

"Pretty much everyone."

"Who?" I demand. Autumn? Katie? My stomach twists. Ronan?

She shrugs noncommittally. "*I* don't squeal on things I might overhear."

It dawns on me. So *that's* what this bitterness toward me is about. She must have found out that it was me in the shower that night she and James had sex, and she obviously thinks I told Lorraine.

Now she's just trying to get under my skin. God, Tillie's so vindictive. And to think I once liked her.

"Hey Tillie, next time you spread your legs for a woman, maybe ask for her name first," I murmur as airily as I can.

I leave Tillie in the bathroom with her mouth hanging open and her cheeks flushed, the moment of pettiness easing a bit of the sting. I head straight for where I left Henry, ready to go back to our penthouse, my mood soured.

He's no longer there. "Did you see where Henry went to?" I ask Katie.

"I think he was heading for the door."

"Thanks." I don't bother saying anything about the bet—there's no point. I weave through the dwindling crowd and out the main door.

"...I should fire your ass right now. I should have fired you months ago," I hear Henry snarl, squared off against Ronan.

Oh, shit. I'm instantly sober.

"If it makes you feel like a bigger man, go ahead. But I'm just looking out for Abbi," Ronan retorts, not backing down, his face equally hard.

"You're just looking to fuck Abbi."

"How could I not want to? She's fucking perfect." Ronan grins wickedly. "And we like the same things. *You* know which kinds of things. Stuff a fucking asshole like you can't give her. *Won't* give her, because you're too damn jealous and selfish and controlling."

Ohhhhh... shit.

I watch as Henry's fist closes tight by his side.

Ronan's not done though, stepping right into his face. "And if you hurt her again like you did last time—"

"I'm ready to go." I dive in between them, forcing them apart, and rope my arms around Henry's waist.

Henry's chest is puffing with anger. The last time I saw him look like this, he had just punched Scott.

"Come on, Henry. It's time to go," I plead. "It's not worth it."

After several long, tense moments, he releases a long sigh and weaves his fingers through mine. He leads me out into the biting night air.

I glance back at Ronan once, to find him lighting a

cigarette, his intense gaze still on us. "What the hell was that about?"

"I was just getting to know your friend," he answers mildly. In his next breath, his voice turns steely. "Do you still want him?"

"No! Why?"

"Are you still attracted to him?"

Ronan still is and will always be attractive. I can't say that to Henry, not in his current state. But I also don't want to lie. "Are you attracted to Margo?" I throw back.

Henry's jaw tightens. He knows he can't deny that without lying, because he's already admitted as much. Every breathing, heterosexual male is attracted to Margo, along with most everyone else.

I'm shivering. Henry shrugs off his checkered jacket and holds it out for me to slip on. "I guess you didn't have a chance to grab a jacket, what with those two assholes coming to my doorstep to throw you over their shoulder and carry you here."

"How do you—"

"Security cameras, Abbi. They're *everywhere*. Don't ever forget that."

I curl my arm through his to bring myself closer to him. "I don't want Ronan, if that's what you're asking. I don't think about being with him again. I don't think about anyone but you. You are all I need or want."

The gravel crunches under our feet as we pass the shower houses, where the sounds of running water and laughter carry.

"And yet I walked in there tonight to find him hanging over you, and you looking like you were enjoying every second of it."

"Ronan wasn't trying anything. I mean, he asked me if I was happy, but after how sad he saw me, of course he would.

We just.... I can't explain our relationship. I guess maybe it's like yours with Margo."

"He has feelings for you."

"No. It's not like that."

"It is. Trust me."

I sigh. "How did that fight start, anyway?" Henry was listening politely to a few of the kitchen staff rave about the chef, and how talented she is, when I left to use the restroom.

"I needed some fresh air. I went out and found him there smoking. He didn't waste any time telling me that you deserve all my love and attention and I better be giving it to you."

"Oh." I frown. "Well, that's not the worst thing for Ronan to say."

"He also said that you don't want to be treated like a good little girl."

I sigh. I remember telling Ronan something about that—about how Henry liked that I was so innocent—way back when I also believed that he slept with that journalist because he *wasn't* satisfied with my innocence. I can't believe Ronan would have the balls to say that to Henry, though.

"It took everything in me to not knock his teeth out. I know *exactly* what you need."

"I'm sorry, Henry. Maybe you were right. It was a bad idea to come here, tonight."

Silence lingers. "They didn't hurt your hip carrying you over here, did they?" he finally asks, more softly.

"No. It's fine. After this afternoon, *you know* it's fine."

He smiles slyly. "Did you have fun tonight?"

"I did, until I ran into Tillie." I tell him about the betting pool, and note the lack of shock or anger on his face. "You don't seem surprised."

"I'm not. And you shouldn't be, either. You can't let those kinds of things get to you."

"Yeah, but they're my friends."

"Friends will disappoint you all the time. That's why I don't keep many friends."

"But they—"

"They're people who came into your life and who will leave just as quickly. You won't remember half their names in ten years. Others, you won't even remember that they exist. They won't come running when you need them, believe me. If they want to waste their time and money betting against us, let them. None of them will be winning a damn dime, that I promise you."

"You're so sure?"

He slows to a stop, to face me. Roping his arms around my body, he pulls me into his chest. "Do you remember the first night we met? When I had to carry your drunk ass home?"

I giggle as I peer up into his beautiful blue eyes, slipping my arms around him. "Some parts, yeah."

A couple heads toward us along the path, and I hear a whisper of, "Is that Wolf?"

Henry ignores them, leaning in to whisper in my ear, "You were going on and on about needing to lose your virginity, and your mouth was pressed up against my neck."

"Yes. Unfortunately, I remember that well," I mutter wryly.

"I carried you along this path, past that," he points to a nearby toolshed, "and I was so fucking tempted to bring you in there and give you exactly what you needed. Right there."

"Why didn't you?"

He gives me a flat look. "Because contrary to what your mother thinks, I do have some morals. But you owned me that night." His alcohol-laced breath skates over my face. "I went home and jerked off—twice—thinking about fucking you. I couldn't tell you the last time I jerked off to thoughts of a woman before that, let alone twice in one night. It'd definitely been a few years."

My breath quickens. "Where?" I whisper.

His eyebrows rise.

"Where did you do it? In the shower? In bed?"

"Once on the couch. Once in bed." He smirks. "Why? Do you like picturing me doing that?"

"Yes," I admit, smiling shyly. Thoughts of watching Henry in the shower that very first time—his legs spread and his arm flexing, his fist gripping his length tightly as he stroked himself—flood back to me. I've watched him touch himself plenty since then, but that first time will always burn in my memory.

A familiar ache throbs between my legs, and my skin starts to flush.

He's hardening against my stomach.

"And were we in that toolshed, in your thoughts?" I ask softly. It's like toying with a dangerous animal now, taunting him and arousing him like this so far from our place, but thanks to the tequila, I can't help myself.

He slides his hands into the coat I'm wearing and then feels his way under my shirt. I squeal with the chill from his hands, but he doesn't stop, sliding them all the way up my back to unfasten my bra.

"We were. The first time." He bends to whisper into my ear. "I stripped you down and fucked your pussy on the work bench. The second time, I bent you over and fucked your ass until you came. You screamed the entire time, but you loved it."

My thighs clench together. Blunt, dirty-talking Henry is one of my favorites. "That would have been a very enlightening night, then."

"I knew even then that I didn't have a hope in hell of resisting you, even though I convinced myself otherwise.

You'd already won me over. And you keep winning me over, night after night. So, yeah. I'm sure that those fools who are betting against us are nothing but fools." He bends down to lay a soft kiss against my lips. It's followed quickly by a much deeper one, stirring every nerve ending in my body.

Behind us, I hear the sound of footfalls on gravel and a few catcalls, but Henry doesn't relent, his one hand sliding down to cup my ass and pull my body flush against his erection.

I'm surprised that he's doing this in the middle of the staff village. Maybe he's more drunk than he's letting on, what with all the Scotch earlier and the shots he just did. Or maybe he's so angry with what Ronan said, he's trying to prove that satisfying my "appetite" will not be an issue. Either way, I'm not about to stop him. Let people see us. Let the jealous bitches like Tillie get a good look at us. I let my hands fist around his hair and I lose myself in the feel of his tongue dancing against mine, no longer aware of the cool temperatures. My desire to get his clothes off and feel him thrusting into me outweighs everything else.

"I need you right now," I whisper against his mouth.

"Then we better start walking, fast."

An impulsive idea strikes me. "I can't wait that long." Breaking away from his mouth, I grab his hand and begin tugging him down the path.

"Abbi, what do you think you're doing?" he asks with amusement.

"You know exactly what I'm doing. If they haven't changed the code...." I punch in the five-digit code I used when I needed a shovel or trowel from this toolshed, surprised that I still remember it.

"I'm not sure you realize—"

I yank open the door to find the dull light already on inside.

"Oh my God!" I yell. Simon the bellhop is bent over the work bench with his pants pushed down to his ankles and Omar from outdoor crew is behind him, thrusting into his ass.

"Holy shit." Omar's eyes grow wide with fear as he pulls out of Simon and scrambles to yank his pants up, jamming his condom-clad, hard dick into his briefs. Simon moves almost as quickly, tucking his own swollen length in with a touch more care.

And suddenly the two of them are staring at the two of us, both of their faces panic-stricken.

Henry nods to the door. "Get the fuck out."

"I'm sorry, Mr. Wolf. We just didn't have anywhere else to go," Omar says, a pleading tone in his voice.

Henry's hand in the air stalls Omar from saying more. "No need to explain. No one will hear about this. Now get out."

The two of them scurry out, tossing a "sorry" as they pass us.

Henry pulls the door shut. And starts to chuckle. "What was that I said, about you somehow *always* finding your way into rooms where people are fucking?"

My giggles follow soon after as I press my face into his chest. "Oh my God, I had no idea...."

"That people used this shed to fuck? Or that those two are gay?"

"Both? I mean, I've overheard some people talking about doing it in the sheds, but those two...." I look up at Henry's secretive smile and it dawns on me. "You knew. How did you... security footage," I answer for myself.

"All these keypads are connected to a main system, so we know when people are going in. Someone's been going in every night around the same time for the last few weeks, so they checked the camera footage on the path nearby. It wasn't hard to figure out what was going on."

"So you've known and you let it happen?"

Henry's lips twist. "People are fucking like rabbits everywhere around here. But I'm guessing it's a lot harder for guys like these two. Some of their roommates might take issue with them bending each other over in the showers. So I told Belinda to leave it alone, as long as no problems arise."

"That was... kind of you." I glance over to where Omar and Simon were and see the bottle of lubricant. "I've never seen two guys like that before."

"Why am I not surprised?"

"Have you?"

"Yes," he answers without hesitation, his hands rubbing and down my arms in an affectionate warming motion. But of course Henry has.

I know he hasn't been with a guy before, he's told me as much. I hesitate. "And does watching two men... *do* anything for you?"

"No. But it also doesn't bother me." A mock frown settles across his face. "So, why did you bring me in here again?"

"I was feeling adventurous, but...." I giggle nervously as I press myself into him. "Who knows who else uses this shed. Maybe we should head back to our cabin."

Henry smoothly grabs a hammer from the rack and jams it through the door handle, stopping anyone from being able to open it. "You know I don't like quitters." With a hand on my back, he guides me to stand exactly where Simon was moments ago. "Not when there's a perfectly good bottle of lube here that shouldn't go to waste." He spins me around and stands behind me, his hands gripping my waist. He dips down to nibble and kiss the crook of my neck.

Shivers course through my limbs, over my breasts, between my legs.

"Are you cold?"

"A little," I admit, even though adrenaline is racing through my veins.

"Then you should leave my coat on. For now." Slipping his hands down into either side of my leggings, Henry eases them down to my ankles, followed by my panties, leaving my most sensitive flesh exposed to the air.

Gooseflesh covers my thighs, and small plumes of hot air sail from my mouth, and yet even with the temperatures, my breath begins to quicken in anticipation, the promise for release under Henry's touch sending a flush of heat through my core.

"Put your arms on the table and bend over."

Just like Simon.

I obey, and find myself studying the smooth concrete floor beneath my feet, and Henry's black work boots as they come up behind me.

My mouth falls open in a slight gasp as Henry slides his hand in between my legs and begins rubbing back and forth. I instinctively set my legs farther apart to give him better access, which he eagerly takes.

Two fingers slip into me and begin stroking in and out, growing the pool of wetness already there. Soon a third finger joins, stretching me wide.

"You're dripping, Abbi."

"Because I want you so badly."

"You made me come all the way out here, tonight. I was expecting to find you warm and naked in my bed. You made me wait," he says calmly. "Maybe I should make you wait."

I rock my body against his hand in the same way I would against his cock if it were there.

"Abbi," he growls, earning my taunting laugh.

I hear the jingle as he unbuckles his belt and unfastens his zipper, and then pushes his jeans down his thighs. Blood rushes to my belly and between my legs. I can feel it pumping into my pussy, making my clit swell with anticipation.

I arch my back and prepare for the sudden thrust into me that I know is coming.

But instead Henry grabs the bottle of lubricant. A moment later, silky liquid hits my tailbone and begins sliding downward in a stream. He uses his thumb to smear it along my tight entrance.

"You want *that* tonight?" I realize with a hint of nervousness. He hasn't done that to me since that night in the truck, at that seedy bar.

"Let's be clear; I want *every*thing, *every* night." He begins prodding with his thumb. It's slick enough that it slides in with only a slight burn. "Open wider."

I move my legs farther apart, and he continues to work me with both of his hands, his right stroking that spot deep inside me that makes heat flare in my belly while his left thumb slowly pushes in deeper from behind. My body responds quickly, the pressure growing and spreading down between my legs.

"Oh my God, this is too intense."

His dark chuckle rattles in my chest. "Babe, I haven't even started with intense." He pulls his three fingers out. I feel the head of his cock rubbing against my entrance. I adjust my stance slightly to welcome it in. His first thrust is so fast and deep that I cry out with surprise.

"Too hard?" he murmurs, not sounding sorry at all.

"No. I want it harder," I dare.

Every thrust after is at a languid pace, in and out, in and out, in no rush to get either of us off it seems, as Henry divides his focus between his cock and the thumb he's pumping in and out of my ass.

The burn is just starting to subside when I hear the bottle

of lubricant compress and a dollop of lube pool over my tight skin. He trades his thumb for two fingers.

"Breathe. I'll go slow," he guides.

I close my eyes and concentrate on my breathing as he very slowly pushes two fingers into me, stretching my muscles. His pelvis barely rocks as he allows my body to adjust to the intrusion.

"Still good?" Henry murmurs, pushing my jacket and shirt up. He loves a good view.

"Yes," I manage to get out, my muscles involuntarily squeezing tightly. There's so much lube on me that it's not long before I feel the press of his knuckles against my skin. He's all the way in.

He folds over me to whisper into my ear, "Do you like it?"

I pant at the pressure this new position has caused. "I like everything you do to me, Henry."

His free hand slips up the front of my shirt to fill with a breast, the bra that he unfastened earlier useless in this position. "Everything?"

"Everything."

"Did you like it when I fucked your ass?"

"Yes," I admit shyly.

"Good." He presses a kiss against my jawline, sending shivers through my core. "Because I'm going to do it now."

My muscles spasm against his dirty words. Am I ready for this again? Right here in a toolshed? "Okay." I don't think I could say no to Henry, even if I wanted to.

He promptly slides his fingers and his cock out of me, leaving me empty. Grabbing me by the waist, he turns me around and hoists me onto the bench.

"How come this way?"

Working his jacket off me, he balls it up and sets it behind me. He lines my hips up with the edge and then guides me down to lie on the table.

"Because it's more intense this way. And I want to see your face." He pushes against the back of my thighs until my legs are practically pressed against my chest. "I want to watch you scream."

He drops to his knees and, leaning in, swirls the very tip of his tongue over my slick puckered skin.

"Oh my God." I gasp, my muscles clenching.

Around and around, his tongue works, his eyes locked on mine as he teases me mercilessly.

I'm terribly exposed in this position, but I guess that's the point. I glance at the door, momentarily horrified at the idea of someone walking in on me like this. But it's barred with a hammer. Even if someone punches in the code, no one's coming in.

Henry doesn't allow my focus to stray for too long though. He stands. I watch with nervous excitement as he coats his rigid length with more lube and then strokes himself to spread it around.

"This table is the perfect height," he murmurs, his eyes flickering from my face to his target as he rubs the tip of his cock back and forth over the tight spot several times. "It's almost like you built it for this very purpose."

"I am a forward thinker." He smiles, his fingers spreading my cheeks apart. "Relax your muscles. Take a breath."

And then he begins sinking into me.

There's so much lubricant on the both of us that my body accepts him much faster than the last time. Still, I wince against the burn, and I find myself wondering how much I could really have enjoyed it. Maybe I was just caught up in the moment.

"Look at me."

Henry settles his thumb on my clit to draw smooth, slow circles around it as his hips rock back and forth, subtly inching in a little deeper each time.

"Do you really enjoy this?" I ask between panted breaths.

He fixes me with an even stare. "I love it. And you will, too. But I need you to relax your muscles and let me in."

"Can you take your shirt off?"

He smirks. "It's a bit cold, Abbi."

"I want to see your body."

Without another word, he reaches over his head to yank off his long-sleeved black shirt.

I focus on his chiseled upper body for the next few minutes as he maintains his slow pace of inching in and out of me, picturing my tongue twirling around his hard nipples, or dragging along that dark line of hair below his belly button. And I try not to flex my muscles.

"How much farther?" I feel like I might split apart.

"Almost there," he whispers through gritted teeth, his eyes dark and full of desire as they watch where we're joined. He slides his hands over my inner thighs, pushing my legs apart farther.

"You're so deep," I whisper through a pant. He was right. This is so much more intense than the last time.

He reaches for the lube.

"Don't we have enough?" I exclaim with a laugh as he squeezes more over me. I feel it dripping along my slit and down farther.

"There's no such thing as too much lube. Touch yourself for me."

I don't hesitate when he asks me to do that anymore. I slip a hand between my legs. My fingers slide easily over my swollen mound and clit.

He begins gently thrusting in and out of me without warning. My hand momentarily stalls with the sting. I bite my lip, trying to keep myself from crying out.

"Don't, Abbi. I want to hear you," he demands. A thin sheen of sweat has formed across his muscular chest.

"But someone else might hear."

"Good. Let them."

"What happened to keeping your private life private?"

"Apparently some of my employees think I can't satisfy my woman. Keep going, Abbi."

Around and around my fingers go, slipping and sliding over my clit, along my slit, dipping in every so often. The burn has subsided and my body is finally loosening up for him. He must feel it too, because he starts thrusting harder into me.

"Oh, God. Henry!" It's getting harder to remain quiet, my lips parting and letting small moans and cries slip out unbidden.

He tips his head back as he pumps, giving me a great view of his jagged Adam's apple.

This cedar table is far from comfortable, even with Henry's jacket offering some cushion for my head, and yet all I can think about right now is what he's doing to me.

"You are so damn perfect. So fucking tight, Abbi," Henry moans. I sense my body producing its own lubricant now as my muscles welcome his intrusion, and my nerves buzz with heady anticipation.

"Harder," I whisper, my stomach and thigh muscles tensing as I start to meet each thrust.

Henry slams his cock into my ass. "You should see yourself right now."

I squeeze my eyes shut. "I don't know if I could handle it."

"You could. You'd love it. Here." He slows long enough to dig my phone out of the pocket of my jacket. Swiping the camera on, he aims it between my legs. He adjusts his stance and begins pounding into me again while recording it.

I suck in a breath as my muscles begin tightening around him, as my clit begins throbbing, as the urge to spread my legs as far as possible takes over.

"So you like having a camera on your pussy." Henry chuckles darkly. "Good to know. Here, watch this." He hands me my phone.

I gasp as I watch his beautiful swollen cock filling my ass, my slickened body stretching around it, accepting him, with each of his thrusts. The video is only fifteen seconds but watching it while he's still fucking me there is all it takes for the familiar telltale tingle to begin in the base of my spine.

"I'm coming," I pant, pressing my palms against the table as if to brace myself, my focus now on the low cedar ceiling above.

I cry out as Henry pushes his fingers deep into my pussy again.

He presses down inside me, against the back of my muscle wall. I can feel his cock stroke the other side.

He picks up the pace of his thrusts. "Abbi," he forces out between gritted teeth.

The first wave explodes through my lower belly and down my thighs. I cry out and still my hips as the sensation flows up my spine, as my muscles pulse around Henry, squeezing against both his cock and his fingers.

"Fuck!" He follows immediately, a deep groan tearing from his lungs, his one hand gripping my ass cheek tightly, his pulsing length working against my muscles to drive me insane. I can feel warmth as his seed flows into me. "Christ, Abbi." He slides his hand out of me, his heavy body falls on top of me. My legs are like Jell-O, splayed to either side.

We lay like that for several long moments, our pants filling the silent night.

"So, was the toolshed as good as you imagined it would be?" I whisper.

"Better. Way better. I didn't have a bottle of lube in my version," he murmurs, earning my giggle.

"I need a shower now. I'm covered in it. I'm all slimy."

He nuzzles his face into my neck and presses a kiss against my throat. “I’ll draw you a bath when we get back. I think certain parts of you are going to need it. I was pretty hard on you.”

My body clenches around his cock, still deep inside me. “I liked it,” I admit shyly. “Especially that last part, when you added your hand.”

“I had a feeling you would.”

I rope my arms around his naked, hot upper body. “I love everything you do for me.”

He lifts himself just far enough to gaze into my eyes. “And I love that you’re so agreeable with everything I want to do for you.”

“I love you.” I reach up to play with the ends of his brown hair. “But can you please get your dick out of my ass? It’s a little uncomfortable now.”

He chuckles. “Sure. Give me a minute.” Very slowly and with care, he slides himself out of me.

We dress quickly, the cold creeping over our damp, flushed skin.

“What about this?” I hold up the almost empty bottle of lube.

He smoothly takes it from my hand. “Probably shouldn’t leave it in here. I’ll pitch it on the way.”

He slides the hammer from the handle and we head out. Three figures linger on the main path, only twenty feet away. Connor and the willowy brunette from earlier stand by the lamppost. The brunette’s eyes widen when she sees Henry. Connor’s face has been taken over by a smug grin.

Ronan is near the trash can. He’s his usual cool self, a lit cigarette in his hand, even though he knows he’s not allowed to be smoking along the paths or other main staff areas. His dark, knowing gaze is on us.

They had to have heard us.

Looping his arm around my waist, Henry leads me past them calmly, as if he doesn't give a shit. He slows just long enough to press the bottle of lube into Ronan's free hand. "Should be a little bit left for you," he murmurs with a smile, just loud enough for Ronan and me to hear. We continue on.

I glance back to see Ronan studying the bottle of lube in his hand. Then, with a shake of his head and a small smile, he dumps it into the trash bin.

"When are you meeting with the engineers?" Morning sun streams through the cracks in the blackout curtains where we didn't fully draw them, allowing me just enough light to study his nipples, hardened by my mischievous fingertips.

"I'm not."

I frown. "Really? I thought they were here today, too."

"They are. But they don't need me there to tell them how to do their jobs," he murmurs sleepily, his voice deep and scratchy.

"Since when do you *not* tell people how to do their jobs?" I press a kiss against his hot, clean skin. It smells of the mint-scented soap from the bath we took together last night.

"So you're in one of *those* moods this morning." He rolls into me, curling his arm around my body to fold me into him. I feel so small when I'm up against him like this. "Since this know-it-all redhead came in to my life and disrupted things." He drags his tongue over the seam of my lips. "Speaking of telling people how to do their jobs, it sounds like Nailed It has all the back end work done for online ordering."

"Yes, I saw that email."

"You need to meet with them next week to make some

decisions. Once they get the production running, you can start selling."

"I know. How'd they get everything ready so fast, anyway? I mean, the regulatory stuff alone can take months."

"It's amazing what an impatient tyrant with a pool full of money can accomplish." Humor laces his words.

"Henry...."

"Don't tell me not to be demanding on your behalf. I'll never listen." His strong, warm hand smooths over my spine.

"But you realize that you're putting all this money and effort into something so small."

"You are getting every advantage. If it stays small, it's because you wanted it to. Is that what you want?"

"I don't know. But —"

"Have more faith in yourself, Abbi."

I burrow in closer to him, curling my thigh around his. "So, what are we going to do today then?"

"Besides this?"

"You can't lay in bed *all* day. You're not capable. Your head would explode." This guy always has pressing matters.

He pulls my thigh the rest of the way around his hip and rolls onto his back. I end up lying on top of him, straddling him, his hard cock nestled between my thighs perfectly.

Instinctively I begin rubbing myself along him, earning a sound of contentment deep within his chest.

"I figured we could grab a nice meal in Lux later." He matches my movement.

"I'd like that."

His finger slides down my spine again, this time continuing farther, down between my cheeks. "How are you this morning?"

"A little sore," I admit. "But not in a bad way." In the way that I love, where I can still feel Henry deep inside me, hours later.

Seizing my hips, he re-angles my pelvis and expertly pushes into me. "Sit up."

I do as requested, letting the covers fall away from us.

He's just close enough that he can reach the light. He switches it on, filling the room with soft light. His sleepy eyes, now a dark heated blue, settle on my full, heavy breasts as I languidly ride him, watching them sway with each roll.

"God, Abbi…." He moans softly, covering his eyes with the palms of his hands momentarily.

"What's wrong?"

Suddenly he's sitting upright, having pulled himself up with an impressive layer of muscle across his stomach. "Nothing's wrong." One hand curves around the back of my skull, the fingers of one hand weaving through mine while the other hand settles on my tailbone, pushing my body flush with his. "Everything is fucking perfect. *You* are perfect for me. How are you so perfect for me?"

It must be a rhetorical question, because his mouth closes over mine before I can answer, and doesn't leave until long after he has come inside me.

"I've never tried lobster," I admit.

"Then have the lobster."

"But what if I don't like it?"

"Then order something else." He says it like that's what everyone else would do.

When I pause over the menu again, hesitating, he tells the waiter, "She'll have the lobster tails and possibly something else after. I'll have the T-bone, rare."

"Yes, sir. Cedric will be here momentarily to help you with your wine selection." The waiter nods politely to me before swiftly moving away.

I let my eyes roll over the interior of Lux. The place is only half-full, its patrons sitting at round tables with expensive white linens and dancing tapered candles. I've been here a few times before, but not in a while, and always as Henry's assistant, fetching things for him or taking notes. "I could never appreciate how nice it is in here. Not from this viewpoint anyway."

"You mean as a guest?"

"Yes."

Henry unfolds his napkin and sets it on his lap. I follow suit. "Get used to it. You're going to see places like this, and nicer than this." He reaches across the table to weave his fingers through mine. "I'm going to give you the world, Abigail Mitchell."

You already have, I feel like saying. "I don't need the world, Henry. I just need you."

Crystal-blue eyes settle on me, studying me for a long moment. "Well, you have me." A small smirk curls his lips. "Bad temper and all."

I shrug playfully. "You're not so bad."

"No?"

"No. Not when I know how to ease that temper."

His brow lifts a touch. "And how is that?"

I kick off my heel and, stretching my leg out, I slide my foot in between his thighs and begin rubbing. He parts his legs a touch more, giving me access. I feel him hardening against my toes. "See?"

He smiles. "But I wasn't in a bad mood to begin with."

I decide now's as good a time as any. "Why didn't you tell me that your birthday is tomorrow?"

The smile sours as his gaze wanders. "I guess I'll need a new assistant after all," he mutters dryly.

"Don't blame Miles. I asked him to tell me. Something I shouldn't have had to do."

"You've never told me when yours is."

"I don't have to. I'm sure you already—"

"March 3."

I roll my eyes at him. "See?"

"It's a regular day for me. I have my meetings at the gold mine." He takes a long sip of his ice water. "Birthdays have never been a big deal in our family."

"Never?" Even Mama, for all she is, always made sure everyone and their dog knew it was my happy birthday.

"My grandmother always made sure we had a cake." He smiles wistfully. "The woman had all the money in the world to buy one and yet she'd always take the time to bake it. She used those boxed mixes, too. They were the best. After she died... it's just any other day."

"That's sad."

"That was my world."

"Well, not anymore it's not. So what do you want?"

"Your mouth around my cock," he says without missing a beat.

"Henry!" I glare at him and flush, searching the two tables within hearing distance. Words like "cock" tend to grab attention. Thankfully, no one is glancing our way. With a rub of my foot, I murmur, "Well, that can easily be arranged. But what *else* do you want?"

He sighs heavily. "Nothing. I'm in Alaska with you. It's all I could ask for right now. Seriously." He slides a hand under the table to grasp my foot and start massaging it. "And you have to stop or we're going to have a real problem when I get up to leave."

Cedric the sommelier appears next to our table then, ending any playful banter I could have thrown back.

I PULL my jacket tight against myself as I follow Henry along the dock toward his fishing boat, our footfalls making a hollow sound against the boards. "Are you sure it isn't too late for a boat ride?"

"We're not going far. Just out into the bay."

"Good, because I didn't take my Antivert." The last time I was on this boat, when Hachiro was here to take photographs of Henry for a magazine, I had to lie down below deck to keep from puking.

"It's good to go?" Henry asks a guy who I've seen working around the dock before.

"Engine's been warming for a bit. Sounds smooth."

"Thanks, Ken." They clasp hands, and then Henry's helping me aboard. Ken unfastens the ropes and we're pulling away slowly, Henry at the wheel.

"What's all this?" I ask, peering over at the pile of blankets sitting in the center of the deck. Two of those tall electric heaters sit on either side, the glowing red telling me that they're on and pumping out heat.

"Lie down. Get comfortable" is his only answer.

To my pleasant surprise, I find a rollaway mattress and a sleeping bag buried beneath the other covers. Kicking off my shoes, I slide into the bag, happy to have changed into sweatpants and a sweatshirt for comfort. "It's warm in here."

"That's the point." Henry's chuckle carries over the low rumble of the boat engine. "I'll be there in few minutes."

I rest my head against one of the pillows and settle my gaze on the sky above us, and the thick blanket of stars. "I used to lie under the stars with Jed when we were kids," I murmur. "We'd make up stupid names for constellations. The only ones we ever got right were the dippers."

"Did the sky down there look like it does up here?"

"No. Nothing is as pretty as it is up here," I admit with a smile.

Henry shuts the engine about ten minutes later. The plunk of the anchor sounds as it drops into the dark water. I sit up long enough to see that he's parked us in a small cove, the closest light from a cabin at least half a mile away.

"What's this place?" I ask as he climbs down. He kicks off his shoes and slips into the sleeping bag, bringing a wave of cold with him that makes me shudder.

"My grandparents used to bring us here at night when we were young."

"To look at the stars?"

"Sure," he answers mysteriously, reaching over my head for something. He produces a bottle of champagne and two flutes from a basket I didn't even notice sitting in the corner.

"Who knew you could be so romantic?" I tease.

"Thank Isabella. She's the one who arranged all this for me. Sit up."

I do, and he props up all the pillows behind us—six in total. I happily settle back against them, his arm curled beneath me, the smell of him wafting around me.

"The water is so calm here." Thank God, the boat's not even rocking.

"Watch the sky out there," he whispers, pointing with his free hand.

We lie there in comfortable silence, sipping champagne and staring off into the sky, my hand dragging back and forth lazily over Henry's chest and abdomen. His body is utterly relaxed against me, something I usually only sense in him in the minutes after he's climaxed.

A wave of pale green light suddenly dances across the sky.

I frown. "What was that?"

Henry says nothing, smiling as his eyes remain locked above and ahead.

A few moments later, another wave skitters across, this one brighter, with a touch of pink.

It dawns on me. "The northern lights!" How had I forgotten about those?

Henry grins. "Aurora Borealis. They're most active in the fall and winter months. With the clear skies, I knew we'd likely see them tonight. This is the best place to watch around here."

I sigh and settle back into Henry, and watch the light show in absolute awe as the waves of green, pink, and purple grow in intensity and frequency. Each one of them makes me gasp and squeal.

"I'm starting to think these lights do more for you than I do," he murmurs, shifting us until his large, warm body is spooning mine, and my head is nestled in the crook of his arm.

"It's my first time with them, so I guess it remains to be seen. Do they last longer than you?" I joke.

I get a playful but sharp slap against my cheek in response. And then his warm hand slips down the front of my sweatpants and into my panties. His fingers stall between my folds. "Seriously. Are you getting off on lights?"

"Shut up!" I softly elbow him in the stomach.

His fingers resume their leisurely exploration between my legs, pulling a sigh from my lips as his index finger pushes inside.

"Hot and soaking wet. Just how I like it." He pulls out long enough to work my pants off my hips and down past my knees. Now I know why he insisted on loose clothes.

I make to roll but he stops me with a soft, "Stay." He buries his face into the back of my neck, his hot breath tickling as he licks and gently bites and kisses along my skin. I feel him shifting behind me and I realize he's pushing his own track pants down.

I raise a hand up and over, hooking it around the back of his head. "I don't want it rough tonight, Henry."

"It won't be rough tonight," he promises. Hiking my thigh up and out with his hand to open me up, he holds it there while fitting himself in behind me. I feel his smooth tip prodding my entrance.

And then he's sinking into me.

I close my eyes as my senses go into overdrive.

"Who knows when we'll get to see this again. Relax your leg and watch. No touching yourself." He settles in, his thrusts unhurried, only breaking every once in a while to press a sensual kiss along my neck and shoulder.

It's a punishingly slow pace that goes on forever. He expertly drags both of our releases out, stalling every time my hip rolls become more urgent, or when his own breathing has grown ragged, a sign that he's about to come. Within the cocoon of blankets, our skin is slick with sweat and every nerve below my waist feels like a live wire.

"Who do you think will last longer? The northern lights or me?" Henry murmurs tauntingly. They've already started to fade.

I close my eyes, feeling another rush into my lower belly. "You, babe. Definitely you."

"Do you want to come?"

"God, yes." My orgasm has been lingering there, just outside of reach, forever.

He releases my leg and slips his hand in between my legs to touch my swollen clit.

I come almost immediately, my cry echoing through the silent bay.

He doesn't quicken his pace but he makes sure the last five thrusts are hard. That's all it takes until he grunts into my ear and I feel him pulsing inside me.

I twist back to kiss him tenderly. "Thank you for tonight."

Henry sighs against my mouth. "We'll do it again next year. Deal?"

I smile. "Deal... wait. What time is it?"

"No idea."

I reach for my phone, cast aside earlier. "It's after midnight. It's your birthday."

"Hmm...." His palm smooths over my bare belly.

"Happy birthday," I whisper against his lips, pulling his bottom lip playfully between my teeth.

He grins. "Is that what you got me? A birthday fuck?"

"More than one, if you're lucky." I chuckle. "I love you, Henry."

He pauses. "Every time you say those words, I can actually *feel* them inside me."

I smile. "I know exactly what you mean." Jed used to say them to me all the time. I thought he meant it, and maybe he did. But I know Henry doesn't love easily. Every time those words slip from his lips, my heart swells.

"And when you look at me like that...." His gaze skates over my face. "You are the gift that I didn't realize I wanted. That I needed. I love you, Abbi." We get lost in a sensual kiss for a few moments, before he pulls out and adjusts himself to stretch out behind me once again. We lie in comfortable silence, our bodies tangled and hot and fully satisfied, gazing up at the Alaskan sky, until I begin dozing off. Somewhere in the sleepy distance, I sense him drawing my pants back up and rolling out from the covers to start the boat. The engine is a soothing rumble. I stay under the warm covers as Henry takes us back to Wolf Cove.

CHAPTER 15

"You can't do this tomorrow? Do they know it's your birthday?"

Henry chuckles through a sip of coffee. "There are hundreds of people who have been waiting for weeks to get back to work. I'm not going to delay that because it's my birthday. We've already lost loyal workers who can't afford not to work."

I huff.

"I'm just going up there to meet with the supervisors and let them see how I work, give a morale-boosting speech to the employees, and walk the mine to prove that the safety issues have been satisfactorily resolved. I'll be back by midafternoon."

I pluck a croissant off a platter and begin pulling it apart. "Fine. I'll just be here, waiting...." I let the ends of my white robe fall apart, exposing my nakedness beneath, fresh from our shower together.

"Jesus Christ, Abbi. We've already fucked three times today and it's only 8:00 a.m.," Henry mutters, unable to resist a long gaze over my body, stalling on my full, round breasts, on the red mark he accidently left from sucking too hard.

"You know, I think your friend Ronan may be right. I might not be enough to satisfy your needs."

"You're right. Maybe I need two men," I quip, earning a flat look. "And I didn't hear you complaining this morning."

"Believe me, you will never hear me complain about waking up to my dick in your mouth." He slides his last piece of toast into his mouth and then, wiping his mouth with a napkin, gets out of his chair. He reaches for my hand and pulls me to him. He cups my chin gently, and presses a soft kiss against my lips. "Thank you for arranging all of this."

"You're welcome. Do you want me to walk you to the helicopter pad?"

"Like this?" He yanks open my robe.

I slide my arms around his waist, his form-fitting black sweater soft against my breasts. His choice of clothing was intentional. He figures showing up at a mine as the new owner in a suit and tie won't win anyone over. "I can change."

"No. It's okay. Stay here, where it's warm."

"And dinner? What do you want to do, Lux again? I can make reservations for us."

He pushes a strand of my long red hair off my face. "Why don't we just stay here? That way I can fail at satisfying you all night long without interruption."

I giggle, my hands trailing over his sculpted back. "Deal."

He leans in for one last, lingering kiss. "Gotta go."

I release him and watch him stroll out the door, grabbing his jacket on the way.

"I love you," I call out, but the door has already shut and he doesn't hear me.

I check the clock again. It's just after eight. If he's back by midafternoon, that gives me a good eight hours. Hopefully it's enough time for the plan that hit me the moment my eyes opened this morning.

I dial the concierge desk and cross my fingers.

"Good morning, Mr. Wolf. How may I be of assistance?" The voice on the other side chirps pleasantly.

"Autumn! Thank God! I need Isabella's number. I need her help with something."

"Hey, Abbi! Sure!"

"You are such a jerk, Connor," I mutter as I hug my chest against the jolts.

"Hey. I didn't put the potholes there," he counters.

"Yes, but you're swerving to hit them!"

He starts laughing, earning my hard slap against his rock-hard chest. It only makes him laugh harder.

Ronan sits on the right side of me as he always does—relaxed, legs splayed, hand gripping the roll handle above. "So, Wolf has no idea you're doing this for his birthday?"

"No. I just came up with the idea this morning, after he left. I called Isabella to help set things up." After her help with the fishing boat last night, I figured she might be willing. I was right.

"*Isabella*," Connor moans with appreciation.

I roll my eyes, ignoring him. "Thank you, guys, for doing this."

"The place was due for a check anyway," Ronan murmurs, his gaze drifting ahead, over the narrow path that serves as a road to the old Wolf cabin.

"I'm serious. Thank you."

Finally he meets my eyes and the look in his softens. I don't know exactly why Ronan went toe-to-toe against Henry the other night; if Henry's right, and Ronan's feelings for me have changed. "Paige sent housekeeping over there a few hours ago, so it should be clean and set up already."

"Awesome. So all we have to do is get the fireplace ready and the wood loaded in and it'll be ready for him."

"I don't get it though. You guys could jump in his plane and fly to Vegas like high rollers for a hot and dirty weekend. Why stay *here*?" Connor lays his cornflower blue eyes on the old cabin that finally appears as we round the corner. The one that Henry's grandfather built on his own. The one Henry has so many cherished childhood memories of.

I smile. "Because this place means something to him."

"YOU JUST HAVE to throw a match in and this baby'll burn," Connor announces, backing away from the expertly stacked pile of kindling and paper in the hearth. "And there's enough wood here to keep you warm all weekend."

"Thank you. Now if you can just help me figure out how to use this." I stand in front of the antique woodstove.

He strolls over, switching on a lamp on his way past to add light to the dim space. He lifts one of the round covers on the surface. "Just stick the wood in here and light it up."

"Right, but how do I bake a cake in it? Wait, it must be in here." I pull on a handle and a door opens to a small compartment perfect for a cake pan.

"Bake a cake...." Connor's face twists up. "You don't bake a cake in this!"

I laugh. "Henry's grandmother baked cakes for him in this thing all the time. I'm going to make a birthday cake for him." I hold up the box of chocolate cake mix as proof. John was kind enough to grab it at the grocery store in Homer on his way in.

"You have a team of five-star world-famous chefs and sous chefs slaving over there in the kitchen, who will whip you up the fanciest cake you could ever imagine with the snap of your little fingers, and you're making him a Duncan Hines cake mix cake?"

I smile. "Yes."

"Because his grandmother baked him cakes here."

"Yes."

Connor frowns. "You want him to think of his grandmother when he looks at you? Is that what Wolf is into?"

"No! You weirdo!" I launch the box at him, missing completely.

"He'll love it," Ronan calls out.

I look up to find him leaning over the ornately carved cedar rail that lines the loft.

"It's all good up here. They only prepared the one bedroom."

"That's fine. We only need the one. Wait, which one?"

He looks knowingly at me. "The one with the balcony."

That's the one that Ronan and I were together in for the first time.

I refocus my attention on the kitchen, rounding the table to pick up the box. "Okay. You start this fire and I'm going to start mixing this so I can get the pan in and...." My voice drifts as a wave of unbalance hits me. I take a moment to try and get my bearings.

But it's not me.

"Are you feeling that?" Connor looks from me to Ronan, to the glasses in the corner hutch. They're rattling and clanking against each other. And the antler chandelier that hangs from the thick beam in the ceiling is swaying. A few moments later, it stills. I feel normal again.

"That was a fucking earthquake!" Connor exclaims.

"They have those here?" I ask in disbelief.

"They have them somewhere." Ronan climbs down the stairs. "Who knows where that one hit, but we definitely felt it here."

"Wow. That was crazy. I've never felt something like that before." Not that I know of, anyway.

Connor's muscular arms curl around me from behind. "You mean besides that time Ronan and I rocked your world?"

I elbow him in the gut and wriggle away, shaking my head. "Help me with this fire or don't, but I'm baking a damn birthday cake."

"I'll help you, Red." Ronan wanders over, chuckling darkly as he punches Connor. "Go and check the cellar."

"Fuck, no! I hate going in there," Connor moans, heading toward the front door. "Why did I have to get stuck with such a pussy for a work partner?"

"Fuck off. I can't help it."

I frown. "Help what?"

"I can't deal with tight spaces," Ronan admits sheepishly. "I panic."

"I can think of a tight place you're fine getting into," I hear Connor mutter before the door shuts.

Ronan sighs with exasperation.

I duck my head to hide my blush. "So they still make the crew come out here?"

"Every single week. And ever since they had a mouse problem in here, we've been having to go into that cellar to make sure nothing's getting in there." Ronan falls into silence as he stuffs kindling and newspaper down into the stove.

I watch him intently. "Are we good?"

"Yeah, we're good."

"What was all that about the other night?"

He strikes a match and sets it inside. "Nothing."

"Didn't sound like nothing." I tear open the cake mix package and dump it into the bowl the kitchen supplied me with. "Henry thinks you have feelings for me. I told him we're just friends," I say as casually as possible.

Ronan says nothing.

"I'm right… right?"

"We're just friends." He sighs, resting his palms on the top of the woodstove. "And yeah, I have feelings for you."

My stomach tightens. "What kind of feelings?"

"The kind I don't want."

I busy my hands with readying the hand mixer, my eyes averted. That wasn't supposed to happen. "Since when?"

"I don't know, but I didn't realize it until you came back."

Finally, I dare look up, to find those piercing green eyes on me. I release a shaky breath. "Ronan, I'm madly in love with Henry. I—"

"I know. I'm not asking for anything, or expecting anything. You asked, so I'm telling you."

Awkward silence hangs.

Finally, Ronan turns back to the woodstove, where flames begin to crackle and lick the open top.

I catch the smirk curling his lips. "What's that for?"

"Handing that lube to me the other night?" He shakes his head. "One hell of a move. That motherfucker crushed me with that one."

I press my lips together, unsure of whether to laugh or cringe. In the end, I can't keep the giggle down, and soon we're both shaking with laughter.

A scream sounds from outside, cutting our mirth.

I drop the hand mixer and race for the door, Ronan on my heels. He grabs me by the biceps and forces me aside so he can open the door and step out first.

Connor's standing beside the truck, holding a rake out in front of him, his face as white as a sheet of paper.

"Dude. What the hell?" Ronan takes the creaky steps down, his puzzled look scanning the area. The old wood door that closes off the cellar is still thrown open. "Bear? Cougar?"

"Raccoon!" Connor hollers, picking up a pinecone and whipping it into the bushes.

That's when I notice the black mask peeking out. The sizeable raccoon chatters back at him before scurrying into the bush.

"I'm done with that fucking cellar! You tell him they need to board that shit up! They're talking about putting fucking solar panels on this roof, but they still want a goddamn hole in the ground. For what! Fucking potatoes? Fuck!" Connor throws the rake to the ground and shudders, visibly shaken and ranting like I didn't even know him capable of.

Ronan doubles over in laughter, and I immediately join him.

"I've gotta say, Betty Crocker, I'm impressed."

"It's not Betty Crocker. It's Duncan Hines, remember?"

"Same shit." Connor pulls onto the road that'll take us back to the hotel. "I'd eat that cake."

"You'd eat anything," Ronan retorts, but quickly adds, "It looks tasty. Especially with the M&M's."

"Well, I'm glad because I was limited on time and materials." I threw the cake into the fridge freezer to cool it enough to spread the chocolate fudge frosting over it, and then I spelled out "Happy 32nd" in colorful candy.

The dash clock reads four o'clock. I glance at my phone to see that I still have no messages from Henry. I guess he's not back yet. That gives me time to change into something nicer and fix my makeup.

The Wolf helicopter is landing on the pad just as we pull in through the gates.

"Oh, perfect! Drop me off here."

Connor eases the truck to a stop and Ronan hops out. He

holds a hand out for me, just like he always did when I worked here, and I take it, just like I always did, even though I've never needed it.

"Thanks again, guys."

"Make him board up that cellar, Red. I don't get paid enough for that shit!" Connor yells.

I smile. "I'll see what I can do."

I turn to Ronan. But he's not looking at me. His intense gaze is locked on the helicopter pad. The pilot is alone and several people, including Isabella, are running toward him. "What's going on?" A sinking feeling is settling into my body.

"I don't know. Come on." Ronan takes my hand and leads me there.

"...they're trying to get an emergency crew in but I don't know what they're going to be able to do. The shaft is completely collapsed. We've lost all radio contact."

Oh my God. Henry.

"What's going on?" I hear someone ask.

Everyone turns to look at me and I realize that it was me talking.

"There was a small earthquake earlier," Isabella begins, her bright doe eyes full of concern.

"Yeah, we felt it. Where is Henry?"

She takes a deep breath. "He was in the mine when it happened, and a part of it collapsed due to that earthquake."

"But... no." A wave of dizziness hits me, and I feel Ronan's arm wrap around my waist in support. "They fixed all the safety things with the gold mine. It should have been safe. It's supposed to be safe. That wasn't even that big of an earthquake. It shouldn't have done anything." I'm rambling.

"The gold mine didn't take any damage," the pilot confirms. "It's the old mine that Mr. Wolf was in."

"What?"

"He asked me to take him over. He said that Scott Wolf

had been paying for some exploratory work and he wanted to see what had been done. The miners who'd done work there went with him." The pilot's face is etched with worry. "I don't know how far down they got, but the entire shaft has collapsed."

"Oh my God." I'm going to be sick.

Voices begin all around me, but I can't focus on any of them, my knees buckling, the world spinning too fast around me for me to stand. Ronan eases me down.

Henry went into a mine.

A mine collapsed on Henry.

Henry might be dead.

I can't breathe.

I don't know how long it takes me to refocus on my surroundings, but when I do, Connor and Ronan are climbing into the helicopter and the blades begin to whir.

"You need to move away," Isabella says, gentle hands settling on my arms to try and lift me up.

"Wait. Where are they going?"

"He's flying them back to the site. They're going to see if they can help at all."

"I'm going, too!" I scramble to my feet and make to run to the helicopter.

Isabella holds me back with surprising strength. "It's not safe."

"Henry's trapped in a goddamn mine! I don't care about safe!" I fight against her grip but she holds on tight.

"Let them go! The sooner they get there, the sooner they can work to free him," she pleads, struggling.

The helicopter lifts off before I have a chance to argue my way onto it. I look up in time to see Ronan peering down at me. He tosses a casual wave, but his face is full of pain.

"Abbi!" From somewhere behind me, I hear Autumn's voice, but I don't turn.

"Can you take her back to her cabin? Stay with her. We'll cover the rest of your shift," I'm faintly aware of Isabella telling her.

"Of course." Another set of hands settle on my shoulders and begin leading me away. My legs move of their own accord.

I hear Autumn's voice all the way back—along the path I've walked with Henry, through the door I've passed with Henry, into the cabin I've shared with Henry—but I don't hear a single word she says.

If Henry is dead....

I make it to the bathroom just in time to heave the contents of my stomach.

CHAPTER 16

"Abbi."

Katie stands at the door to the balcony, my phone in her hand. "It's your mom."

I release the breath I was holding. "What time is it?" It's still pitch black.

"5:00 a.m."

It's been more than twelve hours since the shaft collapsed on Henry, and we've heard nothing yet.

My movements are mechanical when I accept my phone and press it to my ear. "Hello, Mama."

"Abigail! Good Lord, you're safe!"

"Yeah."

Katie comes around to reposition the blanket she wrapped around me earlier, when I came out here to sit on the small love seat.

"This business with Henry and the mine is all over the news!"

She actually said his name. I'm not sure she's ever actually used his name. He was always *that man*. A predator. A wolf.

"Have they told you anything new?"

"They said it was a major cave-in. They're trying to clear the shaft." My voice sounds hollow.

"Gosh. How anyone goes so deep into the ground like that is beyond me. Why didn't you call and tell us about it right away?"

"Why would I?" I say it so simply. "I know how you feel about Henry."

"Abigail!" she exclaims indignantly. There's a long pause, and when she speaks, her voice is calmer, as if Aunt May is in the background, coaching her. "The past is just that—the past. We are goin' to move on from that and—"

"Yeah, because he's probably dead. Is that what you mean by moving on?" The second I say the words out loud, tears spring to my eyes.

"No, you can't think like that. Do not lose hope, Abigail. We're all praying for him. The Reverend is goin' to say a special prayer at service today and tomorrow, and every other day until they find him. God willing, he'll survive this just like your daddy survived. "

"I'm so scared that I'll never see him again." I'm crying openly, unable to contain the emotions that have been dulled by fear up until now.

"I know, baby girl. I wish you weren't so far away. Is someone there with you?"

"Yes, I have friends here. I'm not alone."

At those words, Katie curls up on the loveseat beside me and puts an arm around my shoulder.

"Good. I'm glad. Don't lose hope, Abigail. All of us, we just need to have faith."

I'm not sure what's more shocking—her words or the fact that she sounds genuine. Regardless, it's what I need to hear. I take a deep breath and rub away my tears. Henry doesn't need me giving up on him so quickly. "Thanks, Mama."

"DAMN, NOW *THAT* IS A SHOWER," Rachel murmurs, strolling out of the bedroom in her work uniform, her long hair pulled up into a messy bun. She tosses her makeup bag onto the couch and heads for the table to pick at the platter of fruit and sandwiches that Autumn ordered in. "Thanks for letting me get ready here."

"Anytime."

"You need to make her sleep," I overhear her whisper to Autumn.

"I don't know what to do!" Autumn hisses. "I tried giving her an Ambien but she won't take it!"

"Then slip it in her drink!"

I smirk as I stare blankly at the television screen. Good luck. I'm not eating or sleeping again until they find Henry.

"Okay, well, I have to go to work now, but my shift ends at seven and Katie should be done by three," Rachel calls out louder.

I listen to her heels click on the hardwood and the sound of the door opening. "Uh... hello?"

"*Bonjour*. I was told this is Abigail's accommodations?"

My head whips around at the sound of her voice.

Rachel and Autumn stare with wide eyes as a glamorous-looking Margo strolls in. There's no way they don't know who she is.

Margo sees me on the couch and heads straight for me, her beautiful face twisted with worry. "Do not worry, Abigail. If anyone can find a way out of there, I promise you, it is Henry."

I dive into her waiting arms as a fresh wave of sobs tear through the cabin.

"You're not exactly dressed for Alaska," I note, taking in her red leggings and billowy white blouse. Her black suede booties are lying on the floor where she kicked them off to curl her legs beneath her on the couch.

She chuckles in that laissez-faire way of hers. "I was not planning for a trip to Alaska. I packed for LA."

"Shit. That's right. You had your party last night." Henry helped wrap hundreds of bars with me. It was such a tedious job, and yet he didn't complain once. Bruised and battered as I was, it might have been one of the most calming, pleasant days I've ever spent with him. And it might end up being one of the last I'll ever get.

A fresh wave of tears well in my eyes. I blink them back, and swallow against the hard lump in my throat. "How was it?"

"*Fantastique,* from what I've heard, but I was only there for an hour before news of Henry broke. I am so sorry, I could not get here sooner."

"No. It's okay. I appreciate you coming. Don't get me wrong, Autumn and the others have been great and all. But having you here feels different."

"Of course, Abigail." She reaches forward and squeezes my hands. "You are both important people in my life. If something happened to either of you...." Her flawless forehead wrinkles with concern. "Well, we cannot even think like that. I'm sure they are doing everything they can."

"It's been *nineteen hours,* Margo. How long can someone last down there? What if he was hurt? Is there even any air?"

"I am sorry, I don't know much about how these mines work."

"I don't even know why he went! He said he was going to worry about the gold mine. This other thing was Scott's mess. This is all him! This is Scott coming back from the dead to punish Henry!" And here, Henry was so sure Scott could never hurt me again.

"Sshhh." She pats my hand soothingly. "Do you know how many people are there to help?"

"I don't know." I tell her about how Connor and Ronan jumped into the helicopter to help with the rescue.

She frowns curiously. "And who are these two men to you. Friends?"

I groan. "It's a long, sordid story."

She reaches for the coffee that room service set on the table beside us, and pours us each a cup. "My favorite kind."

"MISS LAUREN, we've brought your things over to Penthouse Two," Isabella announces, standing in the doorway, wringing her hands. Margo makes her nervous. "I can guide you there if you'd like."

"*Merci*. That is wonderful. I'm going to stay with Abigail for now though. I am confident we will hear something soon and I want to be with her."

Isabella nods and then turns to me. "Is there anything I can get you?"

"I'm good. Thank you for everything you've done."

"Autumn mentioned that you haven't slept yet. We could have a doctor prescribe you a sedative to help."

I'm sure she doesn't need Autumn to confirm that. The dark bags beneath my eyes are evidence enough. "Thanks, but I don't want to be drugged out when news comes through."

"Okay. But if you change you mind...." She pauses, head cocked as if she's listening.

I hear it a moment later.

The whir of helicopter blades.

I'm on my feet and running out the door and down the path to the helicopter pad as fast as I can.

Holding my breath the entire way.

The helicopter holds more than just the pilot this time, I note, trying to count heads, to recognize them through the glass. But it's too hard, and so I'm left hugging my body and waiting for the door to pop open.

Connor jumps out first, covered head to toe in dirt. His hair doesn't even look blond. Ronan steps out after him, limping slightly. His eyes search me out immediately.

And he nods.

"Oh my God...." Relief bowls over me as Henry's feet hit the pavement. I stumble a step before I can regain my strength. And then I'm running for him.

He grunts as I plow into his chest. "Hey... it's okay. I'm okay." Warm, strong arms wrap around me, pulling me tight into him as my tears flow freely.

"I thought you were dead. I thought I'd lost you."

"No. Shhh...." He strokes my hair and presses his lips to my forehead. "I'm right here."

"I wanted to go and help but they wouldn't let me."

"Good, because I would have fired every last one of them if I found you on that site when I came up," he warns sharply.

I reach up to grip his jaw, my fingertips reveling in the feel of his scruff as I pull his face down for a kiss on my lips. He's as dirty as Connor and Ronan are. And there's a gash on his forehead. "You're hurt!" I reach for it instinctively.

He flinches. "It's nothing. They've already checked me out and I'm fine."

Now that I'm actually looking, I note that his jacket is soaked in blood. A lot of blood.

Henry notices my panicked look. "One of the guys got hurt pretty bad, but he'll be fine. They've taken him to Anchorage."

"So, what happened? How did you get out? Why the hell were you in there in the first place!" Now that I know he's safe, my anger flares unexpectedly.

He sighs. "I know. It was a stupid move. I figured I was already up there so I may as well check it out. But when that earthquake hit, the shaft crumbled, burying us in there. There was no way we were getting out through there. Derek—one of the guys I was with—knew of another shaft entrance. We headed for that, hoping it'd be clear enough to get through."

"So you climbed out there?"

"With help." Henry's gaze flickers behind me. "When we got there, Ronan and Connor were already inside."

My mouth drops open. "*They* went into the mine after you?"

"Yeah. A miner who'd worked there all those years ago heard about the collapse and came in to try and help. He remembered the other shaft, but he couldn't remember how it connected. The emergency crew decided to focus on the main shaft until more help arrived, figuring that was still their best hope. So those two took off with the miner and some equipment to see if they'd have any luck. Against orders from the recovery team leader, apparently."

"So... Ronan went down there?" I say, dumbfounded. "But Ronan's claustrophobic."

Surprise flashes in Henry's face and his gaze flashes in their direction. "Well, it was definitely ballsy as fuck. There was nothing to say that another quake wouldn't hit and bury them, or that the shaft wouldn't collapse as soon as it was disturbed, or that the miner knew what the hell he was talking about. If they didn't go down, I'd still be stuck in the mine." He shakes his head. "I never thought I'd be so happy to see those two jackasses in my life."

My hands smooth over his chest. "So you're really okay?"

"I'm really okay. I promise."

I bury my face in his chest and inhale deeply. He doesn't smell like my Henry. He smells like earth and dirt and dried blood. But all that can be washed off. "Promise me you will never go into any mine ever again?"

His deep chuckle shakes my body. "I may have trouble keeping that one, given I own one. But I can promise that I'll never step foot in a mine that's been shut down for decades ever again. Give me a minute? I need a word with a few people."

"Okay," I say, even as I'm pulling his face down into another kiss. This one he meets deeply, lingering.

"I was afraid I'd never get to do that again," he whispers.

"Same here." I smile. "Margo's here."

"I see that. Give me a few minutes and then we can head back to our place."

I have to force myself to let go of him, my eyes trailing him all the way over to the small crowd that's gathered.

Henry's alive. And safe.

And I owe it all to Ronan and Connor.

I rush for them.

"Has anyone ever told you that being your friend is hazardous to—" Connor's quip is cut off with a grunt as I barrel into his chest.

"Thank you."

"Thank *him*. He's the nutcase that made me go down in there." He jerks a thumb at Ronan, who stands quietly off beneath a tree, his clothes soiled, but somehow looking as calm and collected as usual.

"I don't know how—" I choke over the rest of the words, unable to get them out. I wrap my arms around his broad shoulders.

With a heavy sigh, he pulls me into his body, burying his face in the crook of my neck.

I finally manage a "thank you" in a rough whisper, and squeeze him tight, not relenting until approaching footfalls sound on the gravel and Henry calls my name.

"Come on, Abbi. I think we can both use some sleep." He looks down at my socked feet. "Where are your shoes?"

I fall against his chest, not bothering to answer, succumbing to the weight of the last twenty-four hours.

Henry leads me over to Ronan. "Make sure you ice that leg," Henry warns him. "And you're taking the next few days off." After a long moment and a heavy sigh, he sticks out a hand.

Ronan clasps it, a smirk curling his lips.

"Holy fuck! What is Margo Lauren doing here?" Connor suddenly exclaims, loud enough for everyone, including Margo, to hear.

"I'll be there in five minutes. I just need a quick shower." Henry tries to steer me toward bed but I smoothly avoid him, and head for the bathroom.

I'm beyond exhausted, I accept, as I gracelessly strip my clothes off, leaving them in a heap on the tile floor.

Henry steps into the bathroom, his tired gaze drifting over my naked body.

I have no energy for words. I quietly begin undressing him, peeling his layers off and tossing them onto the floor. And he allows me, standing still and watching me unbuckle his belt and jeans. I drop to my knees to unfasten his boots and slip off his socks.

It's like I'm operating mechanically as I take his hand and lead him into the giant glassed-in shower. I turn the dials, and streams of hot water hit us from the various angles, earning Henry's deep moan. Grabbing the bar of soap, I begin lathering Henry's chest, my hands slipping and sliding over his hard curves.

"You don't have to—"

"Let me." My fingers touch every inch of his perfect body as I bathe him. By the time I reach his waist, his cock is jutting out. Skipping that part for the moment, I drop to my knees and work on his legs, marveling at his powerful thighs and sculpted calves. I even spend a few moments on his toes.

And when everywhere else is done, I take my time, gripping his length as I soap him up; gently cupping the heavy sac that hangs beneath, full of his virility. I even slide my soapy hand farther back, along the crack that parts two perfect sides of his ass. That earns a sharp inhale from him.

"Rinse off."

He has no clever quips for my demand. He turns into the jets and in moments, his body is clear of all soap. He holds out a hand for me to get off my knees.

But I ignore it, taking him into my mouth instead.

"Oh, fuck. Abbi...." His hands gently clasp my head on either side. "Look up."

I make a point of looking up while I'm sliding my mouth off him, to lock gazes with him. But instead of taking him in again, I grip his cock with my fist and focus my time on his tip, tonguing the tiny hole until I taste the salty liquid beading out.

"No more." Henry reaches down to grab my waist. He lifts me up with seemingly no effort, and after knocking off all the shampoo bottles aside with one quick swipe of his hand, settles me onto the tile ledge.

His mouth finds mine and he starts kissing me with such abandon that I can't breathe. But I don't want to breathe, not when Henry's mouth is on me. I curl my arms around his neck and my legs around his hips, until our bodies are fully together everywhere.

"I thought about this. About being with you. About being inside you. About your arms around me." He reaches between us to fit himself into my entrance. "It's all I thought about. It's all I wanted. I didn't care about the hotel or my money or anything. Just this. Just you." He pushes in slowly but forcefully. My exhausted body isn't ready for it, despite how much I want it. But still he goes, inching his way in, until he's buried deep inside me. He hooks an arm under each of my legs to spread me wide and pin me in place against the wall.

I let my head fall back against the tile and close my eyes.

His mouth slips down to my neck, to my collarbone, to my breasts, sucking in my nipple, his stubble scratching me roughly. I revel in the discomfort of it as he begins thrusting into me.

"Harder," I demand, clasping the sides of his face with my hands to pull his forehead to mine. "I don't want gentle tonight. I want to still feel you inside me when I wake up, two days from now."

"Fuck." He releases one of my legs, letting it hang off the ledge. His fingers coil around my hair at my nape and he pulls my head back to expose my neck to his lips, his teeth. Adjusting his stance, he begins driving into me with his powerful body, over and over again. My cries, my gasps, my moans fill the shower stall as my body opens up for him and ecstasy quickly takes over. As I enjoy what I thought I would never feel again.

When we're done, when we're both clean and fully sated, Henry shuts the water off, wraps us both in towels, and carries me to bed, where I promptly drift off.

CHAPTER 17

"Tell them to fuck off," Henry orders between bites of bacon, his scowl aimed at the iPad screen perched before him. "If they want to interview me, I'll happily talk their ear off about the future of Wolf Hotels. But me nearly dying because I was stupid enough to go down into that mine will not be a topic of discussion."

"Yes, sir." Miles's voice chirps over the speakerphone.

Henry notices me approaching. "Gotta go."

"Will you still be flying back tomorrow?"

"Yeah. Have the plane ready to go by nine."

"Yes, sir."

He ends the call as I climb onto his lap, straddling him. "Reporters?"

He grunts. "There was one here yesterday. See?" He taps the screen. Open on it is a news article about Henry's rescue. And a picture at the Wolf Cove helicopter pad, where a dirty Henry has his arms wrapped around me, and our lips are locked in a deep kiss.

"I didn't even see a camera anywhere. Though I was a little bit preoccupied." In the background is a blurred silhouette of Ronan, looking on.

Our hero.

"It's a good picture."

Henry sighs. "It is."

"Aren't you cold?" I rub my arms up and down his biceps. He was so hungry when he woke this morning—we both were, after not having eaten anything since Friday morning—that he didn't bother putting on a robe after his shower, wandering out to the food-laden table that I requested in nothing but a towel.

"I am, actually." His fingers snag my robe tie. He unfastens it and tugs at the two ends until they're open enough that he can throw them around. Slipping his hands around my waist, he pulls my bare flesh tight against his.

"You may be cold but your skin is hot." I giggle as my nipples pebble—from the cool air or Henry's touch, I can't tell.

"Hmm... so is yours." He dips in to kiss my neck, his mouth a salve for all the anguish of the past two days. "What do you want to do today? It's our last day here."

"You," I answer bluntly.

Beneath the towel, I feel him hardening and instinctively grind my hips into him.

He frees one hand to tug at the tucked end of his towel, releasing it enough to expose himself to me. My hand goes for his cock immediately, gripping his smooth flesh, pressing a thumb down against the tip in a way I'm learning he likes.

My plans for his birthday were foiled two days ago. There is still a cake sitting in the fridge at his grandfather's cabin, a fire ready to be lit, and bedsheets waiting to be mussed. "Just you and me, all day, okay? No interruptions, no phone calls, no—"

A click sounds and then, "Bonjour!" Margo's melodious voice calls out from the open front door. She grins as she strolls into our penthouse, looking as glamorous as ever in tight jeans and a fitted white sweater that she must have sent for.

A wide-eyed Autumn stands in the doorway, looking like she's preparing herself to be flayed.

"I'm gone for a day and this place becomes a free-for-all," Henry mutters, pulling my robe shut and readjusting his towel to cover his erection, though it far from hides it. I climb off him, trying not to flash Margo and Autumn in the process, though I'm sure the former would not mind.

"I promised Autumn that I was the exception, and that she would not get in trouble for allowing me in. *Oui?*" The backs of her fingers trail over Henry's cheek.

"Oui," he mutters.

"You have slept, Abigail. Good." She kisses my cheek and then reaches for a strawberry.

With a wave and a mouthed "I'm sorry,"—and one last look at the back of a half-naked Henry sitting in the dining room chair—Autumn ducks out, closing the door behind her.

"So, Henry?" Margo lifts the crystal lid of the Scotch decanter and bends down to sniff it. Her nose crinkles in distaste. "You have succeeded in dragging me out to Alaska with your antics and yet now you hide in your cabin and sleep the day away. How shall you two entertain me?"

"Do I even want to know what you had in mind?" Henry asks dryly.

"An excursion." Her eyes dance with excitement. "I'd like to see these ferocious American bears. And then dinner here tonight. I have already spoken to the chef and she is preparing a special meal for us."

"You went right down into the kitchen, didn't you?"

"I did. They are lovely down there. And so welcoming."

"I'm sure they were." Henry sighs and reaches for me. I see the question in his eyes. I just finished telling him I wanted to have him all to myself. But Margo abandoned her life to fly up here and comfort me while we waited out news of Henry. We can't just ditch her now.

"That all sounds great to me, Margo. I just need Henry for an hour or two and then we can go."

"*Bon!* The lovely Isabella said she could have a plane ready for us at two. Does that give you enough time to do what you need to do?" She looks expectantly at me, and then at Henry, her sharp almond-shaped eyes drifting down to the noticeable bulge.

"Yes. I think so."

"What have you been up to?" Henry's curious eyes drift over the old cabin as I grab his hand and lead him to the front door and then inside.

The scent of fire still lingers, a residue from the woodstove that burned two days ago. "Isabella sent some of the staff over to clean it up and stage it, kind of like they did during the grand opening. Connor and Ronan set up the fireplace and brought in all the wood. I figured we'd have dinner here." The dishes are still sitting on the counter, unused. "I was going to cook. And then we'd spend the night. I thought that would have been a nice thing to do for your birthday." I'm rambling.

Henry studies me for a long moment, his eyes unreadable. "I would have loved that."

I bite my lip to hide the stupid grin that's threatening. "And there's one more surprise. It's small, but... close your eyes."

He frowns but then complies, his long lashes fluttering as his lids shut.

"Don't look!" I warn, reaching into the fridge to pull out the birthday cake. As quietly as possible, I set it down on the table in front of him and peel off the plastic wrap I protected it with.

"Okay. Open them."

He does, and they settle on the pan in front of him.

"I know it's not anything elaborate, and it might taste horrible. I've never made anything in a woodstove."

His eyebrows rise in surprise. "You made that here?"

"Yeah. In there." I laugh as I point to the polished antique stove. "It was *not* easy. Ronan helped me start the fire and then we watched it like hawks, and argued the entire time about whether it was done." My laughter dies. "Meanwhile you were trapped in a mine and I had no idea...." I sigh. "Anyway, I remembered you saying that your grandmother baked for you, so I thought it'd be nice to make a birthday cake here."

When I look back up, Henry's staring at me so intently and for so long that I begin to squirm.

"How do you get me like no one else gets me?" he asks softly. "How do you know what I need like no one else does, like even I don't? I can read you inside out and yet you surprise me constantly. How do you do that?" He looks genuinely baffled.

I swallow the emotion threatening to spill over. "I don't know, but I promise I'll keep trying to do it every single day that you let me."

He nods, more to himself, his gaze drifting over the interior of the old cabin—the fireplace, the kitchen, the table at the head of the chair. "We're making new memories here, aren't we?" he murmurs softly, echoing something I said to him months ago, the first time he brought me here. Collecting the cake pan, he reaches for me. "Come on. We've got to get back."

MARGO'S silky black hair flutters in the light breeze as she stands on the dock near the readying float plane.

Posing for a photographer.

"What do you think? Would they be good for the Wolf Hotel publicity?" she asks, adjusting her stance.

Henry smirks, his eyes rolling over her ensemble—hiking boots, jeans, a pink-and-beige checked jacket, and thick down vest, the sheepskin collar settled neatly under her bob. She must have had clothes delivered. "In exchange for...?"

"Oh, I don't know." She twists her lips in mock thought. "How about a little boutique castle hotel with a Wolf stamp on it, sooner rather than later?" She grins mischievously at Henry before turning her attention back to the photographer to rattle off a string of French words. He responds with words of his own, along with a wave.

"Abbi! With all this chaos, I almost forgot to tell you. My friend at Nordstrom called me. She is very interested in your Farm Girl soaps for their stores."

"What? Seriously?"

"Yes. You have a meeting with the buyer next Thursday to discuss, but they are very eager."

"But...." I stare dumbfounded at her, wondering if I heard it wrong. She's acting like it's nothing, like Nordstrom even knowing about my product, let alone wanting to put it on their shelves, isn't an impossible feat. "Henry?"

"I had nothing to do with that." He smirks in a told-you-so manner. "We should get going."

Margo holds up a dainty hand. "We are just waiting on two more."

"Two more?"

"Yes. Connor and Ronan."

"You invited Connor and Ronan?" Henry asks in an overly calm voice. "And why exactly did you do that?"

She frowns at him. "Because they saved your life, of course. Stop being ridiculous, Henry."

"So it has *nothing* to do with any stories Abbi might have told you?" He stares expectantly at her.

"Absolutely not. Why? Does that bother you?"

"Doesn't bother me." He looks down at me. "Does it bother you, Abbi? If Margo is planning on fucking both of your friends tonight?"

As surprised as I am by this, I smile up at him, smoothing my hand over his abdomen affectionately and, I hope, to calm him. We haven't stopped touching each other since we woke up—his arm curled around my waist, my fingers woven through his, my lips pressed against any part of his body I can reach. "I'd rather she do it tonight and not while on this excursion. Might frighten the bears."

"There they are!" Margo stands with her hands clasped at her chest, admiring Connor and Ronan as they step onto the dock and head our way. Ronan's no longer limping, at least. "Well done, Abigail," she purrs. "That would have been something to see."

Henry sighs with exasperation.

She spouts off something in French. He retorts sharply, his hand squeezing mine, a scowl forming on his brow. He's annoyed with her.

"What's wrong?" I ask through a sip of water.

"Nothing," he mutters.

Margo's eyes narrow in a wickedly mischievous manner. "I was just telling him that he should invite Ronan into your bed. I am certain that he would be an attentive lover for the both of you."

Water sprays from my mouth.

"Good day, gentlemen!" Margo greets them with warm smiles and two-cheek kisses. "Come, we must hurry." She gestures toward the plane and then hooks her hand around

Connor's arm. He trails her with a star-filled gaze. I can only imagine what's going on inside his head right now.

Ronan hangs back a touch, looking warily at the plane.

"What's the matter?" I ask.

"I hate small planes," he admits.

"You also hate tight spaces."

He smirks. "I do."

Henry comes up behind us, reaching out to slap a hand over his shoulder. "I'm sure it'll be worth every second of fear."

Henry and me in bed. With Ronan.

Margo's words linger. She's right, Ronan is an attentive lover. So is Henry. Ronan *and* Henry?

Their hands, their mouths... their cocks.

All over me.

Inside me.

It's a fantasy I shouldn't even allow—I love Henry! And yet heat begins to pool in between my legs the second the thought enters my mind.

"Abbi?" Henry's staring intently at me. "Are you coming?"

I give my head a shake. "Yup."

CHAPTER 18

I mock scowl. "If I didn't know better, I'd think you were trying to get me drunk."

Henry tops up my glass of white wine. "I am. I think we'll both need it to deal with Margo tonight."

"Oddly enough, I'm getting used to her antics." My gaze drifts over the dining table, set for five. Margo informed us that she invited Ronan and Connor for dinner, too. She informed us with a beautiful, impish smile and a declaration that we of course would be more than happy to have them.

To my surprise, Henry merely nodded.

"At least she behaved today," I murmur through a sip.

"You didn't hear the things she was saying to me in French." He smirks. "Besides, she was busy sizing up her fuck toys. Those two were losing their shit over that fifteen-hundred-pound Kodiak pacing around. Meanwhile they had a hundred-and-ten pound predator sitting between them."

The five of us and Philip the pilot sat on an embankment for hours and watched a family of bears roam the plains below, throwing passing glances our way to let us know that they were aware of our presence, but seemingly unbothered by it.

It was equal parts amazing and terrifying. How Henry doesn't have indents from where my fingertips dug into his forearm, I don't know.

"I'm sure they can handle it."

Henry fills another snifter with high-priced Scotch—his second.

"From what I've seen, those two deviants will be fine."

"What do you mean? What have you seen?"

He holds the sip in his mouth for a moment before swallowing. "Surveillance videos."

"You've been watching surveillance videos of Ronan and Connor having sex with women?" I'm legitimately surprised now.

"One woman."

I frown. "But those two know there are cameras everywhere. Ronan wouldn't do anything like that on a hotel camera."

Henry regards me for a moment. "Not a hotel camera. The cameras in the bedrooms of my grandfather's cabin."

My mouth drops open. "You have cameras in there?" *Oh my God.*

"Relax. I put them in after you left."

I fold my arms over my chest. "You mean you put them in because of me."

"Yes," he says simply. "I didn't want them turning my grandfather's cabin into a fucking brothel."

"And? They were in there again?"

His lips twist. "Once."

I frown. "But you didn't fire them." His mercy on my account can only go so far, I would imagine.

He sighs. "No. Because then I'd have to fire Belinda, too."

"No way!" I gasp. "Belinda?" I think back to the times Belinda crossed paths with us in outdoor crew. She showed them nothing more than subtle disdain. "There's no way."

"Oh, there were many ways. And at the same time." His eyes light up with a devilish look as he sips his drink.

"You *watched* it?"

"She called me to confess when she realized she was caught in the act. The cameras aren't hidden but they're also not overt. She didn't notice the one sitting on the dresser until she was... in a compromising position." He sips at his Scotch again, barely hiding his smirk.

"So you watched Belinda having sex."

"I did."

"And you call Connor and Ronan deviants," I mutter. "Can we say pot and kettle?"

His brow arches. "Are you calling me a deviant?"

"I would *never*," I mock.

He settles that wolfish gaze on me. "I have *never* claimed to be a saint."

"You're enjoying this entire conversation!"

He merely chuckles.

"You deleted it though, right?"

He opens his mouth to answer and then pauses. "Why? Do you want to watch it?"

"No!"

"Does it bother you? Them, with other women?"

"You know it doesn't," I answer honestly. "But you should have told me. I don't like secrets any more than you do."

"Fair enough."

The doorbell rings then.

"You're going to be nice to them tonight, right?"

"When am I ever not nice?" Henry murmurs, strolling toward the door.

"You will have to come to my chateau for a visit. I think you would like it there," Margo purrs between leisurely sips of red wine. The five of us have gone through many bottles, Connor and Margo staking their claim on at least three of them. Margo, because she's Margo, and Connor because he's too excited about having dinner with the supermodel to control himself.

Me? I'm drinking because the unspoken sexual tension in the air is almost choking.

The only two who seem to be practicing restraint are Ronan and Henry. They sit quietly, answering questions when asked, participating in moderate conversation.

And, I feel like, watching my every move.

"Can I clear these plates, sir?" one of the two servers who stood idly by to cater to our every need asks, her almond-shaped eyes taking in the scraps of chateaubriand and fingerling potatoes on Henry's plate.

"Yes. Please." Henry wipes his face with his napkin. "Clear everything, and then you can take your leave. We won't be needing any more service from anyone tonight."

She looks warily at the other server, and then at Margo, who organized this dinner. "What about dessert?"

"Take it back. We already have a birthday cake in the fridge. Right, Abbi?"

"Uh... I don't even know if that's edible. Maybe we should—"

"Perfect! We will all eat Abbi's cake. I'm sure it is delicious." Margo winks at me, her words laced with innuendo.

Oh my God.

It dawns on me that every person sitting at this table has gone down on me at least once.

Worse, I've been with every single person at this table in a sexual way, something none of them can claim.

My face begins to burn as I watch the two servers make

quick work of the dishes, stacking them onto a trolley that's prepped to go back to the kitchens.

"You doing some math in your head, Abbi?" Henry asks, feigning innocence. The bastard has already figured that out.

"Nope." I grab my glass of wine and chug half of it.

And Connor and Ronan are left glancing back and forth curiously, not having caught on to the private joke.

"Give me a minute." Henry follows the two servers out, pulling several bills from his wallet to tip them. I've heard from Rachel and Autumn that he's always generous in tipping the staff when they serve him. It's admirable.

"So?" Margo's elbows are resting the table, her gaze shifting between Ronan and Connor. "Did you two enjoy the meal?"

"Yes. Thank you. It was incredible," Ronan says, patting his belly.

"Yeah, it's been a while since I've eaten like this," Connor adds.

"When have you ever eaten like this?" Ronan challenges.

"Never. I'm not even sure what I ate."

I giggle at Connor's blunt honestly. Oh, how I've missed that.

Margo's musical laughter carries. "Good. Let's retire outside." Grabbing a full bottle of wine and her glass, she beckons. "*Ici*. Come, come...."

Connor doesn't hesitate, grabbing his glass and trailing her out through the french doors. Ronan is a little slower to rise from his chair.

"You good?"

"Yeah." His brow furrows. "I wasn't sure how tonight would go, but it's been fine. He's not such an asshole." He nods in Henry's direction.

I smile. "I should hope not. You climbed down a shaft for him."

"I didn't do it for him," he says softly. He sees Henry approaching, and gets up and heads out to join the others.

Henry's gaze sits on his back the entire way. "He's made it impossible for me to hate him. I hate him for that."

I glare at him. "Would you prefer to be stuck in a mine right now?"

"No." He holds a hand out. "Come on. We're going out there."

My stomach flips. "Henry... you and I both know where that's leading."

"And?"

"And?" I frown at his decanter of Scotch. How much has Henry had to drink? "Just a few days ago you didn't want me anywhere near them. Now you're taking me by the hand to go and watch them fuck Margo."

"Call it curiosity." He watches me evenly, but lets nothing else slip. "Come on. At the very least, it'll be an interesting show. We can leave whenever we want." He pours me another glass of wine—the servers left three full bottles on the table—and leads me toward the door. "Do you think them getting to fuck Margo will be fair trade for going down into that mine?"

"Connor would definitely say so."

"But not Ronan?"

"No, he'd rather fuck—" I cut myself off before I finish that attempt at being wry, cursing the wine and my loose tongue.

I don't need to finish the sentence though. The look on Henry's face says he already knows as much. I just can't tell what he thinks of it.

When we step outside, Connor and Ronan are lifting the cover off the hot tub. Steam swirls off the top and into the cold night air like a thick fog. The tub is set on the ground off to the side of the main porch, enclosed on three sides by a screened structure to give privacy and bug coverage, while opening it up to the rest of the porch. The roof is all screen, and open to the stars above.

I make myself comfortable on the nearby loveseat. The blanket that Katie wrapped round me when I was out here last, fearing for Henry's life, sits in a heap. I cover myself with it now, as this fall maxi dress doesn't provide much warmth. Henry takes a seat beside me.

"How do you... *oui*, like this," Margo murmurs to herself, her fingers dancing over the control pad. A beep sounds and bubbles erupt in the water. Setting her wine glass on a side table, she proceeds to push the sleeves of her dress from her shoulders. The entire thing falls to a heap on the wood floor.

"It's ironic that she makes millions modeling bras and panties, and yet she doesn't own a single pair," I murmur softly, earning Henry's chuckle.

We all watch a nude Margo climb into the hot tub, and it's impossible not to admire her for both her physique and her confidence. While Henry and I completely expected this turn of events, she still gets points for shock from the other half of our group.

Of course, Ronan is so good at hiding his thoughts. His face shows only mild surprise.

"Are you fucking kidding me?" Connor stands there slack-jawed. He's been on his best behavior all day with Margo, biting his tongue against the sexual innuendos, showing his best manners. No doubt he had fantasies about where tonight could go. He just wouldn't have expected it to be so easy for them to turn into reality.

"Are you two going to leave me in here alone?" Margo mock pouts, her eyes raking over first Connor and then Ronan.

Connor turns to look at me, and then Henry. "Are we gonna get fired for this?"

"Considering what you *haven't* been fired for... no, I'd say you're safe here," Henry mutters.

That's all the approval Connor needs, reaching over his head to peel off his shirt.

He's definitely grown stronger than the last time I saw him shirtless, I note, my gaze drifting over his back.

He makes quick work of the rest of his clothing, leaving everything in a heap. No one could find fault with Connor's body and he knows it. He walks confidently toward the hot tub, his cock, long and hard, bobbing with each step.

I feel Henry's gaze on me and I realize that I've been caught looking at another man naked.

I quickly avert my eyes.

"Abbi...."

"Yeah?"

Henry leans in. "You're allowed to watch."

"Ronan, come," Margo taunts, beckoning to him. "Don't be timid."

Ronan's deep, raspy chuckles carries in the air. Amusement over the very idea that stripping in front of us would make him shy. With slower, sleeker movements than Connor, Ronan strips down. Even Henry is watching.

Ronan reminds me of a lion, the way he takes the steps down into the tub, pausing in front of Margo to give her an eyeful of his cock, which she eagerly admires. He's also grown in muscle, his stomach and arms more defined, his ass even rounder. He slips into the water to take a seat on the other side of her.

Margo settles that devious gaze on us. "Henry...." French words sail from her lips.

Henry responds smoothly in French. They go back and forth several times, leaving the rest of us oblivious.

Finally, Margo switches to English. "Abigail, would you like to join us? We will behave."

I give her a doubtful look.

It earns her laugh. "I promise. What is it you Americans say? 'Cross my heart'?" She drags a finger over her left breast. Her nipples sit just at the waterline and the move draws the acute attention of both men on either side.

I look to Henry, who's watching me intently.

"Is that what you *want*?" he asks evenly. "To strip down in front of them and get into the hot tub?"

"No."

His eyebrow rises knowingly.

My stomach tightens. "I don't know."

Below the blanket, Henry's hand slides under my dress, up my thigh, and unceremoniously into my panties. I gasp as he pushes a finger inside me. It slides in too easily. "Really... I think you *do* know." If he's upset by the way my body is reacting to the erotic tension Margo is spinning, he doesn't let on.

"Well... what about you?" I reach out to find his inner thigh, using it as a guide to grasp between his legs.

He's rock-hard.

"*Really...*," I mock.

He smirks. "I never denied anything."

Margo, Connor, and Ronan have started their own conversation and are laughing between sips of wine, paying no attention to us.

"Yes. I do want to," I finally admit, accepting that I'm enjoying this thrill that's coursing through my limbs. "But only if you're there with me."

"Well good, because that's the *only* way that's *ever* going to happen." He leans in to kiss me tenderly on the lips. And then he stands and kicks off his shoes. "Coming?"

Am I really going to do this?

I finish my glass of wine, set it on the side table, and then pull myself to my feet. Henry already has his shirt off.

I quickly pull my hair to the top of my head in a messy bun and fasten it with the elastic I had around my wrist from earlier. Henry disappears through the set of french doors that leads into our bedroom for a moment, leaving me alone with three sets of eyes, waiting quietly for me to undress. When Henry emerges, he's naked.

"Can you help me?" I ask, turning my back to him.

He unfastens the clasp at my nape, the one that keeps my dress secure.

With that undone, I'm able to push the material off much like Margo did. With a deep breath, I let it slide, leaving me in my panties and bra. Cold air bites at my exposed flesh.

Henry's standing knee deep in the tub, his hand out. "A little faster, Abbi. This cold won't do wonders for my ego." He languidly strokes his hard length once with his free hand to emphasize his worry, unconcerned that everyone's watching us.

"She is so beautiful, is she not?" Margo purrs, her eyes like fingertips on me.

Murmurs of assent come from either side of her, their eyes burning into my flesh.

I've been with all of them before, I remind myself.

They've all wanted me, I remind myself.

They've all expressed that they still want me.

With that mental boost to my confidence, I reach back and unfasten my bra. My breasts fall free, full and heavy, my nipples pebbled and not from the cold.

A groan slips from Connor's throat. He always did have a thing for breasts. *My* breasts, especially.

Pushing my panties off my hips, I step out of them. I take a deep breath and, holding my head up with more confidence than I have, I grasp Henry's waiting hand to follow him in.

Margo's eyes are molten as they drift from my face to my

breasts, to the apex of my thighs, where they stall, her lips parting as if with memory.

The water is hot. Borderline too hot. So hot that I'm forced to take extra time, giving plenty of opportunity for enduring looks.

For some reason, I can't bring myself to look at Ronan.

Henry finally seizes my hips and pulls me onto the seat beside him. He settles his arm over my shoulder. "If anyone touches her in here, I will end you." The threat is delivered in his typical smooth, calm fashion.

"What if my foot accidently touches her foot," Margo taunts, her long, slender leg emerging from the center of the tub to flick several drops of water at Henry's face.

He says something back to her in French that makes her throw back her head and laugh, a murmur of "oui" sliding from her lips.

Ronan smirks as he watches her closely.

"What did you say?" I ask Henry.

He leans in to whisper in my ear, "She's going to have her hands full of cock soon enough and to stay away from my pussy."

My eyes can't help but veer to those dainty, very experienced hands. Currently, one is occupied with a glass of wine, while the other absently twirls strands of hair.

"So, hey... Margo. Do you know Giselle Mullock?" Connor asks.

"I do. I know her well." She winks slyly at me. "Why? Do you find her desirable?"

"He jerks off to pictures of her every morning in his bunk. No, not at all," Ronan murmurs, his head tipped back to expose his angular throat.

"You're such a jackass." Connor reaches around Margo to flick Ronan's ear.

"Are you saying you do not pleasure yourself to pictures of her?" Margo's eyes are intent on Connor.

"Well, yeah, but...." He offers her a sheepish grin. "It's not because I *need* to."

"Because you sleep with many women?"

Connor's mouth opens but he stalls, unsure how to answer that, if admitting that he's slept with *many* women will turn her off.

Henry chuckles. "Stop baiting the poor guy, Margo."

She finishes off the wine in her glass and stretches to set it at a safe distance behind them, putting her nipple inches away from Connor's mouth in the process.

He squeezes his eyes shut as if in pain.

"I am not baiting him. I am just getting to know him better." Her hand slips under the water.

I can tell the precise moment that her fist wraps around Connor's cock. His shoulders lift a touch, as if in surprise, and his lips part with a soundless gasp.

"So, tell us about yourself," she says casually, as if she's not giving him a hand job under the water and we don't all know about it.

Connor clears his throat. "Fuck. Well, uhhh... I'm living in Miami. Ronan and I are actually roommates."

"*Really...* for how long?" Margo feigns interest, forcing him to carry on a conversation while she strokes him.

"He's going to unload in the water, Margo," Henry warns.

"He is not. Are you?" she asks sweetly.

"In about ten seconds," Connor admits.

"So soon?"

Connor laughs. "I can't help myself. It's you. You've been driving me crazy all day."

She tsks. "That is not allowed to happen in the water." She leans in to whisper something in his ear and then presses her lips against his. They share a sensual kiss that lasts for a few moments, that all of us quietly observe, and then Connor breaks free and lifts himself up to sit on the ledge, his cock jutting out.

It's impossible not to watch as Margo gets to her knees and fits herself between Connor's legs. Without any licking or otherwise teasing—probably because it's cold out of the water—she takes his full length into her mouth and down her throat in a practiced move, her lips stretched to capacity to accept his size.

The intimate act—the fact that she's doing it in front of all of us—makes blood start rushing down into my belly and along my thighs.

"Jesus Christ. Margo Lauren is sucking my dick," Connor moans, gripping the back of her head with one hand, his eyes on her.

Both Henry and Ronan chuckle. Must be a guy thing.

"How are you doing?" Henry asks quietly, his hand disappearing under the water. I shiver as I feel it slipping between my legs.

"Good."

He slides two fingers into me. And smirks. "I would say so. Open up."

Nerves churn in my stomach as I stretch a leg over Henry's lap, giving him better access. He takes it, sliding in a third finger to stretch me wide. He begins dragging his thumb over my clit in smooth, leisurely circles. "No coming in the water," he warns softly, his gaze on my parted lips.

I reach for his lap, wrapping my fist around his cock and gently pressing the very end of his tip. "Ditto."

He leans in to drag his teeth over my earlobe, and then whispers, "Then, unless you're ready to suck me off with an audience, you might want to stop that."

Connor and Margo aren't paying any attention, but I can

feel Ronan's gaze blazing against my profile. He must know what Henry is doing to me with his fingers.

What would it feel like, to have Ronan's eyes on me while I kneeled before Henry? He watched while I went down on Connor. He watched when Connor's tongue was inside me, too. He watched and I felt his eyes and I loved every moment of it, while it was happening.

If it were Henry I was with while Ronan watched? Henry's cock I was teasing? Henry's tongue inside me?

I seize Henry's hand with a sharp inhale and pull my legs together.

"No? Or just not yet."

"I...." I hesitate. "I don't know."

He studies me quietly, as if he can read my thoughts. As if he can tell that I'm afraid to admit that, yes, I would enjoy it if it was Ronan in that audience. With a kiss on my lips, he settles his hand on my thigh. We turn our attention back to the others, in time to watch Connor gently thrusting into Margo's mouth. A series of low groans escapes his parted lips as he releases.

Beside me, Henry's breathing has quickened.

"Holy fuck. Thank you, sweet Jesus," Connor murmurs as Margo releases his cock from her mouth. He slips his giant body back into the water and lazily reaches for her, touching her somewhere beneath the water.

With a satisfactory smile, she wipes the spit from the corners of her mouth with the back of her hand. "Ronan, darling, would you please fill my glass of wine?"

He glances over at the wine bottle, sitting in the far corner and out of reach of anyone sitting in the tub, and smirks. "No problem." He eases himself out to perch onto the edge just as Connor did.

My eyes automatically go to his jutting length as he

reaches for the bottle and leisurely pours her a glass. He's hard and ready, and yet he hasn't made a move on Margo.

When I look up, I find his heated gaze on me.

"Ronan has an exquisite body, don't you agree, Abigail?" Margo asks, reaching with one hand to accept her wine, while her other smooths over his muscular thigh.

My mouth opens, but I stall on my words. "Yes, of course he does. He knows that." I meet his eyes once more before shifting my attention and body toward Henry. I wrap my arm around his waist and lean in to bury my face in his neck. I run the tip of my tongue along his skin, savoring the saltiness.

"Has Abigail enjoyed...." Margo finishes her sentence in French.

He answers in French, to which she throws something back, and Henry shifts his gaze to Ronan.

I frown. "Have I enjoyed what?"

"Nothing."

"You know, it's really annoying when you two do this. It's like you have a secret language."

"French is a secret language?"

"It is for the rest of us."

"Margo's just stirring trouble." Henry's hard gaze is set across from us.

"What are you afraid of?" she goads through another sip, her steady gaze matching his. "She is highly sexual. She adores you. She will never stray. Do not let your selfishness and jealousy get in the way of what you know she would enjoy." She ends her thoughts in French.

A third voice jumps in, fluently answering her.

And all of our eyes shift to Ronan as he eases back into the tub.

"Dude, you speak French? What the hell?" Connor's face is filled with shock.

Margo slaps him affectionately across the chest and prattles off in her native language and he responds.

"I guess it's not such a secret language after all." Henry studies Ronan as if for the very first time.

"What were they saying, Ronan?" I press, knowing he'll tell me the truth.

He twists his lips. "Margo was asking if you've enjoyed having two men at once, and Wolf told her not in the way she's meaning. And she suggested letting me join you and him tonight," he describes calmly.

My stomach tightens.

"What about me?" Connor exclaims indignantly.

"No. It must be Ronan. Besides, you are already busy for tonight." Margo smiles coyly at Connor, pulling her legs up and apart until her knees are peeking out of the water. His hand is clearly between them, working her over.

It must be Ronan.

Why?

Because I've already had sex with him?

Because I trust him completely?

Because ever since she put the idea out there earlier today, my mind has been toying with it, wondering? Fantasizing? In a way that would never happen with Connor or any other man?

Margo pulls herself out of the hot tub. "It's quite warm in there, isn't it?" She parts her legs to give everyone a full view of her bare pussy, her lips swollen from arousal. "Connor, please help me."

Connor moves fast, as if he's going to lose his chance. He fits his broad shoulders between Margo's slender legs, pushing her thighs apart even farther before burying his face.

She fits one leg behind Ronan's head, so that he can see Connor's tongue working her. He watches quietly, his gaze drifting to Margo's face intermittently. Does he want to have sex with her? Of course he does.

What part will he play in it?

Without warning, Henry grabs me by the waist and swiftly pulls me onto his lap, the move setting my breasts above the waterline. Margo's and Ronan's eyes immediately lock on them, watching as Henry reaches around to cup and knead them.

Ronan says something in French and then Henry is circling my nipples with the pads of his thumbs. Ronan's green eyes flare with fire. Henry pulls me back against his chest and I feel his hard cock between my legs.

"Tell me now... do you want that?" he whispers.

I don't need to ask what he means. "I want you."

"You *have* me no matter what." His hand presses against my cheek, forcing me to turn to him, to meet his eyes. "Are you curious to know what that feels like?"

A soft *yes* curls around my thoughts, but I bite my tongue. "I want... I want your mouth on me and your hands on me, and you inside me. And I don't want anything to happen that will make you love me less, or make you not want me anymore."

Margo's soft moans are growing louder and in frequency. They grab Henry's attention momentarily. He watches as she writhes under Connor's tongue, her gaze now focused solely on Connor. Perhaps Henry's thinking past that, to the time that he gave her exactly what she's pushing him to give me.

"Do you trust me?"

"Yes."

His cock twitches against me, but he says nothing, seemingly content to watch Margo as she grinds against Connor's face, panting. She unravels a few moments later, her head tilted back, her cries sailing into the night, completely unabashed.

Even during orgasm, Margo is beautiful.

Connor climbs out of the tub just far enough to wrestle his wallet from his pants pocket. He pulls out two condoms, tearing the foil package of one of them with his teeth and tossing the other to Ronan, who catches it easily.

"Go inside. I'll be there in a minute," Henry murmurs to me.

I climb out, feeling Ronan's heated eyes on my bare ass as much as the biting cold as I rush through the door and into the warm interior of our cabin. I quickly wrap myself in my robe but the shivers have kicked in, shaking my body. They're all going to be freezing when they come out, I realize. So I dig out a stack of towels from the closet in the liaison's quarters and head back.

Margo is straddling Connor's lap and rocking back and forth. They're alone in the tub and paying no attention to me.

I quietly set the stack of towels there and head back inside.

"Abbi. Come here," Henry calls from the bedroom.

I find him next to the bed, a towel wrapped around his waist.

I frown. "Where did Ronan go?"

"I'm right here," Ronan calls from the chair in the corner, also in a towel that Henry must have given him. The gas fireplace has been ignited, pumping heat into the room.

My stomach flips with nerves.

CHAPTER 19

Silence lingers in the bedroom as the two men quietly watch me process the situation.

Ronan would not be here if Henry hadn't already agreed to this. He wouldn't have the nerve to even suggest stepping inside the room.

"You told him to come," I whisper.

"I gave him a choice," Henry begins calmly. "I told him that he could either stay outside and help his friend satiate Margo, which will keep him busy all night, or he could come in here and watch me fuck you." He glares intently at Ronan. "It was one or the other, and he had to choose."

Ronan chose *this* over a night with Margo? A night likely to push even *his* boundaries, which seem to be nonexistent?

Ronan chose *me* over Margo?

The tension swirling around us is palpable as I glance back at my friend. He's wearing his typical aloof expression. But I see that dark hunger in his eyes. That dark hunger, and something else.

Hopefulness.

Of what, exactly?

What does Ronan really think is going to happen with a man like Henry here?

I clear my throat against the rush of nerves. "What if I'm not okay with it?"

"Then tell him to get the fuck out and he will. He knew that was a chance when he walked through that door." Henry gives me a steely-eyed look. "But I think we all know that's not what you want."

Oh God. He knows me so well. Still.... "Why does this feel like a test?"

"It's not a test, Abbi." He smirks, holding out his hand, beckoning me. "Unless you count me wanting to know if you'll finally be honest with me as a test. Come here." He seizes my hips and pulls me to him. "Are you warm enough?"

I nod. In fact, my entire body is suddenly on fire with anticipation.

Is this really happening?

"Good." Reaching down, he tugs on his towel to release it from its binding. It falls to the floor, showing me how his thick erection stands in wait, his tip adorned by a single bead. I settle my hands onto his broad shoulders, taking a moment to trace the lines of his collarbone with my fingertips before I lean in to replace them with my mouth. Of all my favorite parts to have my mouth on Henry, I still think that might be my top. "I thought you said you'd never share me with anyone," I whisper.

So gently, he cups my face between his hands and presses a tender kiss against my lips. "I also said that I don't ever want you to have regrets." His blue eyes pierce me. "So this is the once for this. You agreed to Margo in France, and now I'm agreeing to Ronan here."

"But I didn't ask for it."

"You don't have to ask. I know you, and I know what you like." Henry's hooded eyes drift behind me. "I wouldn't be agreeing to this with anyone else. I trust you, and you trust him."

I glance back at Ronan and then at Henry. Unspoken words seem to float between the two of them.

Oh my God. This *is* actually happening.

The backs of Henry's knuckles skate over my nape before trailing down to slip into my robe and around my back, to pull my body flush with his. I feel the hard press of his cock against my stomach. "Always so ready, Abbi," he whispers, sliding his hand between my legs and dragging it slowly through my slit, back and forth several times.

"For you, yes. Always." I trail my tongue along the seam of his lips before leaning in to kiss him, hoping he senses how much I mean that. "I love you more than anything or anyone in the world."

He smiles, his confidence dripping from him. "I know that, Abbi. That's why I can do this with you tonight." He bows his neck to kiss me deeply, his lips prying mine open wide, fitting his tongue inside.

I kiss him back eagerly.

From behind us, a soft curse slips from Ronan's mouth. The chair creaks as he adjusts in his seat.

"Something wrong, Lyle?" Henry asks, using his last name, his eyes never leaving mine.

"Nothing. I just thought I was going to get a half-decent show," Ronan mocks, though I can tell from the huskiness in his voice that he's thoroughly aroused by every second of this.

Henry clenches his teeth so hard, I hear a cracking sound. "I can still kick you out."

"Then you'd be unsatisfying your girlfriend on *all* accounts."

"You motherfucker." Henry shakes his head but he's grinning. It's a wicked grin.

My robe loosens and then slips away under Henry's hands, the plush white terrycloth falling to the floor, putting my naked body on display for Ronan.

I shiver.

"Cold?" Henry asks, trailing a fingertip over the goose-flesh coating my breasts.

"No." At least, I don't feel the cold. I don't feel anything except Henry's hard body pressed against me, Ronan's searing gaze on my back, and the low burn of erotic anticipation coursing through my veins.

"Good. Turn around," Henry orders softly.

I do, slowly, to find Ronan's molten green eyes taking in my naked flesh from top to bottom, before following Henry's hand as it slips between my legs again, this time from behind.

For all the times I've watched this happen to others, being the one on display like this is ten times more stimulating.

I can barely breathe.

But why the hell would Ronan want to watch this? If he cares for me the way he says he does... wouldn't this hurt him?

Did Henry make him feel like he had to?

"You don't have to stay," I say gently.

Ronan's gaze flies to meet mine, narrowing slightly. "Do you want me to leave?"

"No. I just mean, if this is too hard...."

Finally, I get a smile.

A smirk, more like, as Ronan reaches over to release his towel and cast it aside. He takes his swollen cock in his palm. "It's *definitely* too hard, Red," he says, his eyes lifting to meet mine for a lingering moment, to show me the amusement in them, before settling down between my legs again.

Henry slides two fingers inside.

My lips fall apart with a moan and I adjust my stance to give him more access, surprised that I'm so comfortable in doing so. But that entire scene earlier—all of us naked in the hot tub, Margo and Connor performing in front of us—has left my body wired, desperate for its own release. And Ronan's eyes on me don't scare me. This is far from the first time he's seen me naked. He already knows my body well.

Henry bows forward to catch my earlobe in his mouth, and I can't help but close my eyes and let my head fall back. "You want to come, Abbi?" he murmurs.

"Yes," I admit breathlessly, feeling my orgasm hovering there, along my spine, just out of reach.

"Not yet." The bed creaks as he takes a seat behind me. Seizing my hips, he guides me back to straddle him in reverse, folding my legs up to nestle against his outer thighs. Keeping me facing Ronan, facing his arousing gaze, as he lifts me slightly to float over his hard cock.

Need pulses in my core as he drags his tip through my folds.

"How badly do you want to be fucked by that right now?" Ronan asks in that way he has, his voice a deep lull. His chin is propped up casually on one hand as he observes.

I hesitate, but only for a split second. "*So* badly." Normally I'd be mortified, talking so openly like this. But whatever this is tonight, the three of us are in it together.

Henry's strong hands grip my hips tightly. And then he's pulling me down onto his hard length, sinking all the way to the hilt with one thrust.

My cry fills the room.

"Fuck," Ronan mutters. "You are so goddamn beautiful, Red." He wraps his fist around himself and begins stroking lazily from root to tip and back again.

The sight of it sends a pulse deep into my pussy. We're definitely all in this together now.

Henry fills his hands with my breasts as he rolls his hips, his thumbs brushing over my peaked nipples teasingly. I arch my back reflexively. "So start fucking me then." His lips are a soft caress against my nape, even with his sinful words.

I grind down on him, and feel his head press deep against me inside. It pulls a moan from my throat with each pass as I begin riding him, my thigh muscles clenching around his hips.

Ronan's strokes suddenly speed up and his thighs fall farther apart, showing off his swollen sac. He looks ready to burst.

On impulse, I reach down to skate my middle finger across my clit.

"Dammit, Abbi!" Ronan grunts, gritting his teeth as milky-white cum spurts from the tip of his cock in streams, over his fist and onto his taut belly.

The sight of him coming—for me, because of me—sends an unexpected wave of heat exploding inside me, spreading through my thighs and belly. My muscles pulse around Henry as I cry out and Ronan milks himself dry, his head fallen back, his Adam's apple jutting out as he jerks in his palm.

"Jesus. I thought you two would last longer than that," Henry mutters through pants, his own breathing growing shallow.

Without warning, I'm suddenly off Henry's lap and lying on my back, on the bed. Henry drops to his knees in front of me. With his hands pushing on my thighs to open me up wide, he wastes no time sticking his tongue into my entrance to begin lapping the post-orgasm wetness up.

Ronan, seemingly unbothered by the sticky substance all over his hand, watches quietly, the angle from his chair perfect for the view.

"You have the sweetest pussy I've ever tasted," Henry murmurs, his tongue slipping through my folds and swirling over my now sensitive clit. He pushes first one finger inside, and then another. And then two more, to allow him to reach deep inside me, to that spot he loves to touch.

I close my eyes and revel in the depravity of tonight. Henry's right. I do like our sordid sex life. I do want Ronan here, watching Henry and me. And I am *so* far gone from the Abbi who stepped off that ferry in May. I'm happy for it, because these carnal nights with him keep bringing me closer to him.

I fist Henry's thick, wavy hair with my hand, tugging on it gently as I roll my hips against his face. I dare look over at Ronan again, to see him stroking himself languidly. The cool mask is gone and raw desire fills his face, his lips parted as Henry's tongue fucks me.

And suddenly Henry's rising and I'm being moved again, being lifted and flipped, to straddle Henry, who's lying on the bed. In seconds his cock is deep inside me again, earning my deep moan as a tingle begins sneaking up my thighs. I'm going to orgasm again, and soon.

It's as if he senses it because he doesn't begin thrusting right away.

Instead, he weaves his hand through my long, red hair to grip the back of my head. "You liked watching him come, didn't you?"

"Yes."

He smirks. "Finally, an honest answer without any hesitation."

I pepper his carved jawline with kisses. "You're not mad, are you?"

"No. I'm not mad." He pauses, his blue eyes studying mine intently. "You have my mouth on you, my hands on you, and my cock in you, and I won't love you any less. I promise you."

"Okay," I murmur as I hear my own words from earlier repeated back to me.

Our lips mesh together in a slow, seductive dance as his

hands slide along the contours of my body, from my knees all the way to my shoulders. I match him stroke for stroke, teasing and tasting his tongue, running my tongue along the seam of his lips, nipping at his bottom lip with my teeth.

Until something grazes my tight back entrance, and I know it can't be Henry because his hands are locked on my hips and his cock is buried deep inside me. I startle, pulling away from Henry's mouth.

His blue eyes blaze as he looks up at me. "Tell me now if you don't want to do this, and it won't happen," he says evenly.

I turn to find Ronan standing behind me, his dark and intent eyes on mine, his hard length jutting out, aimed straight for me.

"Please let me, Abbi," Ronan whispers, his throat bobbing with his swallow.

Oh my God.

I'm speechless.

Henry didn't invite Ronan in here to just watch.

"How? I mean...." My words catch in my throat.

Ronan smiles softly. "I think you understand exactly how."

From beneath me, Henry's lips trace my shoulder, leaving a trail of wetness.

I turn to him, look questioningly at him.

"I want to do this with you, just once. I want you to experience this. *If* you want to. If you're nervous—"

"I am. Nervous, I mean."

Henry hears what I don't say: that I want to experience this with him, too.

"You're in good hands. We'll go slow. And you can stop it at *any* time if you change your mind. Just say the word. Okay?" His mouth moves to feather my jawline, so light that under other circumstances, I might have giggled. But I sense

Ronan approaching and that stifles any silliness. Ronan has a perfect view of Henry inside me, and of my ass in the air.

"Okay," I manage to whisper.

"Do you trust me?"

"Yes." With my body, with my heart. With everything that I am.

"Just focus on me. And don't move your hips until we tell you to," Henry whispers. "As much as you may want to."

With a deep breath, I lean in to press my lips against Henry's.

"Hold still for a bit, Red," Ronan murmurs. "Once I'm in you, you can fuck him as hard as you want."

I hadn't realized now that my hips had been moving; I'd been subtly riding Henry, the feel of him inside me, against me spurring on my natural reaction.

I freeze.

From behind me, I hear a cap opening. Moments later, the familiar drip of liquid hits my skin.

Then there's a second touch on that spot, this time more intentional, lubricated fingers smoothing over the area to wet it.

My heart is racing, and my fists curl around the bedsheets tightly, but I keep my eyes locked on Henry's and focus on his soft lips, kissing them over and over again, conveying how much I love him, despite the fact that Ronan's hand is all over my ass.

Henry smiles. "I'm not worried, Abbi. I know how you feel about me. And I know how I feel about you."

God, to be so damn confident.

Ronan presses down against my tailbone to angle my hips. I hold my breath as he begins drawing circles over my tight entrance with a single fingertip. On the sixth pass, he pushes against it. It slides in so much more easily than last time. "How is that?"

"Fine," I whisper, tightening the muscles back there.

"Good." He leaves his finger there for a moment, while his other hand palms my ass affectionately. And then I feel him sliding it out, only to replace it with another, thicker finger. He does this two more times, before slowly pressing something thicker—two fingers, I realize—in.

I close my eyes as my body accepts them more slowly.

"She's pretty fucking ready," Ronan murmurs.

From below me, Henry smirks. "I guess she really wants your dick in there."

I never thought I'd hear Henry joke like that. "Are you sure you're okay with this?" I whisper.

Henry pauses. "The truth?"

My stomach tightens. "Yes."

"I want to punch his teeth out. But it's also making my cock as hard as a fucking steel pipe."

Behind us, Ronan chuckles.

I can't help my own smile. "Everything makes you hard."

"Everything to do with you makes me hard," he corrects. "And he better hurry the fuck up, because I'm about to blow my load just sitting here inside you, waiting."

The familiar sound of a foil packet tearing fills the room. A few moment later, the edge of the bed sinks with Ronan's weight as he settles a knee on the mattress.

"Open her up for me."

Henry's hands leave their spots—one woven in my hair, the other on my hip—to move to cup either side of my ass. He spreads my cheeks apart.

"Breathe, Abbi," Ronan says softly.

My eyes flare as I feel his tip nudging against me.

"Kiss me. Now," Henry demands softly and I obey, distracting myself from the burn of Ronan slowly pushing into me, with Henry already deep inside the other entrance.

"Oh my God," I groan, as the intense pressure and burn grows.

"Relax your muscles, Abbi, or I can't get in." Ronan's hand smooths over my spine, back and forth soothingly, sending chills through my body, jogging memories of two sets of male hands on my body, kneading my breasts, smoothing over my thighs, rubbing my clit.

Henry latches on to my favorite spot halfway down my neck, his tongue stroking back and forth, his teeth grazing occasionally. Meanwhile, he fits a hand down between us and begins rubbing my clit.

"That's it, Red," Ronan murmurs. "Just keep thinking about how much we both want you. About how hard we both are for you. About how good it's going to feel when both of us are coming in you."

My body begins opening up to him, growing slick from both entrances as my pussy throbs for relief.

A growl of "Fuck" escapes Henry as Ronan sinks in even deeper.

"Start fucking him, Abbi. Slowly."

Henry grasps my hips, giving him purchase so he can lift his pelvis. His cock pushes into me.

"Oh my God!" I gasp. I'm so stretched by the two of them.

Ronan shifts his position and then begins pumping gently into me, too.

I cry out, dizzy, a thin sheen of sweat forming over my skin as I try to focus past the burn to the carnal pleasure that's building deep inside, with so many nerves being stimulated by these two men at the same time.

Henry rocks his pelvis to pump in and out of me. It's different from how he normally fucks me, but everything about this is different.

"Does this feel good for you?" I manage to get out between my ragged pants.

He lets out a weak, breathy laugh. "Yes, Abbi. It feels good."

I turn to look over my shoulder. Ronan's face is tight with concentration, every muscle in his body tense.

"Yes. Abbi. Fucking incredible." He moans as if to emphasize how much.

With my palms resting against the bed on either side of Henry's head, we fall into a rhythm, our groans and cries tangling together with each thrust, each man sinking deeper into me as my body greedily shapes around them, until they're both hitting that spot within me. Until I can't even focus my hazy eyes on Henry, my other senses wild with need. The burn that I felt from Ronan is still there, but it's dulled, replaced with pleasure like I've never felt before.

Ronan's hands slip from my back, to shape around my breasts.

I peer down at them, watching as they tenderly knead my heavy flesh, the pads of his thumbs stroking my hard nipples, before daring look at Henry to see if he minds Ronan touching me so intimately.

"His dick is in your ass, Abbi," Henry reminds me, as if reading my mind. His blue eyes are alight with fire as they watch Ronan's hands. And then he's using his thick wall of abdominal muscle to lift his face to my nipple, his lips parting.

Ronan holds my breast out for Henry's searching mouth.

Henry takes it in, first grazing it with his teeth.

I cry out as I watch Henry's lips wrap around the pink bud and feel him suck hard, the suction borderline painful.

The sting is tempered quickly by a soft feathering at my spine.

Ronan's plump lips and tongue, doting on my body from behind. All while one of his hands slips away from my breast to move between my legs. He begins rubbing my clit.

"Oh my God." I gasp, throwing my head back as his fingertip slips back and forth over the slick, swollen nub. This is too much! Their cocks inside me, their hands and mouths all over me, their grunts and moans carrying into the night, their beautiful bodies....

Pressure begins building in my spine.

Both of them have increased their thrusts in tempo and strength, and I'm moving in time with them, eagerly bucking and moaning with each delicious stretch of my body. Henry has fallen back to the bed, unable to hold himself any longer. He watches me writhe above him, his lips parted, his breathing ragged, his moans deep and raw.

Henry is the first to orgasm, his fingers digging into my hips as he pounds my pussy with hard, erratic thrusts, his face contorted as he groans. It sets off a chain reaction immediately and my body begins quaking with the seismic wave that sweeps through me, every last muscle in my pelvis squeezing around the men's swollen lengths. Ronan's hands find my breasts again, gripping them tightly for purchase as he jerks into me, abandoning all rhythm with his surrendering cries of ecstasy.

I fall against Henry's body, no longer able to hold myself up as the men finish off, pulsing and spilling their hot seed into me, Ronan's contained by his condom.

In moments, the room is quiet again, save for our ragged breaths. I'm draped over Henry's body. His chest rises and falls beneath me; he's seemingly unconcerned that Ronan is bowed over me, his sweat-slick hard chest pressed against my back, his hands on either side of us to hold himself up.

Ronan lays a gentle kiss against my shoulder. "Thank you for letting me have one last time with you, Red."

I twist my neck to meet his hooded eyes, so much tenderness and love in them right now. "That was.... I'll never forget tonight."

"Me, neither." His eyes drops to my mouth. He hesitates for only a second before, almost timidly, leaning in to brush his plump lips against mine once... twice....

He shifts away to meet Henry's sated gaze for a long moment, something passing between the two of them. And then he lifts his spent body off me, leaving my back cold.

"Kiss me right now," Henry whispers, but he doesn't wait for me to act before his fingers weave through my hair and he guides my mouth to his, to deliver a surprisingly hot and hard kiss.

It takes me a moment to respond, and then I'm wincing as Ronan slowly pulls out of me, my entrance burning. The fullness dissipates almost immediately.

The floor creaks with Ronan's footfalls as he disappears out the bedroom door without another word.

"Did you enjoy that?" Henry whispers, his sinewy arms wrapping around my limp body, cocooning me.

"Do you even have to ask?" I press my lips against his neck, tasting salt from his sweat. "Did you?"

He doesn't miss a beat. "Yes. Watching you come apart like that... it was incredible." He pauses. "Are you going to ask me for—"

"No." I shake my head to emphasize my resolve.

"Good, because I don't ever want to share you like that again." His hands begin wandering, over my shoulders, along my spine, down to cup my tender ass. "Every square inch of this body is mine and only mine from this day forward, you understand?"

"Every square inch. Yours and only yours." I run the tip of my tongue over the outside curve of his ear, and feel him shudder beneath me. "I love you more than you could possibly ever understand."

My body shifts as his chest heaves with a sigh. "Believe me, I understand it just fine."

CHAPTER 20

I hug the terrycloth robe tight around my sore body and listen to the hum of the plane's engine fade as the Cessna disappears into the morning sky, shuttling another round of tourists out to admire Henry's Alaska.

I'll always see all of it—the wilderness, the beauty, the peace—as belonging to him.

"Do you want another coffee, Abbi?" Henry calls from inside.

"I would love one." I finish off the last of my first cup with a resigned sigh. We'll be on the helicopter soon, heading for Henry's private airstrip, and then on the jet, heading back to Manhattan where "real life" awaits us. Whatever that means anymore, because life with Henry is anything but normal. It's a completely new life for me, full of deep and peculiar friendships, a business venture that is *mine*—that may actually evolve into something I can't yet comprehend—and more money than I can even fathom.

Though, none of that is important if Henry isn't at the helm of it all.

He's all that's important, really.

I'm staring out at the water as Henry slips my empty mug

from my hand to refill it. I wait patiently, my hand out and ready to accept it back.

Instead of a hot mug, though, I feel something slip over my finger. "Oh my God." I stare down at my hand in dumbfounded shock, at his grandmother's engagement ring.

"Marry me," Henry whispers.

My heart stops for a few beats as I wrap my head around those words. I must have heard that wrong. We've only been together a few months. This is Henry Wolf. But then there's this ring sitting right there, on my finger, staring up at me....

"Marry me, Abbi," he says again, evenly.

"I... but... why?" I stammer.

"*Why?*" With a finger under my chin, he lifts my face to meet his gaze. He stares down at me with such earnestness. "Because I trust you like I've never trusted anyone else. Because you're in my thoughts constantly. Because when I was stuck in that mine, getting back to you was the *only* thing I thought of. Because you know what things—even the most simple things like birthday cakes in a woodstove—will make me happy." He leans down to press his forehead against mine. "Ever since you stepped into my life, you've been in it, for every second of every day. Marry me, Abbi. Let me love you in every way I know how to."

A rush of butterflies flutter wildly in the pit of my stomach. But.... "Henry, you've had a rough few weeks. I mean, your dad died, and then Scott.... And then you almost died, like, two days ago! How do you know you aren't just caught up in it all?"

He smirks. "Do you think I'd propose to you because I was caught up in it all?"

"No." Henry may act quickly, but he does it with clear purpose and smart decision-making.

"I've been thinking about it for weeks. But I kept playing devil's advocate, telling myself that I should wait and let things settle down. But if the last few days taught me anything, it's that I've never been more sure of any decision in my life."

I study the ring on my finger again. It's polished and gleaming, and even more stunning than it was the first time I saw it.

"Be my wife, Abbi. Share my life, have my babies, let me make you moan every single night until we're old and—"

"Yes," I whisper, the pearl and diamonds in the ring blurring beyond the tears now in my eyes. "Yes, of course I'll marry you." I don't need more time to know that I'll never feel for anyone how I feel for Henry. I was ready to throw myself off this porch when I thought I'd lost him.

Henry's throat bobs with his hard swallow. "You know by now that I'm not a traditional man, but if you want me to get down on one knee—"

"No. You're not." I smile up at him. "And you're turning me into a very untraditional woman. But I prefer you just like this." My hot-blooded, foul-mouthed, depraved man who knows how to make me feel like no one else.

Who has shown me a kind of love that I can't live without.

He lifts my hand to kiss my knuckle, just below the ring.

"It fits perfectly." Almost as if it was made for me.

"I know." Henry smirks. "I slipped it on while you were sleeping one night to test it out, and then had it resized a touch smaller."

"You did not!" Now my eyes widen with surprise, earning his chuckle.

"I told you. This isn't a whim." He leans down to press his lips against mine. From his pocket, his phone begins ringing. "That's got to be Jack. He texted me earlier. We need to be in the air by nine to avoid a storm coming through south of here. I'm sorry. I don't want to rush us."

I lean into his firm body, inhaling his intoxicating scent. "It's okay. We can celebrate on the plane."

"Not the way I had in mind."

As sore as my body is from last night, it immediately begins aching with need at his words.

He groans. "Don't look at me like that, Abbi. You'll drive me to bend you over and fuck you right here, standing in the cold. I don't want to defile you like that five minutes after I've proposed."

"Maybe next time then?" I whisper teasingly.

His arms rope around me, squeezing me tight. "Definitely next time."

I let my eyes drift over the dark blue waters below. "Will we be back this year?"

His gaze follows mine. "I guess it depends on when the wedding is, and how fast we have to move on planning it. This is where you want it, right?"

A fresh wave of tears blurs my visions. "Yes." Of course he remembered.

"Then this is where we'll have it." He pauses. "You should probably call your parents and let them know, before news leaks."

"That can wait until we're back in New York," I mutter as my anxiety stirs with that notion. She may have been willing to pray for Henry's safe return, but how willing will she be to accept him becoming a part of our family?

"It's better she hears it from you than someone else," Henry warns. Something that could very well happen, especially given the media attention on him and Wolf Hotels right now, with the recent deaths and the mine collapse.

"I know," I say reluctantly, pulling my phone out of my pocket. I just don't want to give her the opportunity to knock me off this cloud I'm on right now.

Henry presses a kiss against my temple. "Remind her

what this means for getting grandchildren. That should help sway her."

My chest swells. "She'll drive us nuts, asking."

He chuckles. "And I'll thoroughly enjoy the process of trying for them."

I watch Henry's retreating back as he disappears into the cabin, wondering what those arms will look like cradling a baby in them. *Our* baby. Just the thought has my body priming itself for him.

My phone begins ringing in my hand. I look down to see Mama's name pop up, and my eyes widen, afraid for a split second that she's somehow already heard. With a resigned sigh, I answer.

"Abigail! Why haven't you responded to me?"

I sent her a quick text after Henry arrived back, safe, but haven't answered the dozen texts that followed. "I'm sorry. Things have been crazy since Henry came home. We slept for, like, fourteen hours straight."

"That's okay. All that matters is you're all okay."

I swallow my nervousness as I study the ring on my hand and the promise it holds. A life with Henry.

"I'm okay. I'm better than okay."

"What did I tell you? God would deliver, and He has. The Reverend had the whole of Greenbank praying, all day and night. I truly believe that's what made the difference, Abigail. I really do. What about the man who was badly hurt?"

"He had a badly broken leg but he's going to be okay."

"That must have been something, getting him out of there."

I smile. "Henry carried him through the tunnel to another shaft. It was a long way."

"Well, I hope they think twice before going back down. What were they doing down there, anyway? The mine isn't even operational! They were doing exploratory work? For what?"

The news outlets have clearly been thorough in their digging, and Mama has been as eager as ever to get all the information she can.

"It's a long story, but he's not going back into that mine. He's having it sealed off."

"Good. Well, we're all just so happy that they were able to get them out of there in one piece. When are you coming home? And I hope you'll bring Henry with you this time."

"You do?" I can't keep the shock from my voice.

"Now, Abigail, I know we got off to a rocky start, but the Reverend has been helping me see that there is good in him, beyond all those expensive suits and that murderous brother."

I turn back to find Henry leaning against the doorframe, arms folded over his chest, watching me expectantly. "Yes. There's definitely good in him." And a lot of what she'd consider sinfully bad, that I love equally.

I smile.

My future husband.

The father of my children.

The indomitable Henry Wolf is mine.

I bite my lip with a mixture of excitement and trepidation. "I'm really glad to hear you saying this, Mama. Because I have some exciting news."

SNEAK PEEK - SWEET MERCY (EMPIRE NIGHTCLUB #1)

From internationally bestselling author K.A. Tucker comes the dark and sexy Empire Nightclub series.

One visit to my father in prison—convicted for a murder he didn't commit—and I've attracted the attention of the last man I'd ever want knowing that I exist.

Gabriel Easton.

Son of an infamous crime boss. Pretentious liar. Merciless womanizer. A scoundrel to the core.

Worse, he has figured out how desperate I am to protect my father from brutality behind bars. He has the power to grant that protection and he has offered it … for a price.

Me.

I'll do anything for my father, including agree to Gabriel's cruel game. But I won't comply with his every whim and wish.

Unfortunately for me, I think my loathing for him is what he's enjoying most.

That's fine. By the time I'm through with him, he'll be crying my name.

Mercy.

Enjoy this excerpt from Sweet Mercy...

Chapter One - Mercy

"Mercy Wheeler!"

My body, already rigid, stiffens at the sound of my name on the guard's tongue. I've been waiting in Fulcort Penitentiary's visitor lounge for over two hours now, long enough to leave me doubting whether I'd ever be let in.

Shutting my textbook, I collect my purse and rush for the counter with my stomach in my throat, afraid that any dallying could lose me my visit with my father.

The guard staff changed over at some point, because the thin older gentleman with the kind smile who took down my information earlier has been replaced by a burly oaf with beady little eyes and an unfriendly face. His name tag reads Parker. "Who you here to see?" he demands in a gruff tone.

"My dad." I clear the wobble from my voice. "Duncan Wheeler. It should say that on the log?" It comes out as a question, though I can see my father's name written in block letters next to the tip of this guy's pen.

"I like to double-check, is all." He smirks, then recites a long string of numbers and letters. My father's inmate ID number. "This is your first visit here?"

"Yeah." My father only began his sentence two weeks ago, and it took time to get me approved on his visitor list, which is bullshit. I'm the *only person* on his visitor list.

Parker the guard takes a long, lingering scan of my plain, baggy T-shirt. That, along with my loosest pair of jeans, is what I carefully chose to comply with the prison's visitor dress code policy. No tank tops, no shorts, no miniskirts.

Nothing tight. Nothing to "provoke" the men serving time behind these bars.

His eyes stall on my chest for far too long.

I fight the urge to fidget under the lecherous gaze. He's at least twenty years older than me and unappealing, to say the least. Just imagining what kinds of thoughts are churning in his dirty mind makes my skin crawl. Then again, *everything* in this place—the barbed wire fences, the heavily armed guards, the long and narrow hallways, the constant buzzing as door locks are released, the fact that I'm about to sit in a room with murderers, rapists, and God only knows who else —makes my skin crawl.

"What's your old man in for?" Parker finally asks.

I hesitate. "Murder." Are prison guards even supposed to be asking these types of questions?

"Yeah?" His gaze drops to my chest again, and he's not trying to be discreet about it. "And who'd your daddy kill, sweetheart?"

I'm not your goddamn sweetheart. My anger flares, at the invasion of my privacy, at the term he so casually tosses out, at the lustful stare. "Some asshole who wouldn't take no for an answer from me." A mechanic named Fleet who worked at the same auto repair shop where my dad worked, a slimy guy who smelled of motor oil and weed and apparently jerked off to cut-and-paste photos of my face atop porn mag bodies. Who cornered me one night with the full intention of experiencing the real thing.

My father didn't mean to kill him and yet here he is, serving twenty-two years because of a freak accident. Because the prosecutor was convinced otherwise and decided to make an example of him. Because we hired the world's most ineffective lawyer. It's the first thing I dwell on when my eyelids crack every day and the heaviest thing on my shoulders when I drift off at night.

I'm exhausted by guilt and anger, and it doesn't seem like it's going to let up any time soon.

Pervy Parker smirks. "Lock your things up in number seventeen and then head to security screening." He slaps a key onto the counter with his meaty paw. "Phone, car keys, coins, belt. Don't forget so much as a coin, unless you wanna get strip-searched." His mouth curves into a salacious smile. "And you won't get to say no to that if you ever wanna see your daddy again."

My face twists with horror before I can smother it. They wouldn't *actually* strip-search me for forgetting to take out a penny from my pocket, would they?

The prick laughs. "Welcome to Fulcort Penitentiary."

Who is she here to see? I wonder, watching the shriveled old lady fidget with her knuckles, her hair styled in tight gray curls, her wrinkled features touched with smears of pink and blue makeup. A husband? A son?

I've kept my eyes forward and down since I passed through the airport-level security screening process and was led me to this long, narrow visitation room. I've set my jaw and ignored the hair-raising feel of lingering looks and the stifling tension that courses through the air. My father warned me against attracting attention, that having inmates knowing he has "such a beautiful daughter" would only make his life harder in here. While I rolled my eyes as he said that, I also decided to heed his warning the best way I can, so as not to ruin his life further.

So, no makeup, no styled hair—I didn't even brush it today—and minimal eye contact.

Except this sweet-looking grandmother who sits at the cafeteria-style table across from me has caught my gaze and now I can't help but occupy my mind with questions about her while I wait. Namely, how many Saturdays has she spent sitting at Fulcort waiting for a loved one, and what will *I* look like when I'm sitting in this chair twenty-two *years* from now?

A soft buzz sounds on my left, pulling my attention away from her and toward the door where prisoners have been filtering in and out.

An ache swells in my chest as I watch my father shuffle through. It's only been two weeks and yet his face looks gaunt, the orange jumpsuit loose on his tall, lanky frame.

He pauses as the guard refers to a clipboard, his gaze frantically scanning the faces at each table.

I dare a small wave to grab his attention.

The second his green eyes meet mine, his face splits with a smile. He rushes for me.

"Walk!" a guard barks from somewhere.

I stand to meet him.

"Oh God, are you a sight for sore eyes!" He ropes his arms around my neck and pulls me tight into his body.

"I missed you so much!" I return the embrace, sinking into my father's chest as tears spill down my cheeks despite my best efforts to keep them at bay. "They made me wait for hours. I wasn't sure if I'd make it in today—"

"That's enough!" That same guard who just yelled at my father to walk moves in swiftly to stand beside us, his hard face offering not a shred of sympathy. "Unless you wanna lose visitation privileges, inmate!"

Dad pulls back with a solemn nod, his hands in the air in a sign of surrender. "Sorry." He gestures to the table. "Come on, Mercy. Sit. Let me look at you."

We settle into our seats across from each other, my father folding his hands tidily in front of him atop the table. A model of best behavior. The guard shoots him another warning look before continuing on.

"So?" I swallow against the lump in my throat, brushing my tears away. I've done so well, hiding tears from him up until now. "How are you doing?"

He shrugs. "You know. Fine, I guess." He quickly surveys the occupants of the tables around us.

That's when I notice that his jaw is tinged with a greenish-yellow bruise. "Dad! What happened to your face?" I reach for him on instinct.

He pulls back just as the tips of my fingernails graze his cheek. "It's nothing."

"Bullshit! Did someone hit you?"

His wary eyes dart to the nearby inmates again. "Don't worry about it, Mercy. It's just the way things are inside. Someone thinks you looked at them funny.... Pecking order, that sort of thing. It's not hard to make enemies in a prison without trying. Anyway, it's almost healed."

My eyes begin to sting again. This is *my* fault. I should never have told him about what Fleet did that night. It's not like the dirty pig succeeded in his mission; a swift kick to his balls gave me the break I needed to run inside and call the police. Now, had the police done their goddamn job, Fleet never would have strolled into work the next morning with a smug smile on his face and a vivid description of how firm my ass is, and my normally mild-mannered father wouldn't have lost his temper.

Two weeks in and he's already been attacked? My father is one of the most easygoing guys I've ever met. The fact that he went after Fleet the way he did in the garage was a surprise to everyone, including Fleet, according to what witnesses said.

"Hey, hey, hey.... Come on. I can't handle watching you cry," my dad croons in a soothing voice. "And we don't have time for that. Tell me what's going on with you. How's school? Work?"

I grit my jaw to keep my emotions in check. We're supposed to have an hour, but the guard already warned me that Saturdays are busy and this visit will most likely get cut short. So much for prisoner rights. "Work is work. Same old." I've been an administrative assistant at a drug and alcohol addiction center called Mary's Way in downtown Phoenix for six years now. The center is geared toward women and children, and there never seems to be a shortage of them passing through our doors, hooked on vodka or heroin or crack. Some come by choice, others are mandated by the court.

Too many suddenly stop coming. Too many times I feel like we're of no help at all.

Dad nods like he knows.

Because he *does* know, thanks to my mother and her own addiction to a slew of deadly drugs. Heroin is the one that finally claimed her life when I was ten.

"And school? You're keeping up with that, right?"

I hesitate.

"Mercy—"

"*Yes*, I'm still going." Only because it was too late to drop out of my courses without receiving a failing grade. Though, given my scores on my recent midterms, I may earn a failing grade anyway.

He taps the table with his fingertip. "You need to keep up with that, Mercy. Don't let my mess derail your future. You've worked too hard for this, and you're so close to getting that degree."

I've been working toward my bachelor's degree part-time since I was eighteen, squeezing in classes at night and wherever I could find the time and money. At twenty-five, I'm two passing grades away from achieving it. Up until now my intention has always been to become a substance abuse counselor, to help other families avoid the same anguish and loss that my father and I live with. That's why I took the job at Mary's to begin with.

But shit happened, and now I have another focus, and it is laser-specific.

I swallow. "I'm looking at taking the LSAT."

"LSAT?" My dad frowns. "That have something to do with being a counselor?" My father isn't a highly educated man. He spent his teenage years working on cars and skipping class to get high. At some point he decided school wasn't for him, so he wrote his GED and then got a job in a mechanic shop. It took years, but he finally got licensed.

"No. It's for getting into law school." I level him with a serious gaze. "If you'd had a better lawyer than that shyster, you would have gotten involuntary manslaughter at most. Your sentence would have been a sliver of what you're facing now—"

"No, wait." He pinches the bridge of his nose. "What are you saying, Mercy? That you're going to give up on your plans and go to law school just so you can try and get me out of here? I mean, do you even wanna be a lawyer? I thought you hated lawyers." He chuckles as if the idea is amusing.

Nothing is amusing about this. "I want to be able to hug you without some guard breathing down our necks." My voice has turned hoarse. "I want my kids to be able to play and laugh with their grandfather." It's going to be years before there are actually tiny feet running about. But will my fifty-year-old father even live long enough to see the outside again?

"I don't like this at all." Dad shakes his head. "How many years of school is it, anyway?"

"A lot less than what you have to serve right now." Three full-time, plus articling. If I even get accepted anywhere. I've always excelled in my courses, but this is a new direction, one I've never spent a second considering. And then there's the whole "how do I pay for tuition and survive for three years while I'm going to law school full-time" question. All of our savings went to that joke of a lawyer who screwed my father.

It's a lot to figure out, but I *will* figure it out, because there is no way I'll accept coming here every Saturday for the next twenty-two years to watch my father slowly wither away.

"This isn't the life I hoped for you. But I know better than to argue with you." Dad sighs, his shoulders sinking. "So... what's the weather like? I haven't been outside yet today."

"Sunny. Hot."

"Shocking." He offers me a wry smile.

Despite my mood, I can't help but chuckle. It's always one or the other in the desert. A lot of the time, it's both, and in July, it's oppressively so. But the eternal sunshine is the main reason we moved to Arizona from North Carolina after my mother died. It's a natural mood-booster, my father says, and he has always worried about me inheriting her depression. "I had to change in the parking lot." The dented blue shitbox that I drive has never had working air-conditioning, so I pulled my T-shirt and jeans on over my shorts and tank top. "Figure I'll leave these clothes in the car for Saturdays. It'll be like my prison uniform."

He makes a sound. "Good call. Maybe bring a paper bag to wear over your head too."

"Dad."

"Trust me, I've heard the way the men in here talk about women, especially pretty young women like you...." His eyes narrow on a guy three tables over whose dark eyes flitter curiously to us—to me—while a ready-to-burst pregnant woman sitting across from him babbles away. "I don't want anyone giving you grief when you come visit me."

"Nobody is going to give me grief." Except that guard, Parker, but there's no way I'm telling my dad about him. "And if anyone says anything, *ignore* it. They're just words."

He harrumphs. "How's the new place?"

I avert my gaze, dragging my fingertip across the table in tiny circles. "Fine."

He sighs. "That bad?"

"It's... lacking charm," I admit. Anyone who has lived in Phoenix for long enough knows which areas of the city to avoid, and when my dad's conviction was passed and we accepted the fact that I'd need to downgrade from the two-bedroom apartment we were sharing—a downgrade from the house we had before that—we started looking for cheap one-bedrooms closer to work and campus. We found one. A relatively clean, quiet twelve-unit complex with decent management and minimal needles littering the parking lot. A diamond in the rough, my dad called it.

Turns out it's more like a diamond in Mordor.

The couple two doors down—Bob and Rita—fight like they're sworn enemies. I've watched her launch glass from their fourth-storey balcony, aiming for his head as he runs to his car. The cops have been there twice that I know of. It's only a matter of time before an ambulance is wheeling someone out—my bet is it's Bob.

And then there's my next-door-neighbor, Glen, a hairy-chested guy who I hear every morning through the thin walls masturbating to the tune of my 7:00 a.m. alarm and who likes to knock on my door in the middle of the night, bleary-eyed and wearing nothing but his boxers. He always asks for Doritos. I tell him I don't buy Doritos—I *hate* Doritos—but he keeps coming back. I'm beginning to think Doritos is code for something else.

I don't open the door for him anymore.

And I'm not telling my father any of this. He has enough to worry about in here.

The guards come around, tapping several inmates on the shoulder to let them know that their time is up. That earns countless pained expressions from both prisoners and visitors alike. My dad and I watch as people embrace, some adhering to the rules while others hold on until they get a bark of warning.

That'll be us before long, and then it'll be another week before I make the hourlong drive up here.

My heart sinks. "So... what's your cellmate like?"

Dad smirks. "His name is Crazy Bob. And yes, they call him Crazy Bob to his face. Haven't asked what he's in for, and I don't think I wanna know. He likes the violin and NASCAR. Hasn't tried to shank or rape me in my sleep yet."

I frown my disapproval for the poor joke. "The violin and NASCAR. That's an odd combination, right?"

"Yeah. You could say that," my dad agrees. "But Crazy Bob is odd. He seems all right so far. Been in here over ten years now. Knows everything about everything. He's been giving me the lay of the land, so to speak. Where the minefields are, so I can avoid 'em."

"That's good. And the food?"

"The peas are mushy, the potatoes are grainy, and I've fixed tires that had more give than the meat they served last night." He chuckles. "So, kind of like your cooking. In fact, did you take a job in the kitchen that I don't know about?"

"Har. Har. Har." I roll my eyes. Leave it to my dad to try to make jokes in terrible circumstances. But he's always had a natural ability to defuse any tense situation.

So how did he end up getting punched in the face?

I bite the inside of my cheek, wondering if I should push. Finally, I can't help it. "Dad, why did someone hit you?"

He waves it off. "Aww... it was nothing—"

"So then tell me about it, if it's nothing," I challenge, wielding that sharp edge in my voice that Dad swears is like listening to a recording of my mother.

The longer he studies the smooth surface of the table, the more I'm convinced that my gut is right and it's not just a matter of a pissing contest or a funny look.

"Dad...."

"Apparently Fleet's got family or something in here. He wanted me to know he wasn't happy with what happened to Fleet, is all." Dad shrugs nonchalantly. "So now I know. I'm just gonna stay out of the guy's way and everything'll be fine." His jaw tenses. He's more worried about it than he's letting on.

Rightfully so. My father is locked up in here with a family member of the guy he killed and he's already attacked him.

I think I'm going to vomit.

"We need to tell the guards—"

"No." He shakes his head firmly. "Trust me, *no,* Mercy. That won't do me *any* good in a place like *this*. Fulcort's known for.... Well, let's just say I'm a guy with no friends, no affiliations. I'm best to fly under the radar."

I frown. "What do you mean, affiliations?"

His gaze drifts around the room. I follow it, taking in the various men in orange jumpsuits. The population of Fulcort penitentiary is made up of every age and skin tone—short, tall, fat, skinny, clean-faced, scruffy.

How many of these men are like my father, I wonder.

How many of them don't belong in here?

Probably a lot less than the number of men who earned their cell.

My dad drops his voice to a murmur. "You see that guy over there? With the tattoo on his face? Don't be too obvious."

I shift my gaze to my left, spotting the guy in question

easily. Half his face is marred with ink—a scaly dragon with talons—making him look downright scary. He's sitting across from a young pretty Latina girl with fake nails long enough to be used as a weapon in a place like this, I'd hazard. "Yeah."

"Crazy Bob says he's high up in some notorious LA gang. Anything that guy wants in here, he gets. Anything."

"So become his friend."

Dad chuckles. "That's not how it works." He glances over his shoulder at the group of inmates filtering in. "See that one there? The third in line?"

I watch a heavyset man with pock-marked cheeks and unkempt gray hair stroll in. He must be in his seventies, with a belly that strains the waistline of his prison garb. "Okay."

"He's got the warden and plenty of the guards in his pocket. Even dragon-face stays away from him. He could put a hit out on anyone and it'd be done in a day, inside these walls or not. That's what Crazy Bob claims, anyway."

I watch the man lumber along. Maybe it's the jumpsuit and shaggy mop on his head but I'm picturing him stretching pizza dough or selling car insurance from behind a chunky old desk circa 1970, not swimming at the top of the food chain in a maximum security prison, scaring LA gangbangers.

"What's his deal?"

"Mob boss. Big into the drug trade."

I feel my eyebrows pop. "As in, like, Al Capone…?"

"As in, you betray him, he takes out your entire family and then you, and then he pisses on your ashes." Dad's voice drops to a whisper. "Crazy Bob told me that some clueless do-gooder guard came in here last year, stirring the pot against the corruption. He didn't last long."

"As in fired?"

"As in stopped coming in. His family hasn't heard from him since." Dad gives me a knowing look.

"I feel so much better knowing you're spending your days with these kind of people," I mutter, nausea stirring in my stomach. I study the mob boss as he passes. He walks with ease, as if he owns this room and he knows it. And maybe Crazy Bob isn't blowing smoke. Maybe he does own this place.

Curious about who he's here to see—one of his mobster minions, probably?—I let my gaze follow him to the four-person table in the far corner.

And find myself suddenly ensnared in a storm.

Chapter Two - Gabriel

I was fully prepared for two things when my eyelids peeled open this morning: one, that I'd be nursing a fucking epic hangover for most of the day after last night's festivities, and two, that I'd be in an extra-pissy mood by the time I made it up to this shithole.

What I did not expect was to be sitting in Fulcort with a raging hard-on for some chick visiting her old man.

But there you have it.

Fuck.

I've been coming here once a month for the last three years to see my father and I have *never* laid eyes on that woman before. I'd remember. Those sharp cheekbones, that thick jet-black hair. Those fat fucking lips, the kind that were made for wrapping around my cock and sucking slowly. She's hiding her body in baggy clothes—standard protocol, though she's taken it to the extreme; she's one step away from men's sweatpants—but her arms are toned, her neck is slender and long, her olive skin looks silky soft. I'm a betting man and I'd bet there's a tight ass and tits that sway when she's riding hard hiding beneath all that.

I didn't even notice her at first. I came in, settled into my dad's usual table in the corner of the room, and started surveying all the degenerates filling the room on this fine Saturday afternoon, killing time until Dad decided to grace me with his presence.

And then I spotted her over there, her pretty brow furrowed in worry as she leaned over the table to get as close to the man as possible without setting off the guards, and I haven't been able to peel my gaze away since.

It's been forever and a day since a woman has stirred my blood like this.

What's even more interesting is that she and the guy she's visiting—her dad, maybe?—leaned in to share a few whispered words and then those big, brown eyes of hers shifted to the inmates coming in.

To my father.

With wariness, she watched him stroll all the way over, and that's how, bingo, we're now eye-fucking each other. At least, that's what *I'm* doing.

Until I can get out of here, track her down, and switch to straight-up fucking.

My dad settles his girth into the stiff chair across from me. Somehow he's managed to pack on fifty pounds eating shitty prison food peppered with the odd steak dinner. "You're late," he mutters in his typical gruff voice.

"You have somewhere else you need to be?" I throw back before I can bite my tongue. If he wasn't going to complain about that, it'd be about something else. Still, he doesn't take too kindly to attitude, and Dad's bad side is not one you ever want to be on, blood-related or not. "Got caught up with work," I lie. "Who's that new guy over there? Number seven." I nod toward the table.

"What do I look like? Fucking four-one-one?" he snaps back, irritated.

I shrug, acting all nonchalant. "He seemed interested in you when you came in, is all."

Dad's bushy eyebrows furrow with the glare he shoots me before peering over his shoulder. "New fish. A nobody," he declares.

It's at that precise moment that my future lay glances our way. Her chocolate-brown eyes flare and then snap back, her face paling. Yeah, I'd say she got the skinny on who my father is, and it scares her. But will she be scared of me too? If so, what can I do to ease her fears?

My dick twitches with eagerness.

Dad shakes his head. "How's the club doing? You and Caleb haven't run it into the ground yet?"

I roll my eyes. "It's running smooth." Better than smooth, and he knows it. He likes to talk about Empire like it's his club, like it was his idea in the first place. He had nothing to do with it. My older brother and I purchased an old factory warehouse and converted it into a nightclub eight years ago. It's gone through several identity transformations but it's found its stride, catering to high-end clientele with cash to burn and people to impress. A one hundred percent legitimately run business, as far as any law enforcement is concerned. And, trust me, they've tried to prove otherwise. That's the downside of being the sons of Vlad Easton: you have the Feds and the IRS crawling up your ass on the regular.

"Peter was here last week." His cold gray eyes watch me. "He said our *friends* have been causing problems for Harriet again."

By friends, Dad means the cartel, aka nobody's friend, and by causing problems for Harriet, he means venturing farther into US territory and encroaching on my family's foothold in the lucrative cocaine and heroin trade, a business that my father and his brother, Peter, have been nurturing for decades, originating with a supply arrangement from "our friends" down south.

A business that has amassed us impressive wealth and power.

"So what's Peter going to do?" I ask carefully. My uncle is a crazy fuck—almost as crazy as my dad, who isn't quite as crazy as the cartel.

His sagging skin contorts with his sneer. "What's *he* going to do? How about what are my sons going to do!" He stabs at the table's surface with his meaty index finger. "It's time you two stop fucking around like a bunch of playboys and act like you're ready to take care of the family business."

I bite my tongue against the urge to remind him that we've laundered millions through Empire for "the family business," and that it's Caleb and me who keep the highly lucrative underground fight ring going. We can't talk openly about it here, and besides, he doesn't want to hear that. He definitely doesn't want to hear the thoughts Caleb floated after the handcuffs landed on Dad's wrists almost four years ago—that it's time to let the cartel move in, wash our hands of the dirty drug business, and invest all this money in other, legitimate things. Things that won't land us in this shithole with him.

But it's like Dad reads my mind. "What do you think, that you two could afford any of your cars and your houses and your fucking club if not for all the sacrifices your uncle and I have made? All the blood and sweat that's poured. The tears?"

I highly doubt any of those tears came from my father. He didn't even cry when my mother died. The guy's tear ducts probably don't work. And I damn well know none of that pouring blood was his, though there's been more than enough spilled thanks to "Harriet."

He's right though: we've gotten filthy rich off junkies shooting their veins with heroin and partiers filling their nostrils with cocaine.

I sigh reluctantly. "We'll go talk to Peter."

"Good." He nods slowly. "Because I want things running smoothly for when I get out."

You're not getting out of here. Dad's pushing seventy-five—he was in his midforties when Caleb and I were born—and he has another six years to serve for the witness tampering and money laundering convictions the Feds nailed him on. A drop in the bucket compared to what they *could* put him away for, if they could find their assholes in the dark.

Harriet alone would put him away for life three times over. Could put *all* of us away, something my brother and I are not so keen on risking. Sure, when we were younger, we felt invincible. But Caleb's thirty-one, I'm twenty-nine, and I'm looking at the indomitable Vlad Easton in an orange jumpsuit, sitting in a place where he swore he would never end up. And my brother and I? We've done the math. A lifetime behind these walls isn't worth it, not when we're already living like royalty.

I'd say we've been smart, for the most part, keeping our hands relatively clean. Or looking clean, at least. That was always the strategy. But what Dad's demanding now is the opposite of keeping our hands clean. He's telling us to sink our hands deep into Harriet's dirty, disease-riddled cunt.

No fucking thank you.

And then there's the matter of dealing with the goddamn cartel. I wouldn't say I'm *afraid* of them—we have our own network of proficient "fixers" to deal with threats, and I've learned to hold my own. I would just rather not wake up one morning to my head separated from my body.

Caleb and I have discussed the future of the Easton empire already. Neither of us trust Dad's judgment anymore. He and Uncle Peter are old-school, where giving your word is an iron-clad agreement and going against your word earns you a brutal punishment; where R-E-S-P-E-C-T isn't just a catchy song, it's a way of life. They put way too much stock in the belief that blood breeds loyalty.

Caleb and me? We live by one rule: don't trust *anyone* but each other.

That's where Dad made his mistake, bringing Marek, some third cousin born to a whore back in Russia, into the fold. Dear cousin Marek is now feeding worms in an undisclosed location, but before he ended up there, he gave the Feds just enough of a smoking gun to tuck my father away for almost a decade.

A guard passes through, stalling at table seven. The crestfallen look on my raven beauty's face tells me that her visit is over. *Shit.* If I can duck out of here early and cut her off in the parking lot, I could earn myself a blow job before the drive home—

"We need to go over some things," my dad says, slipping a wad of paper out from somewhere unseen and sliding it across the table to me. Prisoners aren't allowed to bring anything in with them, but the guards look the other way when it's us.

I unfold it to reveal a full eight-and-a-half by eleven sheet covered in encrypted codes that only Caleb and I and our accountant can decipher to hidden overseas accounts that the Feds didn't manage to turn up in their investigation.

This is going to take forever.

I sigh heavily as I watch the woman wrap her arms around the man's neck and squeeze tight, tears running down her cheeks. Her father, I'm guessing. Or uncle. Family. Definitely not her husband.

The guy's shoulders sink as he's led back to the cells with her watching him the entire way.

Not until he's out of sight does she move for the visitor entrance, her gaze drifting over mine in a slow pass. It's only for a second or two, just long enough for me to note the way her lips part, the way her dark eyes skitter over my chest and arms, the way her cheeks flush deeply, and then she swallows hard, ducks her head, and walks stiffly and quickly for the exit, those baggy jeans doing nothing for the tight ass I'm imagining.

"Gabriel!" my father barks, spearing me with a glare. "Chase pussy on your own time."

I plan on it.

"Parker. Hey." I rest my elbows on the security desk.

The sweaty, overweight guard leans back in his chair. "Gabriel Easton… what can I do for you today?"

I've never liked this dumb fuck, but I tolerate him because he's as pliable as putty. He's also worse than a twelve-year-old girl when it comes to spreading gossip, but he knows better than to chirp about me. "There was a woman in here, visiting an inmate. She left a half hour ago. About five eight, long black hair and—"

"Say no more." A shit-eating grin stretches his ugly mug. "Damn, that was a fine piece of ass. At least, I'm guessing. Sounds like she's coming back next Saturday. I'm gonna get her into a room to find out exactly what's under—"

"Yeah, yeah." As if he'd be conducting a strip search himself. They have female staff for that. But he's already given me one vital piece of information—she'll be back next week. "What do you know about her?"

"Why do ya wanna know?"

I level him with a severe look.

It has the desired effect. "Let's see. Her name is…" Parker lifts a page on his clipboard. And smiles. "Oh right, how could I forget... *Mercy* Wheeler. As in 'have mercy on my soul.' And my dick." He lets out a loud snort-laugh.

I ignore his idiocy, unable to stop the smile that slowly stretches across my lips.

Mercy.

My sweet, sweet Mercy.

You will be mine.

Read Sweet Mercy, Empire Nightclub #1 now

ALSO BY K.A. TUCKER

The Wolf Hotel Series:

Tempt Me (#1)

Break Me (#2)

Teach Me (#3)

Surrender To Me (#4)

Dirty Empire Series:

Sweet Mercy (#1)

Gabriel Fallen (#2)

Dirty Empire (#3)

Fallen Empire (#4)

For Contemporary Romance, Women's Fiction, and Romantic Suspense by K.A. Tucker, visit katuckerbooks.com

ABOUT THE AUTHOR

K.A. Tucker writes captivating stories with an edge.

She is the internationally bestselling author of the Ten Tiny Breaths and Burying Water series, He Will Be My Ruin, Until It Fades, Keep Her Safe, The Simple Wild, Be the Girl, and Say You Still Love Me. Her books have been featured in national publications including USA Today, Globe & Mail, Suspense Magazine, Publisher's Weekly, Oprah Mag, and First for Women.

K.A. Tucker currently resides in a quaint town outside of Toronto. Learn more about K.A. Tucker and her books at katuckerbooks.com

Printed in Great Britain
by Amazon

77887969R00174